THE WATERS OF ADAMAH

P J BROWN

Publisher: **Speight Street Media**

Book Cover by Kelly

eBook ISBN: 978-1-965192-75-7

Paperback ISBN: 978-1-965192-76-4

Hardback ISBN: 978-1-965192-77-1

To Deb Smith

Best friend and my beta reader

I am forever grateful.

Prologue

October 1981.
Somewhere in a rural part of the country.

The stranger appeared dazed, barely lucid, and unsteady on his feet. There had been an almost deafening booming noise, which sounded like the loudest thunderclap ever heard, and an immensely bright radiance of light had engulfed him, blinding him temporarily.

He was still shielding his eyes as the thundering noise dissipated into silence, and the intense light faded, revealing the surroundings. His focus was returning as he lowered his hand from his eyes, but he still felt unsteady on his feet. Looking around, taking in the surrounding forest, nothing seemed familiar. The trees, the sounds, the smells, even the sky, peeping through the forest's canopy, seemed new to him.

He didn't know where he was – couldn't seem to remember. It was as though the thunder and lightning had taken his memory.

Was it even thunder and lightning?

He wasn't sure.

What is going on? Where am I?

Suddenly he was cold and shivering, his teeth starting to chatter. It was the beginning of the colder months in this area. The temperature was dropping rapidly, and standing there in this unfamiliar place, looking down at himself, he realized that he was almost naked. He was wearing nothing except for some sort of cloth wrapped around his hips covering his front and back parts, and no footwear.

The sun was getting lower because the light was fading fast, which meant the temperature was going to drop even quicker soon. Oddly though, none of this panicked him. His head had cleared now, and his eyes were focused again.

He remembered his purpose.

His senses tuned into the surroundings, and he could hear a river or stream not far away. A river would lead to where he needed to go, he reasoned. He started in that direction but stopped when he heard vehicles approaching from the opposite direction. He listened as the vehicle noises got louder and then faded away. He looked ahead to where the river may be, contemplated his choices, then turned and headed to where the vehicle noise was coming from.

He nodded to himself.

This was a better idea.

ONE

Henleyville
Present day – September 2023

Henleys Diner was unusually quiet for a Saturday. Usually, the lunch crowd would be filling up the place by now, but today was the annual parade at midday - the Henleyville Timber Festival Parade. Almost everyone in town was out lining the streets, jostling for the best vantage points.

Well not everyone.

Lesley Jones was sitting in the diner with her daughter Amy, having a late breakfast. It was just after eleven am. Lesley wasn't hungry, but she had promised her daughter they would have breakfast at the diner before joining the rest of the town folk to watch the parade. Amy had chosen blueberry pancakes, her favorite, and was busily tucking into them while her mother just sipped her coffee.

Lesley put her coffee cup down on the table.

She didn't feel well at all today, worse than she had been feeling recently. When she got out of bed this morning she collapsed, her head hitting the floor so hard she knocked herself out. Then after she regained consciousness, she'd felt her head for blood but fortunately, there was none. No cuts or contusions.

Sitting opposite her daughter now, she was still feeling the effects of the fall, her head a little foggy, and a headache pounding its beat at the back of her eyes.

I might have a concussion, Lesley thought.

This wasn't the first time Lesley had blacked out.

The episodes were becoming more frequent.

The doctors told her the tumor was getting bigger and her symptoms would worsen. There was nothing they could do they'd informed her. Surgery was not an option this time. The neurologist she had been sent to at City General Hospital – how ironic Lesley had thought - had told her the tumor had grown into the temporal lobe and the cerebellum, and if they attempted to remove even a tiny section, Lesley could end up in a vegetative state or even worse, she could die on the operating table.

Lesley knew she was getting worse, and that hiding her symptoms from Amy was becoming harder. Her daughter was smart, very smart for a thirteen-year-old.

Lesley would often catch Amy staring at her, her eyes seeming to look right inside her and seeing the monster growing in her head, but she would never say a word. She would just stare. Lesley would notice the look on Amy's face, a resigned look, a look of knowing, and it would unnerve her.

Did she know?

How could she know?

I've told her nothing about this, Lesley would think to herself.

Today was different, though.

Today she couldn't hide the pain she was now feeling, and it was worrying her.

Lesley rubbed her forehead and grimaced. The throbbing headache was almost unbearable. It was the worst headache she'd had since she started feeling ill about two months ago.

"Are you okay, Ma?" Amy asked, looking intently at her mother.

Amy had always called her mother 'Ma.'

It was the first word she had spoken as a child.

And Lesley still remembered that day like it was yesterday.

....

14th October 2010

It was Amy's first birthday, and it was breakfast time.

Amy was in her highchair and Lesley was spooning porridge into Amy's mouth when the phone rang. It was Doctor Mac with the results from the scans.

Lesley had been getting a lot of headaches lately and she had been feeling dizzy and unwell at times too, so she'd spoken to Doctor Mac at Henleyville Hospital, where she worked as a registered nurse. Even though the symptoms were familiar to her, Lesley knew she wasn't pregnant this time around because, well, she just knew.

She wasn't dating anyone.

She hadn't dated anyone since Steven.

And besides, she wasn't interested in romance anymore. Amy was the love of her life now.

....

Lesley had moved to Henleyville when Amy was three months old. In an odd twist of luck, the nursing vacancy at Henleyville Hospital was still available twelve months after she first saw it online, so she had sent off an application, not expecting to receive a response because she hadn't worked since she'd lost her job at City General Hospital.

However, less than an hour after she'd clicked 'SEND', she received a phone call from Doctor Gareth Mackenzie at Henleyville Hospital and after a twenty-minute phone interview, he offered her the job there and then.

Doctor Mackenzie told her that accommodation would be provided with the job, and all she would have to do was pay the utilities. The salary they offered was remarkable, Lesley thought, considering she was still a young nurse at only twenty-six years old. Doctor Mackenzie must have read her thoughts because he told her that her experience in the City General emergency department, and her top marks at medical college, meant she had all the qualities they needed.

Everything seemed to happen very quickly from then.

Lesley excitedly accepted the offer, packed, and moved her and Amy to Henleyville within two weeks.

2010 was going to be a good year, she said to her young daughter when they left Capitol City.

....

That morning on the phone, Doctor Mac – everyone called him Doctor Mac – who had suggested an MRI just to rule out anything abnormal, gave Lesley the news. The results, he had told her, showed a small tumor about the size of a walnut on the cerebellum, and the neurosurgeon at City General wanted to do a biopsy as soon as possible.

"Tumor?" Lesley replied, only hearing bits and pieces of what Doctor Mac was telling her.

"Henry Jurgensen is the best neurosurgeon in the country, probably one of the best in the world. You know that. I sent the MRI scans to him for consultation. It's not my area of expertise Lesley," Doctor Mac had told her.

Lesley was looking at Amy.

She was playing with the spoon, making a mess of the porridge, and giggling to herself.

"When, Doctor Mac?" Lesley asked.

"Tomorrow, Lesley. They have you scheduled for nine in the morning. I know it's very short notice, and we can handle a few days here without you, I promise. But you need to get on top of this now," he urged.

Lesley was due to start her shift at ten am that morning and the babysitter was coming any minute.

What about Amy, she thought.

"Amy," Lesley mumbled into the phone. "I can't take her with me."

"We've got everything covered, Lesley. Jennifer Henley said she would take care of Amy till you get back. And Mrs. Robinson, our midwife, will take care of the clinic office duties for the time being," Doctor Mackenzie told her. "We have no pregnancies at the moment, which is quite strange I must admit."

Shocked, stunned, and trying to process everything in her mind, Lesley ended the call and looked at Amy. She was smiling brightly at her mother. She lifted the little spoon from her bowl of porridge, held it out for her mother, and said "Ma."

Lesley broke down and cried.

....

Present Day

"Ma?" Amy said again. "Is everything okay?"

Lesley snapped out of her memories to the here and now, as a tear trickled down from her right eye.

She looked at her daughter, who had stopped eating and was waiting for a reply.

"What, sweetie?" Lesley said, wiping away the tear.

"Ma, you look like you're in pain. Is it another bad headache?" her daughter enquired, watching her mother carefully.

"Yeah honey. Double shift yesterday catching up, I guess. Don't worry. I'm fine," Lesley lied.

"Mmm. You always say that," Amy replied, unconvinced, not taking her eyes off her mother.

Lesley felt guilty under her daughter's intense gaze.

She hated keeping secrets, and it was obvious that lying to her daughter no longer worked in her favor.

She looked away and saw a man sitting alone in another booth. He had a baseball cap on, and his head was down slightly, hiding his eyes. Underneath the baseball cap, Lesley noticed his hair was about shoulder length and brownish in color. His face, what she could see of it, looked unshaven, but it was hard to tell because the headache was affecting her vision today.

Everything was a little blurry.

She couldn't tell how old he was, but she guessed maybe around forty. He seemed unremarkable but rugged, she thought.

He was eating what appeared to be the all-day breakfast of eggs, bacon, sausages, baked beans, mushrooms, tomato, and toast.

Healthy appetite, Lesley thought.

She continued watching as Jennifer Henley, the diners' owner, approached his table carrying a pot of black coffee.

"Need a refill, Joe?" Jennifer asked him.

When he lifted his head to respond to Jennifer, Lesley got a better look at his face, but she didn't recognize him. She thought she knew almost everyone in town.

Working at the Henleyville Hospital you get to know lots of people and their families and friends, but Lesley was sure she had never seen this guy before. There was something familiar about him, though, that feeling suddenly dawned on her.

No, I don't know him, she thought, shaking her head slightly.

Maybe he is just passing through, she convinced herself, *or he's here for the parade and I've seen him on the street.*

The man nodded at Jennifer and smiled.

"Yes, thank you," he said.

Jennifer refilled his cup with hot coffee.

At the same moment, he looked straight over at Lesley, their eyes locking. He nodded once and smiled at her.

Lesley had that familiar feeling again.

Startled, she looked away, back to her daughter, who was still staring at her mother. Amy just lifted her eyebrows at her mother, waiting for a response.

"I'm fine honey," Lesley tried to assure her as she glanced back at the man, but he was no longer looking over at her.

She looked at Amy and said, "And I don't need to see a doctor. I know that's what you are going to say next. You always do… It's just a bad headache."

Amy looked disappointed and confused and maybe a little upset.

She averted her eyes from her mother, stabbed her fork into the last mouthful of blueberry pancake on her plate, and shook her head ever so slightly.

Lesley saw it.

Does she know, Lesley wondered?

But how could she know? I haven't told her anything, she thought to herself.

Amy is smart though. And intuitive. Maybe it's time I told her about it, Lesley pondered. *Maybe tonight after the parade.*

Maybe, she thought, *but how do I even begin to tell her that I'm going to die?*

They both sat in silence as Amy finished the last of her milkshake and Lesley drank the dregs of her coffee.

The headache was not getting any better, so Lesley reached into her handbag, took out a couple of the strong prescription painkillers she had gotten from the hospital pharmacy, downed them with water from the jug on their table, and headed off to pay for their meal.

"You ready, honey?" Lesley asked Amy when she got back to their table.

She noticed Amy was staring over at the man in the baseball cap.

Amy nodded, got up, and headed for the door without looking at her mother.

Joe turned and watched as Lesley headed for the door and followed Amy outside.

He'd seen the girl looking at him – well, felt it, actually. That feeling you get when someone is watching you - an intuition. He'd turned his head just enough to catch a glimpse of her in his peripheral vision. He knew it was her daughter. He'd heard Lesley call her 'honey' and 'sweetie', so it was an educated guess on his part, but he was certain he was right.

After they'd exited the café, both mother and daughter headed in the direction of the parade.

Turning back to his now empty plate, he caught the attention of Jennifer Henley, lifted his coffee cup, and wiggled it for her to see. Jennifer smiled and grabbed the coffee pot on her way to his table.

Outside, Lesley couldn't be certain, but she was sure the man in the baseball cap – I think Jen had called him Joe, she recalled - had been watching them leave the café.

It's hard to say, she thought.

She tried not to make it obvious she was looking back into the café through the glass windows and doing it without turning her head proved quite tricky. But even with the blurry vision and the pounding in her head, she was sure the baseball cap man had been watching them as they left.

Am I being paranoid?

No, she reassured herself. *I don't know him, so you can't be too careful.*

I'll ask Jen next time I'm in the café, she thought.

The Henley family have owned the café for three generations, so if they didn't know who the man was, then he was not from around these parts, that's for sure.

They reached the parade, and Amy saw some of her friends from school.

Lesley knew them all.

They were all good kids, and their families had been here for as long as Lesley herself had lived here, probably longer because Lesley had only moved here for work not long after Amy was born.

A new start was what she had wanted back then.

Capitol City had too many bad memories for her.

"My friends are over there. Can I go with them, please?" Amy asked.

"Sure, honey," Lesley replied and smiled at Amy.

She knew her daughter was responsible.

"Message me when you're done, and I'll come get you, okay? I'm going to drop by work for a while, so I'll be there if you need me. Do you have enough money?"

"Yeah, I'm good, Ma. I've still got my allowance from 2020," Amy replied, grinning at her mother, then headed off to her friends.

"Don't forget. Text me," Lesley called after her, waving her phone in the air.

She watched as Amy met up with her friends, and then they all disappeared into the crowd lining the streets. The parade was just beginning. Lesley knew she could trust Amy and her friends.

Trust, she thought, and as she stood alone on the footpath, her mind wandered back in time – to more than fourteen years ago.

TWO

Capitol City - March 2009

Working in the City General Hospital emergency department in Capitol City was a big deal for Lesley. City General is a world-renowned hospital in one of the largest cities in the country.

It was her dream job, and her first posting after medical college. It was like she had hit the jackpot: great pay, great staff, great opportunities. But after working there for almost three years, doing double shifts more than twice a week, she wasn't happy anymore.

The hospital board had recently appointed a new administration team, brought on to manage the hospital out of the effects of the Global Financial Crisis, and immediately funding was cut drastically to a lot of "unnecessary services and areas in the hospital," they had been told.

There were wholesale staff cuts and redundancies as well, with the remaining staff having to pick up the slack by taking on extra shifts frequently and regularly losing rostered days off. Everyone was burning out, and Lesley gradually lost her passion for the job.

She hadn't had a day off in three weeks.

And to make things worse, even Emily, her best friend, seemed to be a little stand-offish lately.

Lesley had seen an online job ad for a registered nurse at the hospital in Henleyville about a week before she found out she was pregnant. She had been scouring the Internet for job vacancies absent-mindedly when she came across the listing. If she applied for it and got the job at Henleyville Hospital, it would mean a move to another state.

But it didn't matter to Lesley.

She loved being a nurse, and she figured that a new start in a small-town hospital might be an opportunity to really make a difference again.

She had Googled Henleyville and found it was a beautiful picturesque old town surrounded by lush forests to its north and farmlands to the south and west. There were several small creeks and a river that fed into a massive dam to the east. Henleyville seemed to have everything that was required of a smaller town and its surrounding region.

'Henleyville Hospital adequately services the population of approximately 3,500 people,' one article said, 'including its own paramedic service based out of the hospital.'

'Henleyville also has two schools, catering for all ages, and many small businesses that have been operating since the town's early days,' the article continued.

The old timber mill, which was founded by the original settlers in the area, had closed many years ago due to newly introduced conservation laws, Lesley had read.

The next day, she had mentioned the job to Steven, her boyfriend. He had returned inside after finishing 'another work call', as he'd said. Steven had his own business as a builder, and he'd been out of town a lot recently.

"I have to go where the work is, Lesley," he'd told her a few months back.

He seems a bit weird today, Lesley thought as she watched Steven rummage through his work bag.

"What do you think, Steven?" Lesley asked again, referring to the job in Henleyville.

"If you're not happy at City General anymore then apply for it," Steven replied, matter-of-factly, not looking at her.

Lesley continued to watch as Steven apparently found what he was looking for, headed back outside to his work truck, got in, and drove away.

That night when she got home from another double shift at the hospital, she told Steven she would think about it, but she wanted to talk to Emily, her best friend, first before she decided to apply.

"Why do you want to talk to Emily?" Steven asked, with an odd look on his face.

"She always gives the best advice, Steven. I trust her instincts," Lesley replied.

Emily was ten years older than Lesley, and a more senior nurse, so Lesley valued her wisdom and advice. Plus, she knew she could trust Emily to keep it to herself. But Lesley felt it was odd that Emily seemed distant lately. Normally, Emily and Lesley worked the same shifts, but for the past few weeks, their rosters had not matched. Emily had been doing a lot of night shifts, while Lesley was stuck on the day shift and frequently doing double shifts, not finishing until ten pm.

The last time Lesley had seen Emily was at a change of shift after finishing another double shift. Emily was just starting the night shift and seemed flustered when Lesley saw her. Lesley had called out to her, but Emily turned away and got on the elevator before Lesley could catch up to her.

That incident still bothered Lesley a week later when she discovered she was pregnant.

She hadn't had a period cycle in months, which generally was not a worry for her because she'd always had erratic cycles.

Lesley was fourteen when she had her first period cycle.

She had 'become aware' as her mother had put it.

From then on, Lesley's cycles were few and far between, and when they did happen, she suffered excruciating pain and debilitating illness. At Katharyn's insistence, their doctor put Lesley on birth control, which helped alleviate almost all the symptoms.

But lately, Lesley had not been feeling well, with bad headaches and severe nausea at times. She had been having a few dizzy spells too and sometimes she would wake up feeling groggy and lethargic. So, she did one of those home pregnancy tests. It showed a positive result.

She was pregnant.

But I take birth control, she thought, *and more importantly, Steven is infertile.*

Two more home pregnancy tests over the week gave the same result: Pregnant.

Steven flew into a rage when she told him that night. He accused her of cheating on him, lying about taking birth control and trying to trap him with another man's baby. He told her he couldn't have kids, and she knew that.

When they first started seeing each other, Steven told her he'd damaged both testicles in a motorbike accident when he was fifteen. The doctors had told him the damage meant he could never produce sperm. After that, he'd decided he wasn't the fatherly type anyway, so kids were not a part of his future. Lesley wasn't happy about this because she wanted kids one day – just not yet - but she had accepted it and decided to keep seeing him anyway.

Besides, when they started dating, she was only twenty-three, and her nursing career was just taking off. Steven was handsome, tall, and athletic because of his manual job. His business was going great, he'd told her, and he'd just hired another licensed contractor to help him because he was getting so many jobs.

She thought her relationship with Steven, who was almost thirty, worked well and fit into her career-first plans.

Until it didn't.

Steven wouldn't calm down.

He was pacing around the apartment, yelling at her, saying he couldn't move to another state because his business was too important. He had jobs lined up for the next six months, and the clients were depending on him, and how could she do that to him. Lesley could accept that his business was important to him, but she couldn't accept the blatant accusations he was hurling at her. And, of course, he didn't believe her when she told him she hadn't cheated on him, and he also said she was lying about her reasons for taking birth control.

"I don't trust you anymore," he had yelled, and that hurt Lesley a lot.

But the biggest shock was yet to come.

Steven stopped pacing and yelling and stood right in front of her, a slight smirk on his face. He told her he'd been seeing someone else, a nurse at the hospital where she worked, one of her closest friends, Emily.

Lesley was stunned.

She couldn't believe Emily would do this to her. She said as much to Steven. He told her he and Emily had been seeing each other for ages but didn't know how to tell her.

He seems to be enjoying this, Lesley thought watching his performance.

He stopped and looked at her with a smug look on his face.

It was off-putting.

She pushed him away, not wanting to believe what she was hearing. She needed to get away from him, so she ran into the bedroom, slamming the door behind her. Steven yelled at her from the other side of the closed door that the pregnancy betrayal had removed any guilt he felt about cheating, and then he spat out his full confession about the affair.

Trust, Lesley thought, *I'll never trust anyone ever again.*

Steven packed his things and left that night.

Lesley hadn't cried at all when he left. She was in shock more than anything. Shocked that she had trusted Emily and Steven and thought she had loved him.

Did she love him?

She wasn't sure anymore if she did or didn't or if she had ever really loved him at all.

Is that why I didn't cry? she'd wondered.

She didn't know.

Nor did she know how she was pregnant.

Everything changed after that night.

Emily wouldn't answer Lesley's calls. She avoided her entirely and quit her job at the hospital a few days later. Then somehow, City General Hospital found out Lesley was pregnant and put her on administrative leave pending review.

Two weeks later, her contract with the hospital was terminated.

"What am I going to do now?" she said to herself after receiving notification of her termination.

She was alone, with no job, and expecting a child in about seven months. Nobody would hire her now. She would be a single mother, raising her child on her own, she thought, just like her own mother had done.

Mother.

I need to call her, Lesley realized.

She hadn't spoken to her mother since she'd told her she was pregnant. Her mother had reacted strangely when Lesley told her the news. Lesley was at work, sitting alone in the staff break room when she made the call to her mother.

"No!" her mother gasped in horror down the phone when Lesley told her she was pregnant.

"Mother!" Lesley exclaimed, a little shocked by her response.

"I'm sorry Lesley. It's… um.... just a surprise, that's all. Are you okay? How do you feel?" Katharyn Jones asked.

"To be honest, mom, I'm struggling a bit. I've been having dizzy spells… and I just feel worn out," Lesley told her. "Maybe it's work, I don't know, but something just doesn't feel right."

Her mother said nothing for a while.

"I know. Are you going to tell Steven?"

"I have to. I will try tonight. After my shift," Lesley replied.

"Are you sure he is the father?" her mother asked.

"What?" Lesley responded, not sure if she had heard her mother correctly.

"You told me he can't father children," Katharyn said.

"No, he can't, mom. I don't understand it either," Lesley replied, a little despondent.

"Mmm. I'll call you tomorrow, Lesley. I must go," her mother said and hung up.

Lesley still had her phone to her ear.

"Mom? Mom?" she said then looked at her phone. 'Call ended' it said.

"What the hell, mother!" Lesley said to the empty room.

Hanging up on her daughter, Katharyn Jones collapsed onto her sofa because she knew how and why Lesley was pregnant. There would be dire consequences now, meaning Lesley and her unborn child were no longer safe.

THREE

Present day – September 2023

Instead of dropping by the hospital like she had told Amy, Lesley went home and lay down. Her headache had eased a little, thanks to the painkillers she'd taken, but her vision was still affected.

Work can wait, she'd decided.

Besides, it's my weekend off. And I must pop into the hardware store, she thought, *to see old John Miller. His left knee is getting worse. Maybe I can persuade him to see Doctor Mac.*

....

Old John Miller is a stalwart of Henleyville, been there forever, it seemed, and a town favorite. Everyone who knew him called him 'Old John'. It was a running joke because nobody knew exactly how old he was. He'd been in Henleyville since 1980, he'd tell people, and they would be dumbfounded because even today, he still looked like he wasn't a day over fifty years of age. Tall, handsome, and muscular, John Miller could easily pass for a much younger man.

"Good genetics," he'd always respond with a smile.

John had worked in the old Henley Mill before it closed about thirty years ago, then started his own hardware store. It was there that Lesley had met him not long after she had arrived in town. The kitchen tap in her new residence was constantly dripping, and she figured it needed a new washer.

Confronted with numerous containers of washers in the hardware store, Lesley had asked the nice man behind the counter for help.

"What size washer do you need?" John Miller had asked Lesley that morning.

"I don't know. I didn't realize there were different sizes. I thought they were all the same," she had replied.

John Miller just smiled at Lesley and said, "I'll come take a look if you like. You're in the old Cooper place, aren't you?"

Confused, Lesley asked, "The old Cooper place?"

"Yeah. On Old Mill Road, near the school. Nice old home with a black roof and green shutters on the windows. It's got the letterbox attached to that big tree next to the driveway," he said, smiling at her.

Lesley was still confused.

"Um, yes. How did you know?" she asked.

"That place has been vacant for a long time. And when someone new moves here, word spreads around very quickly," John Miller said.

He noticed the distraught look on her face.

"Oh, don't worry. The old Cooper place is as solid as a rock, and we look after our own in Henleyville. You are part of this town now," he'd reassured her.

"But I've only been here a week," Lesley replied.

"We knew you were coming, Miss Jones. The hospital clinic has been trying to fill that nursing position for almost a year now," John Miller explained.

He shook his head in wonder, thinking about something Carol Wilson had told him back when she had first arrived in Henleyville. She'd been on a road trip around the country, and she'd said that something drew her to Henleyville, so she decided to stay. That was more than twenty years ago.

"Anyway," he continued, "when your application came through, we were all excited. It's been hard on the doctors since Nurse Wilson retired."

Lesley was feeling embarrassed and didn't know what to say. She had always been a very private person, but this man – and most of the town apparently – already knew a lot about her. He was saying something else now, but Lesley seemed lost in her thoughts, staring at the scar on John Miller's neck.

"Are you okay, Lesley?" John Miller asked, reaching across the counter, and touching her arm.

Surprised by the touch, Lesley refocused her mind.

"Yes, yes. I'm fine, sir," she replied, recovering slightly. "I just need a tap washer please."

"Call me John. John Miller is my name," he said and smiled. "And I need to take a look at that tap of yours to figure out what you'll need. Is that okay? I can come by after lunch if you like. Not much happens in hardware after one pm."

"Um, yes. Thank you, Mister Miller… Yes. I'll be home then. I don't have any tools in the house, though," Lesley said.

John Miller smiled.

"Don't you worry about tools. I think I can find some somewhere," he said, looking around his store.

Lesley looked embarrassed.

"Oh…Yes, of course," she said. "I don't know what's in the house yet. I've barely had time to unpack."

John Miller nodded.

"One thirty okay then?" he asked.

"Yes," Lesley replied, "thank you, Mister Miller. You are so kind."

"John," he said. "Please call me John."

Lesley nodded, smiled, and left the hardware store, the bell above the door jingling as she exited.

....

Lesley woke up when the message notification sounded on her phone. The room was getting dark. She sat up and instinctively felt her head. The headache was gone.

Thank God, she thought.

And as she looked around her bedroom, she realized her vision had cleared, and she could see normally again. She picked up her phone and checked the time. It was after six thirty pm. Lesley had slept for more than six hours, and she started to panic because Amy had texted her several times.

Amy was at Henleys Diner, ready to be picked up, and 'Could my friends get a lift home too, please Ma?'

'Ma, are you there?'

'Ma, where are you???'

'I've rung the hospital. You are not there!' the messages had read.

'Sorry. I was sleeping. Be there in 10' she texted back.

They got home about an hour later.

Amy went upstairs to shower and change while Lesley went into the kitchen to make some hot chocolate. When Lesley arrived at the diner to collect Amy and her friends, Amy told her mother they had already eaten. Lesley wasn't hungry anyway, so she was happy that Amy had eaten. Jennifer Henley had told Lesley that Amy had helped her clear the tables, load the dishwashers, and refill the napkin dispensers.

"She's an angel, that girl of yours," Jennifer had told Lesley.

Lesley was standing at the sink, looking at the tap and thinking about old John Miller, when Amy came downstairs and into the kitchen.

"I'm glad you're feeling better, Ma," Amy said to her mother's back as she sat at the table.

Lesley turned and smiled at her daughter.

"Me too, honey. I'm sorry I didn't answer your messages earlier. I must have been in such a deep sleep, I guess," she replied.

She brought the hot chocolates over to the table and sat down opposite Amy.

It's now or never, Lesley thought to herself.

"Amy... I need to talk to you about something," she said, looking at her daughter.

Amy was staring into her cup of hot chocolate, not looking at her mother.

"I know, Ma," Amy said softly. "You're sick again."

Lesley breathed in quickly with surprise.

How does she know?

Amy looked at her mother.

"It's the same as before, isn't it?" she stated rather than asking.

"Before?" Lesley asked. "What do you mean 'before'?"

"When I was a baby…. The tumor. It's back, isn't it?" Amy asked, her eyes locked on her mother's.

This, too, was more of a statement than a question.

Lesley was caught off guard.

How could Amy know about that?

Hardly anyone knows about that.

Only Doctor Mackenzie and the specialists at the hospital back home know about it.

She hadn't even told her mother yet.

Lesley was starting to panic inside.

Amy must have seen the look on her mother's face.

She said, "Mom, I found your hospital records when I was looking for something in the spare room. I read them. And I know you've been having episodes lately. It's the same as back then, isn't it?"

Amy has never called me 'mom,' Lesley thought.

Hospital records? Oh my God. I'd forgotten about them, she realized.

"No," Lesley replied softly. "No. It's not the same Amy."

"I've Googled your symptoms, Ma!"

Amy was back to calling her mother 'Ma,' but she was getting visibly upset.

"Symptoms?" Lesley asked. "What symptoms?"

Amy listed them off with her fingers.

"Severe headaches. Blurred vision. Dizzy spells. Blackouts."

Lesley was shocked and Amy saw it.

"Yes, Ma. I know about the blackouts. I've found you passed out on your bathroom floor a few times, plus in the lounge room and on the floor next to your bed. Who do you think put you back into your bed each time?"

Lesley didn't know what to say.

"I… I just figured I'd managed to get up off the floor by myself without knowing," she mumbled.

She was looking at her daughter differently now. Her thirteen-year-old daughter. Well, almost fourteen. It's her birthday next month.

I guess it's possible, Lesley thought. *I'm not a big person because nursing keeps me fit. Plus, Amy is almost as tall as me, and she is very strong for her age, so it is possible.*

"The tumor?" Amy asked, snapping Lesley from her thoughts. "It's back, isn't it?"

"Yes," Lesley admitted, tears filling her eyes now. "But it's not like back then, Amy. They can't remove it this time."

Amy looked down at the table.

Her hot chocolate had gone cold.

She pushed the cup away from her.

"Why not, Ma?" Amy said, her voice cracking with emotion and tears welling in her eyes.

Lesley reached across the table and took her daughter's hands in hers. Amy looked at her mother. Both struggled to hold in their tears, and Amy's chest was heaving with each stifled sob.

"It's too dangerous, sweetie. The tumor is too big, and it's grown into more parts of my brain now. There's nothing they can do."

Amy pulled away from her mother's grasp, got up, and ran upstairs to her room. Lesley sat there, put her head in her hands, and cried like she had never cried before.

FOUR

Capitol City - Present day - September

Lenora Jackson was sitting at her desk, scrolling through old newspaper articles online.

The Capitol City Times offices were abuzz with excitement this morning. There had been new developments in the war in Eastern Europe, and everyone was glued to the news feeds on the various television screens throughout the building.

Not Lenora, though.

Her focus was on the computer screen in front of her.

Lenora Jackson handled cold cases for the Capitol City Times. It had been her specialty for the past twenty years, and several of her in-depth investigations of cold cases had resulted in new vital evidence being discovered, leading to the arrests of suspects who were eventually tried and convicted of their crimes. Lenora had won several awards for her journalistic investigations and was often a guest speaker on crime podcasts and true crime shows. To date, Lenora Jackson has helped solve four long-standing Capitol City cold cases.

What Lenora was working on now was not an official cold case as such. Not an unsolved murder, not a robbery where the suspects were never caught, not an old hit-and-run death with no suspects. This was a different type of cold case investigation. There were no victims of crimes. No actual crimes had ever been committed – that she was aware of.

Quite the opposite, in fact.

As her investigation deepened, and her search parameters widened, Lenora had discovered that six people from various walks of life had encountered a person – a shadow person, they all had said – who had apparently saved their lives, spoken to them, then simply vanished.

Several things seemed to tie all these events together, Lenora realized.

The first was what this shadow person had said to them: "Be ready. Your time is coming."

None of the individuals could comprehend what the shadow person meant by this, and not one of them could get a clear view of him either, but they all attested he spoke to them in their respective native languages. Among the bemused were a Romanian tourist, a Japanese immigrant, an Indigenous woman, an individual of Ghanaian heritage, and a Jewish couple.

This 'shadow person' speaks many different languages, Lenora noted. That's the second odd thing with all these cases, she was thinking.

The third coincidence was that each of these people was seen as a leader in their community, and held in very high esteem by their peers, almost like religious leaders.

Was it a coincidence? Probably, Lenora speculated.

This link was the odd one though, Lenora had thought, because she knew someone who'd had an encounter similar to these other five cases, and that person was not a leader in his field or very religious. In fact, he hadn't stepped foot inside a church since his school days. Lenora knew this for a fact because the man was her Irishman husband, Simon.

Although she just remembered, Simon had once told her he did have Gypsy blood in him, and Gypsies were powerful, mysterious folk in his homeland.

On July 22, 2009, Simon O'Reilly had been on his way to work to start his afternoon shift at City General Hospital, when he was involved in a single-vehicle car accident.

Heavy dark clouds filled the sky that day due to a massive storm front which had moved in over the city and its surroundings. Vision was poor because of the torrential rain, and Simon was struggling to see barely ten feet in front of him when his vehicle hit a large puddle of water and lost control. The vehicle spun and went careening into a guard rail, flipped several times, throwing Simon through the front windscreen, before eventually coming to a rest upside down about twenty meters away from where Simon lay on the road.

He had not been wearing his seat belt.

Simon had told Lenora that when he was lying on the road, he knew he had sustained traumatic injuries, and he could feel himself drifting away. He said his only thoughts were of her.

A short distance away from where lay, there was a flash of light and a loud crackling noise. Someone was approaching him, but he couldn't make out who it was because his eyes wouldn't, or couldn't, focus.

"It was just a shadowy figure," he explained to Lenora.

Simon told her that the person knelt down next to him and placed a hand on his wrist. Almost immediately, an intense heat surged through his body for what seemed like ages but was probably only about twenty seconds. Then the person leaned close to Simon and said "Be ready. Your time is coming," in Gaelic.

The next thing Simon remembers is waking up in hospital with Lenora standing next to the bed. The only injury he had sustained was a burn mark on his right wrist, probably from landing on the road, the doctors had told him.

Simon had no other injuries.

"Unbelievable," the doctors had said. "Your car is a write-off. You should be dead."

Simon was discharged the following morning.

Lenora didn't know what to think when Simon told her about the accident and what he had encountered. Quite frankly, she didn't know whether to believe him or not. She figured he had suffered a bad knock to the head, and the doctors hadn't picked it up, but Simon had no injuries, visible or otherwise, they had assured her, apart from the burn mark on his wrist.

It was about a week after the accident, when Lenora was at work, still processing in her mind what her husband had told her, that she found herself scouring the Internet for 'miraculous survival stories'.

This enquiry brought up approximately half a million search results.

Browsing through a number of these, Lenora found articles about family pets who had saved their owner's lives, people who'd had an intuitive feeling not to go somewhere, or get on a bus or train, a decision that had saved their life, and stories of people surviving being lost in the woods. But she found nothing that had any similarities to her husband's story. She guessed Simon must have sustained a bad concussion and had been hallucinating, so she gave up.

That was then.

This morning that all changed.

Lenora's assistant, Serena, had brought in a magazine that was full of stories most people never believed because they seemed so far-fetched. The front page of this magazine normally had headlines about alien abduction, or fishermen finding Atlantis, something along those lines. Serena had left the magazine, called the Capitol Enquirer, on her desk, and Lenora had spotted it when she arrived at the office.

On the front page, the headline read, 'Man says "Alien saved me." Told him to be ready.'

Lenora had stopped abruptly after seeing those words in the headline.

"Be ready," she had repeated after reading it, remembering what Simon had told her years ago.

Lenora took the magazine and read the article.

It was about a Japanese man in his thirties, an immigrant, Haruto Tanaka, who had lost his wife in a tragic house fire two years earlier. Tanaka had been consumed with guilt since his wife's death because he was unable to get her out of the house in time. Haruto Tanaka was a very spiritual man and a successful business owner. He was in his shed building wooden toys for underprivileged kids when the fire started in the basement of their house. The fire had quickly engulfed the house before he even realized what was happening.

His wife was trapped inside, unable to escape, and perished in the fire.

Tanaka had started drinking heavily after his wife's death and suffering poor mental health, he'd decided to end his grief by taking his own life. Haruto said he couldn't swim so he'd decided to jump off a bridge that crossed the river near his town. After jumping off the bridge, Haruto says he remembers sinking to the bottom, gulping in water, and knowing he was drowning and losing consciousness.

The next thing he remembers is lying on the bank of the river, with what he described as a 'shadow being' kneeling next to him. He said the being was shrouded in a dark, cloudy mist, which made it difficult to focus on it, but he was certain it was male. He said the shadow figure grabbed his right wrist then he felt an intense heat surge through his entire body for about thirty seconds, after which the shadow figure said, "Be ready. Your time is coming."

Haruto Tanaka said he woke up in the back of an ambulance sometime later.

"When did this happen?" Lenora said to herself after reading the article.

Checking the magazine cover, she saw it was dated October 2016, seven years ago.

That was what Lenora was doing now: searching online for any other articles or records of Haruto Tanaka.

She quickly realized the name was quite common, so more detailed information was needed about this Haruto Tanaka in the magazine article. Lenora had contacts everywhere, even at the Capitol Enquirer, so it was easy to get put through to their archives department, where she hoped they could answer her questions.

They could and did.

After getting the additional information she was hoping for, Lenora narrowed down her search and found two more articles about Haruto Tanaka, one of them a missing person report from six years ago.

Several hours later, and after extensive research on the other five people who had similar stories to tell, Lenora discovered there was another anomaly that tied all these people together, including her husband Simon: they all had mysteriously disappeared without a trace, all presumed dead.

All these people had something else in common, something Lenora didn't yet know about: They all had the same burn mark on their right wrists.

With all the information she had collated so far, Lenora was able to put together a timeline of events.

She knew Simon had his accident in July 2009, then vanished in October 2010. Haruto Tanaka apparently drowned seven years ago in September 2016 but survived, then was reported missing a few months later.

It was eerily similar for the other cases on her list too.

The Ghanaian man had survived a fifty-meter cliff fall in dense bushland, on July 31, 1981, while bushwalking alone and suffered no injuries. He returned home then disappeared a few months later while he was on a business trip. His wife had reported him missing. That was in late October 1981.

An Indigenous woman was supposedly bitten by a deadly poisonous snake three times in September 1988, survived, and went missing in January 1989. Nobody has seen her since.

A Romanian national traveling on a tourist visa, was mugged and then stabbed six times in an alley next to a nightclub he had just left in October 1995. No witnesses ever came forward, and the CCTV cameras in the alley were apparently not working that night. The man miraculously walked out of the alley sometime later after he was discovered by a security guard doing his rounds. The guard had found the man unconscious but with no injuries. The man's family in Romania had reported him missing in early 1996 when he failed to return home after his visa was due to expire.

The Jewish couple had committed suicide in early December 2002 after church elders discovered they had been embezzling funds from the Synagogue accounts. They had both ingested a lethal dose of ricin. However, both husband and wife woke up later alive in their bed, unharmed, except for a burn mark on their right wrists and a memory of a shadowy person telling them to 'be ready'.

The wife's sister reported them missing in January 2003 after they failed to return from a New Year's Eve trip to Capitol City.

Looking at the timelines now, Lenora saw that each 'death-life' event occurred in the second half of one year, then each of them had vanished within a few months – except Simon.

Additionally, she noted that there was seven years between each death-life experience.

This could be significant, she figured, but how and why? Lenora speculated that there must be some importance to the months as well, but why seven years apart?

Now, something else troubled her.

"Wait a minute," Lenora said out loud, but to no one.

She looked at the timelines again.

"1981, then every seven years to 2016?" she mumbled thoughtfully, then said, "Nothing for this year though."

And she was right.

There were no articles describing a 'shadow person' or being told to 'be ready' after Haruto Tanaka disappeared.

None that she could find anyway.

Maybe there *was* an incident, but it wasn't in the news or tabloids yet, Lenora pondered, or perhaps it hadn't happened yet. Another fact occurred to her: There are no death-life stories pre-1981.

What happened in 1981? Lenora jotted in her notebook.

Are there other mysterious disappearances before then?

If so, when? Shadow person?

Seven years apart, Lenora wrote, circled it, and added a big question mark.

FIVE

Capitol City, October, 13 Years ago.

By the time Lesley had arrived for her appointment at Capitol City General Hospital, her scheduled biopsy had turned into major surgery.

The attending neurosurgeon, Doctor Henry Jurgensen, after reviewing the MRI scans again, advised Lesley that this was the only course of action with this type of tumor, considering its position on the cerebellum.

Time was critical, he had told her, because of its size.

"Okay," a stunned Lesley had agreed, and all the paperwork and consent forms were then filled out.

Calls were made to Doctor Mac and Jennifer Henley, and they both assured Lesley that everything was under control and taken care of and not to worry about Amy because she was in good hands. Lesley called her mother too. Katharyn told her daughter she would be there.

Within the hour, Lesley was in the operating room and under anesthetic.

Lesley was dreaming of doves and butterflies. She could see two white doves flying around near some trees by a pond. She was sitting on a porch. The pond was glistening in the morning sunlight, and she saw a mother duck and her ducklings paddling on the other side towards the bank. Then a beautiful butterfly flew around in front of her, and when it landed on her stomach, she realized she was pregnant, maybe about six months along, and this made her happy. She smiled as she watched the butterfly open and close its colorful large wings several times.

Curiously, it looked as though the butterfly was watching her.

It flew off when a voice nearby called Lesley's name.

She watched the butterfly as it disappeared into a garden in full bloom near the porch, then she turned to see who was calling her. But she couldn't make out who it was because her vision was blurred by an intense light. The light then started to fade, and she felt herself drifting off somewhere. But the voice kept saying her name, an enquiring voice she realized, and she tried to refocus.

She closed her eyes and reopened them to see a man standing next to her.

"Lesley? Can you hear me? Lesley, wake up."

It was Doctor Jurgensen.

"Butterfly," Lesley mumbled as she came out of the anesthetic.

She stared at Doctor Jurgensen as if she didn't recognize him, confusion on her face.

"Lesley, you're in the ICU," he told her.

He glanced at the monitor, checking her vitals, then looked back at Lesley.

"The surgery went well…We were able to remove most of the tumor via craniotomy, as we discussed, and we have confirmed it's benign," Doctor Jurgensen explained, "so that's good news. We'd like to start a course of targeted radiation treatment as soon as possible, provided you are healing properly and have gained some strength."

Doctor Jurgensen looked at the two ICU nurses in the room.

"We'd like to get you up on your feet tomorrow and see how your balance is and if you feel any nausea while standing. Okay, Lesley?" Doctor Jurgensen asked, then nodded to the nurses, not waiting for a response from Lesley. "I'll check back in on you in the morning."

The doctor left the room.

Lesley was feeling sore and a bit foggy in her head, still not fully awake, but the pain was minimal because of the IV medication. She had heard some of what the doctor was telling her, although the details were vague in her mind. The ICU male nurse was checking Lesley's vitals and IV lines, while the lady nurse was performing stimuli response tests, checking that Lesley had feeling in all her limbs and extremities.

"Can you feel that, Lesley?" Nurse Amanda asked, rubbing a metal object on the sole of Lesley's left foot.

"Yes," Lesley responded softly, her eyes closed.

"What about now?" the nurse asked again, this time rubbing the sole of her other foot.

"Lesley? Lesley, can you feel that? Where am I touching?"

"Yes," Lesley answered, "my right foot."

The nurse continued her tests on other parts of Lesley's body: thighs, torso, arms, hands, fingers, and face. Lesley was asked to wiggle her toes, wiggle all her fingers, and move her head slowly from side to side. This last request was quite painful to perform, but she managed to do it. And after the nurse was done, Lesley was happy because it meant she had not lost any of her motor functions, which was great news.

"Brain surgery always poses risks," Doctor Jurgensen had advised Lesley at her pre-surgery consultation. "There are no guarantees."

"Is my baby okay?" Lesley mumbled, looking at the male nurse.

She saw his name badge.

It read 'Simon'.

"Baby?" Simon, the male nurse, enquired, looking confused.

He looked at Amanda for help, but she just shrugged and shook her head.

"Um…Yes," he replied hesitantly, looking at Amanda and shrugging also. "Everything is fine."

Lesley smiled and closed her eyes, feeling relieved.

When she opened her eyes again, Simon was checking the bandages around her shaved head, and she spotted an odd mark on his right wrist. It looked like a bird, but maybe it was a scar, she thought.

A swallow? A dove? Who knows, she wondered.

My head hurts and I'm feeling groggy. Could be any type of bird really. No. I think it's a scar, not a tattoo, more like a burn mark, she kept thinking while looking at Simon's wrist.

It's hard to focus now, she realized.

Her eyelids were getting heavy, the intravenous meds were doing their job, and Lesley was grateful for the pain relief.

As she was drifting off to sleep, she thought she heard the nurse called Amanda whisper, "Baby? What the hell was that all about, Simon?"

But Simon wasn't listening to her.

He was just staring at Lesley's bald head and at the birthmark on her neck behind her right ear. If her hair had not been shaved off before the surgery, it may not have been noticeable. But there it was, and Simon was staring at it with a very strange look on his face. Somehow, he recognized the birthmark – and what it meant.

It was the symbol of the 'Mother of Life'.

How do I know that? Simon wondered.

"Your time has come," a voice whispered in Simon's ear.

He spun around quickly, the voice familiar to him, but there was nobody in the room. Amanda had left, and Lesley was fast asleep. He looked down and touched the mark on his right wrist – the symbol of the Corvus – knowing what he now must do, then left the room.

Ten minutes later, Simon returned to Lesley's room.

He stood in the doorway for a moment, watching her as she slept. He wanted to be sure she was still asleep before he went in. He looked up and down the hallway. Nobody else was around. The nursing station was unoccupied as well.

His time had come, he was told.

Now was his chance.

In his pocket, he had a syringe containing fifty milligrams of Novolin, an insulin drug for type one and type two diabetes. Lesley was *not* diabetic.

Simon moved over next to Lesley's bed, watching her intently. Satisfied she was still sleeping, he removed the syringe from his pocket, then looked towards the door of the room, listening for noises.

The coast was still clear, he thought to himself.

He turned and reached for the IV line, which was supplying the Morphine to Lesley. Just as he was about to inject the Novolin into the IV line, he felt a presence behind him. Without warning, the syringe was knocked out of his hand, and it fell to the floor.

Simon spun around, anger and rage quickly building inside him, then immediately froze.

A stranger was standing in front of him.

He was tall, broad shouldered, with facial hair from not shaving for several days and longish brown hair. He was wearing nursing scrubs, but Simon had never seen him before. In that instant, Simon reacted, rushing forward, attempting to attack the stranger, but the stranger was too quick. He was behind Simon in a flash and picked up the deadly syringe. Simon turned and faced the stranger, seeing the syringe in his hand.

"My time has come," Simon snarled at the stranger. "She has the mark."

Lesley had stirred due to the commotion in her room and was groggily looking at the man with the syringe in his hand.

The stranger glanced at Lesley, their eyes locking momentarily. Simon lunged at the stranger again, but it was pointless. The stranger was too quick. He grabbed Simon on the left shoulder near his neck with one hand, stopping him instantly where he stood. The stranger turned back to Lesley, nodded once at her, and pressed the button on her IV station to give her a small dose of Morphine.

"You are safe," he told her, his voice a soothing melody.

A moment later, the stranger and Simon disappeared in an intense flash of light so bright it engulfed the entire room, temporarily blinding Lesley. When her eyes were able to focus a few seconds later, there was nobody in the room, no evidence that anyone had been there.

What just happened? Lesley wondered, as she drifted off to sleep again.

Down the hall from Lesley's room, the stranger entered the visitors' waiting lounge, stood tall, then bowed his head at the lady seated alone in the room.

"It is done. She is safe," he said.

Katharyn Jones got up out of her seat, nodded at the stranger, and said, "Thank you, Joshua."

She then left the visiting room, Joshua's eyes following her, and headed off to check on her daughter.

Lesley remembered nothing from that night, not even her mother being there.

....

A few months later, back in Henleyville, life was back to normal for Lesley.

It was early 2011, her hair was growing back, and she had finished the last of the radiation treatments at the larger regional hospital four hours' drive away. The tumor was gone, they had told her. Doctor Mac had requested they perform a final MRI just to be certain. The regional hospital had sent the scans over to City General Hospital at the request of Doctor Mac, and Doctor Jurgensen had given Lesley the all-clear.

It meant no more long drives back and forth on her days off to have the treatments, and she could now spend more time with Amy, just doing normal things again.

Immensely relieved and overjoyed at the news, Lesley organized a small thank-you party at Henleys Diner for those who had helped and supported her during her whole ordeal.

Almost everyone in town turned up that day.

Even her mother had come back from Capitol City to be there.

Katharyn Jones had spent most of her time in Henleyville looking after her granddaughter Amy while Lesley had been recovering. But she had returned to Capitol City a week ago to "attend to some business," she had told Lesley. Now, Katharyn was back in Henleyville, and Lesley noticed her mother seemed to be getting along quite well with John Miller.

Someone else was there too.

Someone Lesley didn't know.

He lingered around outside the diner for a while, watching Lesley through the windows, but she never saw him.

He was glad of this.

He didn't want to be noticed because people asked too many questions, and he always had to be vague in his answers, which annoyed him.

But Katharyn Jones saw him.

She knew who he was, too, and she acknowledged his presence with a slight nod.

SIX

Henleyville, Late September 2023

It was late in the evening, an hour to midnight. Amy had already gone to bed, leaving her mother alone in the lounge room watching a show on one of the streaming channels but barely paying any attention. Weary from the daily drudgery, Lesley yawned and looked at the clock on the wall. Noticing the lateness of the hour, she reached for the remote to turn off the TV and head off to bed, when the book on the coffee table caught her attention. Clicking off the television, Lesley picked up the book and sat back in the lounge, as if all her fatigue and sleepiness had now vanished.

Her mind was now completely occupied by the thought of reading the book. The unusual occurrences and her mother's words echoed in her head. Katharyn had instructed Lesley to read the 'Book of Adamah' because there was much her daughter did not know.

"There are things we need to discuss, Lesley. Family secrets," Katharyn told her daughter, knowing it was time Lesley learnt the truth.

"What family secrets, mother?" Lesley asked.

"The book, Lesley. Please read it first then I will tell you everything," Katharyn told her.

Lesley's imagination ran wild, thinking about what the book could hold.

She could not have estimated how old this ancient book was. A weathered, reddish-brown leather cover, its thick texture binding the archaic pages together. On the front of the book was an intricate design, a fusion of a tree of life motif intertwined with butterfly-like wings. She was fascinated and mesmerized by the book, however, at the same time, she was uncertain. Perhaps because of the mysterious nature of the book, she was unsure of how she would handle the information contained in it.

Nonetheless, intrigued by the design and her mother's words, she decided to read it as she ran her fingers over the elaborate symbol carved into the thick leather, wondering what it meant.

Taking a deep breath then exhaling, Lesley opened the book and began reading...................

The Legend of Adamah

In the beginning, there was only one realm: The Heavens.

Not satisfied with this, the Creators formed two more realms: The Light and The Darkness.

In The Light realm, the Creators made countless great celestial bodies shine in all its regions. And on one of these celestial bodies, which they called Adamah, they gave life to the terra with vast rivers and oceans of water. Many great creatures evolved from these waters to walk the lands and swim in the seas.

Eons passed, and the lands became silent.

The great creatures had gone.

Adamah needed new life.

So, from the waters, the Creators imagined a being: a woman, immortal, born of purity and with ageless beauty, and with the essence of nature, life, and death.

They named her Aryanna, and she bore the mark of the 'Mother of Life' over her heart, as decreed by the Creators.

Time passed, and Aryanna grew unhappy in The Light realm because she was lonely even though Adamah was bursting with the life that nature had created.

So, the Creators put life inside her, and she bore two children of purity: a girl child, born with the mark of the Swan, and a boy child, born with the mark of the Ouroboros.

She named them Adanne and Athanasius.

As they grew older, Athanasius became increasingly jealous of his sister Adanne because she was gifted with the ageless beauty of her mother, whom he worshipped and loved. Wanting his mother's love for himself, Athanasius decided to kill his sister, but in the act of doing it, his mother came between them, and she was mortally wounded by Athanasius. As she died in his arms, her life essence flowed back into the waters of Adamah from which she had come.

The Mother of Life was gone.

The Creators were furious.

For his crime, Athanasius was banished to The Darkness for all eternity.

Adanne was inconsolable after her mother's death.

Darkness filled the skies of Adamah as Adanne cried for seven days, then drowned in the flood of her tears, which had covered the lands.

The Creators had failed.

They had given no thought to evil intentions and their consequences, so they decided they would no longer be the creators of new life.

Instead, they passed into law that Nature was now the only giver of life, and all life could only be created in The Light. Evil now lived in The Darkness and no life should ever be created or fostered in it.

After many thousands of years, the darkness cleared, and brilliant light once again filled the skies of Adamah.

The floods, caused by the tears of Adanne, receded leaving rivers, oceans, and a great inland lake.

And out of the waters of the great lake came a woman, born in the light, and born of purity and with ageless beauty.

The 'Mother of Life' was reborn.

Aryanna had returned. And Nature had returned all her essence.

The Heavens rejoiced.

In celebration of Aryanna's return, the Creators ignored their own law and filled Adamah with many thousands of creatures born of the lands and seas. They also sent many Guardians down to Adamah to live as mortals, their goal to populate the lands and evolve.

But Aryanna was not happy, so the Creators asked her why.

She told them her heart was empty because her daughter was gone.

"And what of your son?" they asked her.

"I have no son," she replied.

In The Darkness, Athanasius heard these words spoken by his mother. His screams of sadness and pain echoed across all the realms.

"How can we heal your heart, Aryanna?" the Creators asked.

"I wish to grow life inside me again. A girl, born of no man," she said. "But she, and all who shall come from my blood, must be mortal. I shall not see another suffer for all eternity. This is my only request."

The Creators granted her wish.

And a girl was born of Aryanna, a child born of purity and with ageless beauty. And Aryanna was pleased. Her heart was filled with love again. She took her newborn daughter to the sacred waters of lake and bathed her clean.

A crowd had gathered to watch this.

Aryanna kissed her daughter on the head and said, "I name you Medora, and I give you my life. You shall bear a mark, a symbol of your purity, grace, and beauty. And no man shall ever create life with one who bears this mark."

Then Aryanna touched the head of her daughter, and a mark appeared where she had laid her hand.

It was the mark of The Dove.

"You now have my essence, my sweet child," Aryanna said, then turned and handed Medora to one of the people who had gathered there.

"The time will come when I shall return," Aryanna vowed, then exposing the birthmark on her chest for all to see, the mark the Creators had given her, she proclaimed, "I will be reborn in the pure one who bears this mark and avenge the sorrow of my first-born daughter."

Aryanna then walked into the sacred waters and disappeared into its depths, her essence returning to Nature once again.

Again, Athanasius screamed from The Darkness upon hearing his mother's words.

With evil and hatred now his only comfort, he vowed that any girl child born of his mother's blood shall die by his hand.

The Creators were watching from The Heavens, and having heard Athanasius' vow of revenge, they sent two new Guardians to Adamah, immortals, to protect, raise and guide Medora.

....

After reading the story for the third time, Lesley closed the old book her mother had given her for her fortieth birthday a few weeks back.

"It's just an old fable," she said to herself, staring at the cover.

Then, suddenly, she gasped because she remembered that Amy had a birthmark on her left hip. And the more Lesley saw it in her mind's eye, the more she came to realize it looked very much like a swan.

SEVEN

The planet TELLUS
Many thousands of years in the future

"We don't have much time left, Katharyn. The rift will close soon. We need to leave," Jonathon called to her from the terrace doorway, but she didn't hear him.

Tellus is so beautiful, Katharyn was thinking.

Her home, a magnificent structure, was perched high up on a mountain. As she stood there on the terrace, Katharyn gazed down into the valley and city below, surveying the lands the people of Tellus had called home for more than two thousand years. She loved it here, the same as her ancestors had loved Adamah before they were forced to leave it and find a new home.

Athanasius' reach seemed limitless.

And now, because of him, she was being forced to leave her homeland, the only home she had ever known.

How could she leave now and abandon the people she loved?

But Katharyn knew she had no choice.

The Corvidaens, Athanasius' death-dealing creatures that lived in The Darkness, would stop at nothing to ensure they acquired the power of 'The Pure' for him, the means by which he could escape The Darkness realm.

And that meant killing Katharyn.

She was the last of the pure-borns and a direct descendant of Aryanna, along with Athanasius. With Katharyn out of the way, Athanasius presumed he would be gifted the powers of The Pure, as was written in the ancient Book of Laws, a book created after the birth of The Light realm.

By ancient law, The Pure, the seven powers of the Creators, could only be passed down to a pure-born child in one of two ways: If the Creators willed it, or, 'if the child of the dove, the mother of the swan, takes no breath.'

To Athanasius, this meant he had found a way that he could receive the power of The Pure. He knew his mother, the mother of the swan – the swan being his sister Adanne - had died by his hand. And he knew Medora bore the mark of the dove, so he assumed if he was to kill any child born after Medora, then The Pure shall pass to him, as the only remaining pure-born child.

At least, that was his interpretation of the laws.

However, Athanasius was wrong in his assumption.

It was, in fact, a prophecy, foretold by the Creators and written into ancient law, but Athanasius didn't know that. He had spent every moment of his eternal existence seeking out every pure-born child and trying to end their life, not realizing it was pointless.

Even so, Katharyn and her Guardian, Jonathon, were no longer safe because they both knew Athanasius would not stop until he had achieved his goal.

Katharyn was born on Tellus, pure of heart and soul, gifted with ageless beauty and the ability to create life born of no man. She bore the mark of the dove, and Katharyn knew the blood of Aryanna, the 'Mother of Life', ran through her veins.

Her Guardians had told her this when she was old enough to understand, at her age of awareness. And they'd also told her of Athanasius' vow, screamed from The Darkness, which to date had proven true. From Adamah to Tellus, many generations of pure-borns had suffered the fate of Athanasius' deadly hand, each death marked with the symbol of the Ouroboros burned into their forehead, a reminder to all that his reach from The Darkness was infinite.

Now, as a young woman, Katharyn was nearing the age when she could fulfill her birthright by creating life inside herself and give birth to a pure-child born of no man.

Katharyn is a stunningly beautiful woman, more beautiful than any other on Tellus, and it is said the old Guardians believed she is the image of Medora.

Well, that's the story Jonathon had told her.

Jonathon looked at the wormhole in the sky beyond the valley. It was starting to close.

"The ship is ready," Jonathon said, coming up behind Katharyn on the terrace. "We must go now, Katharyn. The Corvidaens are near, and the ground forces are struggling to hold them off."

Katharyn turned to face Jonathon, her Guardian since birth. She noticed he was holding a large book in one of his hands. It looked very old. She put her hands to his bearded face, then kissed him on the cheek.

"You have always taken care of me, Jonathon," Katharyn said, her eyes a little teary. "It is one of the many reasons why I love you."

Jonathon had always struggled internally with his love for Katharyn. It had consumed him since his first moments with her here on Tellus the day she was born but in a good way.

Jonathon and Athena were Katharyn's Guardians.

But Athena was killed by the Corvidaens while she was trying to protect Katharyn's mother. Jonathon had managed to fight off and kill the creatures and save Katharyn, but sadly not her mother.

During the battle, Katharyn's mother had been infected by the 'Touch of Death' from a Corvidaen and died within two days. Jonathon had also sustained a life-threatening injury to his neck during the battle but managed to survive.

That was when Katharyn was fourteen years old.

And now, the Corvidaens were coming again.

They came each time Athanasius opened the rift from within The Darkness.

But this time, it was a battle Jonathon knew he could not win because he was the last Guardian, and the Corvidaens were always many. Even with the help of the soldiers of Tellus and their highly advanced weaponry, Jonathon knew it would take just one Corvidaen to get past him and the soldiers, and that would mean Katharyn's death.

Jonathon loved Katharyn as if she were his own daughter, and he would continue to protect her for as long as he had breath - this was *his* vow to her.

Katharyn watched him intently, knowing what was on his mind. She turned to see where his eyes were now focused on the sky and, more importantly, the rift in the time continuum that was slowly closing.

"Come on," Katharyn said. "Time is wasting. And we must destroy that thing."

They headed for their ship, one of several new galactic spacecrafts built specifically for this type of journey. Time spent on Tellus meant technology had advanced to astonishing new levels. Life had been good here.

Until now.

Another swarm of Corvidaens came out of the rift just as Katharyn and Jonathon got to their ship. The Tellus defense alert system sounded its warning again, and dozens of fighter ships took off and started firing at the swarm. The creatures were everywhere now. A large group of Corvidaens split from the main swarm and headed for the command center base, while the battle in the sky raged on. The creatures had located Jonathon and Katharyn and were homing in on them.

"Are you sure you can fly this thing?" Katharyn asked, looking around the flight control room of the ship.

"How hard can it be?" Jonathon replied, not looking up.

He was busily working the instruments of the flight console in front of him, then smiled at something that appeared on a small display screen.

"Yes!" Jonathon said loudly with excitement, then looked at Katharyn. "My friends have contacted us. They've found our new home and sent co-ordinates for a safe landing place, but…" he hesitated, looking at Katharyn as she strapped into her seat.

She looked at him when he stopped speaking.

"But what?" she asked, knowing she wasn't going to like the answer.

He grinned at her now.

"We might have to swim," he said.

Just as the swarm of Corvidaens reached the base, Jonathon engaged the drive engines, and the ship took off, heading straight for the rift in the darkening sky. They entered the wormhole just as it was starting to close. Jonathon pushed a button and released several massive explosive devices into the rift. They exploded, killing the Corvidaens that were trailing them, and the wormhole began to implode.

Their ship was struggling to stay ahead of the blast waves, and the shrinking abyss behind them seemed to be reaching out, trying to keep them inside it. The collapsing wormhole was now all around their ship, darkness engulfing the craft as it shook violently from the enormous blast wave that was now pushing them.

Katharyn looked at Jonathon with a look of impending doom on her face.

"Jonathon!" she cried out, gripping the arms of her seat tightly.

Looking over at her and seeing her face, Jonathon said, "Not going to happen," and he pushed the ship's speed control to maximum.

Within a few moments, they escaped from the rift just as another enormous explosion caused it to expand rapidly then implode into a void, creating a sound like an anguished scream that echoed across the sky.

Jonathon slowed the ship and it stabilized and stopped shaking.

"Wanna go again?" Jonathon said coyly to Katharyn, who was still gripping the arms of her seat and staring straight ahead.

Smiling to himself when Katharyn didn't respond, he looked to see they had emerged from the rift into a clear blue sky above an open stretch of land surrounded by dense bushland. In the distance was a vast body of water, a lake the size of which they had never seen before. It seemed to go on forever and was bordered by mountains and magnificent forests.

"That's it," Jonathon said, pointing to the lake. "Beautiful isn't it."

"We're landing on that?" Katharyn asked.

"No," Jonathon said. "In it."

Jonathon touched the control panel in front of him, and their spacecraft changed course and headed straight for the deepest part of the lake.

"Hold on," he said.

Their ship broke the surface of the lake in silence and descended slowly towards the bottom, where they saw a massive underwater cavernous structure, which was their destination. Carefully, Jonathon steered the ship deep inside the water cave, then swung it around to face out towards the opening. Satisfied the ship was far enough inside the cave depths, he shut down the drive engines and put the ship into standby mode.

"Welcome to Gaea," Jonathon said, looking at Katharyn.

"Gaea?" she replied.

"I'll let them know we've arrived," Jonathon said, ignoring Katharyn's obvious unspoken question. "We'll be safe here. It's a little primitive compared to Tellus, but we should blend in fine."

A short time later, Katharyn and Jonathon were standing on the shore of the lake, where a small group of people were waiting for them. Katharyn touched the side of her helmet near its neck panel, and it disappeared into the body-fitting space suit she was wearing. Jonathon did the same, then smiled at the waiting crowd.

Their welcoming party was six of Jonathon's closest and oldest friends he had not seen since they'd left Tellus during a rift cycle, hoping to find another planet suitable for them to live on and safe from the Corvidaens.

Francis and Mariangela, two of Tellus' most gifted and respected scientists, were the oldest and most senior. Raphael and Aniela, interstellar technology flight engineers, were a little younger, and Samuel and Laila, both skilled fighter pilots, were the youngest. But nobody could tell because they all looked very similar in age.

"It's good to see you, Francis," Jonathon said to the man at the front of the crowd. "All of you," he then said to the others.

Jonathon started taking off the backpack that he'd attached to his suit for the swim from the ship. Katharyn was doing the same.

Francis stepped forward.

"Jonathon, it's been a long time, old friend. I'm glad you are both safe," he said, embracing Jonathon with a warm hug, then looking at Katharyn.

But Katharyn wasn't looking at him or the other people.

She was looking up at the mountain to her right.

She stood silently surveying it, then looked back at the lake for a moment before returning her attention to the mountain again.

Something odd about that mountain, she thought.

Shaking off the feeling, Katharyn turned to Francis and the others who were watching her intently. They all looked different to the people back home on Tellus. It's the clothing, she concluded.

"Hello, Francis?" Katharyn said to the man next to Jonathon.

Francis held out his hand in greeting.

"Katharyn," he smiled at her as they shook hands. "Welcome. It's been a long time. You were just a young girl when I last saw you."

Francis then introduced the others to her.

After many uncomfortable hugs and shared greetings, Francis said to Jonathon and Katharyn, "There is much to tell. Grab your things. We must go. That explosion might have attracted attention."

The welcoming party all turned and headed to where they had parked their transport vehicles.

Jonathon picked up his backpack and looked at Katharyn, who was again looking at the mountain. She stood there a moment longer, then picked up her own backpack and headed in the direction the others had gone. Jonathon watched her walk off, then turned and looked at the same mountain. He seemed to recognize it and nodded slightly as he stared at it for a few seconds before running to catch up with Katharyn.

The transport vehicles were very primitive, Katharyn observed, as was the structure they were now standing in. None of the others seemed bothered about it. Even Jonathon was not fazed by any of this, she noticed. Francis saw Katharyn just standing inside the doorway, taking in her surroundings, and obviously not understanding anything of the past couple of hours.

"Katharyn," Francis said, getting her attention. "Come sit," he urged, waving a hand towards a long lounge. "Please."

Katharyn followed his instructions and sat down on it.

"Where are we?" she asked.

"This is Gaea," Francis replied, looking at the others seated in the room, "but they don't call it that here."

Katharyn looked at Jonathon.

"Welcome to Earth," he said, spreading his arms.

"Earth?" Katharyn replied, dumbfounded, looking back at Francis.

Francis moved and sat down next to Mariangela.

He glanced at her, then turned to Katharyn and said, "This *is* Gaea… but it has not been called that for many thousands of years. Well, actually, Earth people think Gaea is only a mythological name, so, historically, it has never officially been called Gaea."

Francis looked at Jonathon for a moment.

"But we know different," he continued, looking back at Katharyn. "Our history predates Earth's documented history, Katharyn."

"Earth," Katharyn repeated to no one in particular but then looked at Jonathon for more information.

"Yes," Jonathon said in response to her look. "This is planet Earth. It is called 'The Earth,' but it is also Gaea. They are the one and the same. Just in a different time."

Katharyn continued to look at Jonathon, waiting for more of an explanation.

He shrugged and said, "I'm a Guardian. I know things."

Katharyn kept staring at him, unconvinced.

"I've been around since long before you, Katharyn," Jonathan protested at her stare.

"A *very* different time," Francis stated, drawing back Katharyn's attention. "Your ancestors fled Adamah many millennia ago, as you know. They were a very skilled race of people, even back then."

Francis looked at Jonathon, who gave a slight nod of his head.

Francis continued, "When they arrived on Tellus, it was the Tellus you know of that they encountered, with a far superior advanced civilization living there."

He paused and looked at the others in the room who had remained silent.

"Your ancestors had traveled more than a hundred thousand years into the future, Katharyn," he told her, "Through a rift."

Katharyn was struggling to comprehend all this information.

She sat forward, put her elbows on her knees and her head in her hands. She remained like that for a few moments, not saying anything, then started shaking her head slowly in disbelief.

"One hundred thousand years?" Katharyn mumbled, then lifted her head out of her hands to look at Francis, then at Jonathon.

"Yes," Jonathon replied, in a gentle voice. "More than that, in fact. Time on Tellus is the same as time here."

"Then why is this place so… primitive?" Katharyn asked, looking at everyone in the room.

"Because we've gone back in time a few thousand years," Jonathon said. "… And there's something else you need to know. Adamah… is Tellus. Tellus is Gaea… and Gaea is Earth. It's all the same place."

Katharyn got up, shaking her head in disbelief, and started pacing the floor. Everyone watched her but nobody said anything. Katharyn then stopped, turned, and faced them all.

"*When* are we?" she asked.

"1980," came a chorus of voices all at once from everyone in the room.

EIGHT

Francis and Mariangela had prepared some food for Katharyn, Jonathon, and themselves. It was dark outside now, and the others had gone home.

"Going home?" Katharyn had queried when Raphael, Aniela, Samuel, and Laila had said they were leaving. "To Tellus?"

"No, our homes here," they told her, and left.

Katharyn remained on the front porch of the house, after watching the others drive away in their primitive transport vehicles, standard automobiles for 1980 Earth, though. Jonathon noticed Katharyn was looking up into the clear night sky, which was filled with millions of bright stars.

It was very familiar to Katharyn.

She had gazed into the very same night sky many times during her life, and seeing it here in this different time period, gave her some comfort.

"Beautiful, isn't it," Jonathon had remarked.

When they came back inside, Katharyn and Jonathon were taken upstairs and shown to their rooms. Katharyn took a long overdue shower to freshen up before coming back downstairs for the evening meal.

"At least there's hot water in 1980," Katharyn joked as she sat down at the table, joining the others.

She saw that Jonathon had also showered and changed his clothes, with his long hair now tied back.

The food Mariangela had prepared was wonderful.

"It's a beef stew with lots of vegetables," she told Katharyn.

Jonathon seemed to be really enjoying it because he was gulping it down like a starving warrior. They all stopped what they were doing to watch the spectacle. He looked up from his plate and saw them all staring at him.

"What?" he said, to their incredulous stares, holding his fork at the ready. "I'm hungry. Immortals have to eat too. This is good, Mariangela."

He then continued shoveling the food into his mouth. Katharyn shook her head at him, and they all laughed.

The food was good, Katharyn had to admit, and she said as much to Mariangela who thanked her. It was rich and hearty, and it filled them all up. Jonathon enjoyed it so much he asked for a second helping and then a third.

After the meal was finished, and the table was cleared, they sat there drinking hot beverages and making small talk.

Katharyn put down her cup and asked, "Francis, how long have all of you been here?"

"Well… we left Tellus the last time the rift appeared, which in Tellus time, was seven years ago. But, in the rift, time is relative… and irrelevant. Wormholes bend time and space, Katharyn, so unless you have exact time-space co-ordinates," he said, looking at Jonathon, then back to Katharyn, "you could end up anywhere... and in anytime."

When he didn't continue, Katharyn said, "So…?"

"So…" he said, drawing out the sound of the word, "We were supposed to arrive in the twenty-fifth century, but something happened inside the rift, and… we landed in the twentieth century instead. 1970 to be precise."

"You've been here, in this time, for ten years?" Jonathon asked, astonished.

"Yes," Mariangela responded.

"But you look exactly the same as the last time I saw you both," Jonathon stated.

Mariangela said, "It's in our DNA. Remember?"

With a sudden realization, Jonathon nodded.

They all sat in silence, processing what had been said.

Katharyn was the first to speak.

"I felt something strange when our ship was going through that thing, Jonathon," she said to him. "It felt like something, or someone was trying to get hold of me. But I was so scared at the time, I wasn't aware it had happened till now."

Jonathon just nodded in silence, looking at Katharyn knowingly.

"I think we destroyed the rift," Jonathon eventually said.

"Hmm," Francis said, "they have a saying here: time will tell."

It was getting late, and there was a lot of new information for Katharyn to absorb. Everyone was tired. So, they got up to head to their rooms for the night. Katharyn stopped in the doorway of the dining room and turned to Francis.

"This place where you all have been living, what do they call it, Francis?" she asked.

"Henleyville," he replied.

....

The following morning, at breakfast, Francis was explaining to Jonathon that there was still much to discuss and plans to be made.

"Where is *your* ship?" Jonathon asked Francis.

"In the lake. Same as yours," he replied. "Don't worry. They are both safe. The lake is only used for fishing and swimming. Nobody knows about those hidden caves way down in its depths."

"Why didn't you come back?" Jonathon asked.

"We couldn't," Francis said. "The ship sustained some damage going through the rift. The control system for the main drive engines was destroyed. We only just managed to escape the rift before it closed."

"Couldn't Raphael and Aniela fix it?" he asked.

"No. Not with 1980's technology. Unfortunately," Francis replied.

"I thought you were all dead," Jonathon told him.

"No, my friend," Francis said smiling, "Just stuck… We've sent numerous communications since we arrived here, but we've had no response."

"Hmm. I asked for help many times, Francis, but none of your powerful colleagues would listen," Jonathon told him.

Mariangela handed Katharyn a hot beverage when she came into the kitchen. Katharyn accepted the drink and was looking strangely at Mariangela's attire. Over her dress, Mariangela had another garment wrapped around her. It had pictures of plants and flowers on it and was tied at the back and around her neck.

Katharyn thought it looked very odd.

"What is that you're wearing?" she asked.

"It's called an apron," Mariangela replied, smiling. "Come. Let's all sit at the table. There's more for you to know."

They all sat down, then Francis began talking.

"It's very different here than it is on Tellus. Obviously," he quickly added, seeing Katharyn's raised eyebrows. "Firstly, our names."

Mariangela continued the conversation.

"Everyone has two names here. A first name and a last name," she told them.

Katharyn had a blank look on her face.

"On Tellus," Francis said, "we have one name only… as you know, but here you need a second name. A last name, or surname, as they call it here, to distinguish between families and other people with the same first name."

"So, you have two names now?" Jonathon asked them.

"Yes," Mariangela replied. "We are the Coopers," she stated happily, smiling at Katharyn and Jonathon.

Francis quickly added, "Frank Cooper and Marie Cooper."

"Frank and Marie?" Katharyn repeated.

"Yes," Frank said. "We shortened our names to fit in more with the time here. Everyone does it."

"You can be John," Marie said, smiling at Jonathon. "And you could be Kate or Kathy," she said to Katharyn.

Katharyn was mortified at this suggestion, and her facial expression clearly displayed this.

"My name is Katharyn," she said firmly to everyone. "I will not be changing it."

The others nodded, accepting her decision, not wanting to upset her.

"But you will need a last name, Katharyn," Frank urged gently. "For things like identification documents, bank accounts, obtaining medical assistance, and other things like that."

Jonathon asked, "Cooper? How did you come up with that name?"

"We have a small business here in town where I make buckets, barrels and other storage containers out of wood I get from the timber mill," Frank explained. "A person who makes those kinds of things is called a cooper apparently, so we decided that would be our second name: Cooper."

Katharyn and Jonathon both said nothing.

Frank added, "And that's another thing. You both need to get jobs. Nothing here is free like it is on Tellus. Everything costs money… and the only way to get money is to earn it."

"Money?" Katharyn parroted.

Frank explained, "It's a currency that has value, and everything here has a price or cost. If you want or need something, you must buy it… with money."

"Frank makes the wooden containers," Marie said, "and we sell them in our little shop in town. That's our business. People pay us money to buy the things Frank makes."

"We both worked in the timber mill at first and saved most of the money we were paid so we could start the cooper business… We've done alright for ourselves, too," Frank said, smiling at Marie, "which is how were able to build this house."

"It's important that you fit in," Marie told them. "Try to look and act like an average person, and dress like the locals, so nobody bothers you. That's the goal."

Frank got up and went over to a hall stand, picked up a large book about three inches thick, brought it back, and dropped it down in the middle of the table.

"You need to pick a last name. Pick one out of this," he suggested, pointing to the book.

"What's that?" Katharyn asked.

"A phone book. It's got hundreds of thousands of last names in it," he said. "I suggest you pick one that a lot of people have. The more common, the better."

Katharyn pulled the phone book over to in front of her, opened it near the beginning, and saw that names were listed up and down each page in rows. Hundreds on each page. She flicked through the pages quickly to see it was the same throughout the whole book.

"I'm not changing my name," Katharyn said, then opened the phone book at a random page, closed her eyes, and dropped her right index finger onto the page.

She opened her eyes and looked at the page.

Frank leaned over to see where her finger was touching the page.

"Okay," he said, straightening back up, "Katharyn Jones it is."

....

A little while later, Frank took Jonathon to his shop in town while Marie and Katharyn stayed at the house. Marie had suggested she could help Katharyn pick out some clothes to wear and give her more advice and information about Henleyville and the requirements of living in these new times. Frank had agreed.

There were people everywhere in the town center.

It was a busy day in Henleyville, and Saturday was his best business day, Frank had told Jonathon on the drive to the shop.

And he was right.

Customers had not stopped coming into his store this morning, buying pieces that Frank had made recently. Jonathon had watched the comings and goings with amusement because everyone had looked at him strangely when they first entered the store, then made an obvious effort to keep clear of him.

Frank was writing something down in a large book on his counter after having just sold a couple of items to a nice gentleman who had chatted with Frank for ages, all the while glancing at Jonathon with an alarmed look on his face.

"People are friendly here," Jonathon said deadpan when the man left the store.

"What were those things he purchased?" he asked.

Frank stopped and looked at Jonathon, knowing full well why the good folk of Henleyville seemed very wary of Jonathon. He turned back to his notebook and made another entry.

"Napkin holders," Frank replied. "I make all sorts of things here, Jonathon."

Frank closed the book he'd been writing in.

"Come," he said, looking at the clock on the wall. "I'll show you out back. I'm due for a break anyway."

The back of the store was a workshop full of timber, benches, tools, and items Frank was making or had finished making. It smelled like nature in the workshop, and Jonathon noticed it, taking in the aroma. He smiled and nodded with pride at Frank.

"You have many hidden talents, Francis," Jonathon said. "And it smells great in here."

Frank looked around his workshop, at his creations, his livelihood, and smiled in pleasure.

"I really enjoy this life, Jonathon… And you must start calling me Frank. Okay?" he said, the smile fading.

Jonathon held up his hands, surrendering to the request.

Frank said, "Remember. It's important you blend in."

He paused for a moment looking Jonathon up and down.

"Which is why you need to change your name. Jonathon is too formal… This is a small country town. People here don't like *formal*," Frank explained, emphasising the last word.

"O…K," Jonathon replied, rolling his eyes because he knew one of Francis' famous lectures was about to begin.

"You need to find work, also," Frank went on, ignoring Jonathon's sarcasm.

"I have a job, *Frank*," Jonathon said, the sarcastic emphasis on his name not going unnoticed by Frank. "I protect Katharyn."

Frank shook his head.

"You and Katharyn can stay for as long as you need, Jonathon, but you need an income, a way of earning money," Frank said, waving his hand at the workshop, "to support yourselves, to purchase necessities, and live in this time period."

Frank stopped and looked at Jonathon, who did not like any of this.

"There's something else too," Frank said, then hesitated. "…. Here, in Henleyville, you shouldn't live together unless you are married."

Jonathon reacted angrily.

"I'm a Guardian, Francis. Sent to protect the pure-borns. Guardians can't marry!"

"I know, I know," Frank said, putting his hands up, trying to calm Jonathon. "But they have a weird moral code in this town. Unwed people living together is frowned upon here."

Frank then paused, a thought coming to him.

"Or…" he began.

When Frank didn't continue, Jonathon asked, "Or what?"

Frank looked at him.

"You could just tell everyone Katharyn is your daughter."

Jonathon opened his mouth to say something but stopped, contemplating the suggestion.

Frank walked over to one of his work benches and picked up an item he had not finished making yet. He turned it over in his hands and pretended to adjust something, wrestling with his conscience about how to bring up the next subject - a very sensitive subject.

"You haven't told her, have you?" Frank said without looking at Jonathon.

It was a statement rather than a question, and Jonathon visibly bristled as the words found his ears.

"Told who what?" Jonathon replied, pretending he didn't know what Frank was talking about.

But he did know.

And that unspoken truth still burned hard in his heart. Because how could he tell the woman he thought of as his own daughter that he had failed many times since the beginning?

Frank had finished pretending to fix the little wooden object. He put it back down on the bench and walked over to Jonathon, who was clearly distressed.

"I know Katharyn is very special to you, my friend, and I know why too. You told me, remember?" Frank said, putting his hand on Jonathon's shoulder, not lecturing anymore. "But I think it's time she knows everything."

The bell above the front door of Frank's store jingled several times, indicating a customer had come in. Hearing the bell, Frank turned and headed towards the door between the workshop and the store.

"Break's over," Frank said, then stopped as he got to the doorway.

He turned back and looked at Jonathon, who was still lost in his thoughts.

"One more thing, Jonathon…" he said, pausing so Jonathon would look at him, "you need to get a haircut."

Frank then disappeared through the doorway and into the front section of his store to attend to the customer. Jonathon lifted a hand and ran it through his long messy locks. You couldn't blame the townspeople of Henleyville for being wary of Jonathon. After all, he did look like a homeless mountain man who hadn't seen civilization for decades.

NINE

Frank closed his shop just after midday and took Jonathon for a tour around the town center. They had lunch at Henleys Diner, one of several small businesses owned by the Henleys, apart from the timber mill just outside of town.

Walter Henley inherited the timber mill his grandfather had built back in 1875. Walter was a young man of thirty in 1940 when his father died suddenly of heart failure, and Walter, being the only son, had to step in and take the reins of the family business.

Since that day, Walter Henley had done marvelous things in his forty years at the helm of the family business. Henleyville had prospered enormously off the back of the mill's success. The town had a hospital, a library, several churches, a massive community hall, a county courthouse, and a municipal building, all built by Walter Henley. The main street and town square had become a small thriving metropolis, and the population had grown to what it is today courtesy of the Henley family's generosity.

The town, and most of its residents, loved the Henleys.

With the short history lesson over, Frank and Jonathon left the diner. They were walking back to Frank's vehicle when they came to the barber shop, so Frank, thinking quickly, ushered Jonathon inside and introduced him to the owner, Gill McBride.

Silence fell over the shop like a heavy blanket the moment Frank and Jonathon walked in. No one spoke or moved. It was as if time had stopped, and Frank noticed that all eyes were clearly focused on Jonathon.

"Gill. Hi," Frank said in greeting. "This is my cousin John. He's come for a visit."

Frank looked at Jonathon and shook his head slightly.

"He was hoping for a shave and a haircut, if you can fit him in," Frank told Gill.

Jonathon stood still, bemused, and caught off guard.

"Well, good afternoon, Frank," Gill McBride replied. "Sure, I can."

He walked over to them, smiled, and greeted them both with a handshake.

"Nice to meet you, John. Come take a seat here," he said, gesturing to the only unoccupied barber chair.

The shop had four barber chairs, each facing a mirror so the customer could watch while the barber did his work. The other three barber chairs were taken, their occupants watching with wide eyes as Jonathon walked over and sat down in the chair.

Gill McBride wrapped a large dark sheet around Jonathon's shoulders, secured it around his neck and clipped it in place. The sheet covered his arms, body, and the tops of his legs, Jonathon noticed.

"So," Gill said, looking at Jonathon in the reflection of the mirror and clicking the scissors in his hand, "let's see what we can do."

A couple of hours later, Frank and Jonathon walked through the front door of Frank's house and were met with curious stares from Katharyn and Marie. Marie smiled and kissed Frank on the cheek, then they both stood watching as Katharyn silently stared at Jonathon, who was becoming more self-conscious the longer the silence continued. Much of his long wild hair had been cut off and styled into a cut most of the men in town wore, and his face was now clean-shaven, revealing his manly jawline and handsome features.

Katharyn was awestruck and gaped in wonder at Jonathon's transformation.

"I'm hideous!" he exclaimed, then turned and walked back outside. "Athena would be ashamed of me."

"No, Jonathon," Katharyn said, catching up to him on the porch. "Athena would be proud of you because you did this for me... for us."

The scar on Jonathon's neck just below his jawline was obvious now. Katharyn had not seen it before because Jonathon's beard and long hair had hidden it. She looked at it now, knowing its cause, remembering that day and the days after when she had cried for her mother, and prayed for Jonathon's survival.

"I'm proud of you, too," Katharyn said, tears welling in her eyes from the memories. "And I think you look handsome."

Jonathon sighed and looked down at Katharyn standing next to him. He saw her eyes were wet with emotion, so he put his arms around her and hugged her, his chin resting softly on the top of Katharyn's head.

After a few moments, he whispered, "I miss them, too."

Later in the afternoon, Katharyn was in the kitchen helping Marie prepare the evening meal. The men were sitting on the front porch, watching kids go by on their bikes and the neighbors out walking their dogs. They waved at Frank as they passed by the big tree at the end of his driveway. Frank waved back.

"Katharyn enjoys being around Marie," Jonathon said, waving to the neighbors as well. "I can see it."

Frank smiled and said, "Marie is in her element, my friend. She told me she gave Katharyn some of her dresses that don't fit her anymore. She thinks they will be perfect for Katharyn."

Jonathon just nodded, now deep in thought.

Frank looked at Jonathon, who was clearly a few sizes too big for the shirt Frank had given him, and said, "And we need to get you some new clothes as well."

Jonathon looked down at the clothes he was wearing and nodded in agreement.

"The timber mill you were telling me about at lunch," he said, looking at Frank, a thought coming to him. "Does it smell like your workshop?"

Frank smiled and nodded.

"Yes. Why do you ask?"

Jonathon turned in his seat and faced Frank.

"Do you think I could work there?" he asked.

"Sure," Frank said, "they're always hiring."

"What do they call the people who work in a timber mill?" Jonathon asked, his mind ticking over.

"Well..." Frank said, thinking, "There's machine operators, timber cutters, laborers, millers..."

"That's it!" Jonathon exclaimed, startling Frank a little. "Miller! That's what I'll be."

"A miller?" Frank stated rhetorically. "Good. I'll take you down to the mill on Monday,"

"Yes. I'll be John Miller," Jonathon proclaimed with a big smile on his face.

....

Monday morning, The Henley Timber Mill hired John Miller on the spot and put him to work straight away, which pleased Jonathon immensely. The timber mill did smell like Frank's workshop but much better. Jonathon loved the smell of the freshly cut timber and the forest smells from the tree logs piled up around the mill yard. He was in his element and by the end of his first day, he'd made friends with all the other timber workers who were amazed at Jonathon's strength and agility.

Over the next few weeks, Jonathon – now called John Miller – settled easily into his work routine and, from his wages, bought several sets of new work clothes. He'd also given some money to Frank and Marie for food, and he offered the rest to Katharyn to go shopping in town. She had refused at first but, seeing the look on Jonathon's face, she accepted his gift. Marie was excited too because the ladies' shop in town had stocked up with some new clothing lines, and she told Katharyn they must go there.

"You can buy a dress for the opening of the new school," Marie excitedly told Katharyn.

At the end of Old Mill Road, on a massive block of vacant land, Walter Henley built a brand-new school for Henleyville, and its grand opening was coming up on Saturday. Frank had told them the whole town would probably be there, as well as various newspaper journalists and several photographers from a big city television network because the mayor himself, old Walter Henley, would be cutting the ribbon at eleven am.

On Saturday morning, Frank and John stood in the front hallway, dressed immaculately, waiting for Marie and Katharyn to come downstairs. John felt very uncomfortable wearing the new crisp shirt and tie Frank made him buy for this occasion. He kept pulling at the neck of his shirt, feeling like he was choking. Marie came down first, and she looked wonderfully radiant with her hair done differently from how she usually wore it. Both men complimented her, and Frank kissed Marie on her cheek.

Frank looked up and saw Katharyn at the top of the stairs.

He looked at Marie who was smiling and nodding.

Frank tapped John on the arm, nodding in the direction of the stairs, and John turned to see Katharyn slowly coming down, a vision of pure beauty and glamour. The new dress was sheer and light and hugged Katharyn's svelte frame as if it were made for her. Her hair, normally pulled back in a ponytail, was newly styled and loose, flowing down over and around her shoulders.

John's eyes widened at the vision of Katharyn descending before him, and his mind instantly transported him back to a time long ago.

"Medora," John said, barely audible.

He was stunned.

He thought his eyes were deceiving him because Medora, the daughter of Aryanna, was coming down the stairs.

Frank heard what John had said.

"Katharyn," Frank said loudly, to snap John out of his memory, "Wow!"

John was amazed by Katharyn's transformation and remained still, silently gazing at her.

Katharyn was beaming, a smile spread across her face.

"Thank you, Frank," she said, "But Marie deserves all the credit."

"Nonsense," Marie said, smiling at her. "I just played with your hair a little."

Katharyn noticed that John was just staring at her, saying nothing, with a look of horror on his face.

"Jonathon. You don't like it?" she said, turning around where she now stood, showing off her dress.

"Yes," John said, weakly. "Yes. Sorry… Katharyn, you took my breath away that's all... I've never seen you like this before. It... suits you."

Katharyn is the spitting image of Medora, John was thinking. *Medora, the first of many I have failed to save.*

With this realization, John was almost overcome with long-suppressed emotions.

Seeing John struggling and with an understanding of why, Frank said, "Ready? Let's go, shall we."

From the Cooper house, it was a short walk to the end of Old Mill Road where the new school and its grounds encompassed several hectares of prime real estate. Frank had been right. It seemed like everyone in Henleyville was there. Dozens of newspaper reporters, two television vans, food trucks, and market stalls filled the grounds to the left of the school. Near the front entrance to the main building a small stage had been set up. It had a podium with several microphones attached and on the stage were about a dozen chairs for the invited dignitaries.

The reporters were busily preparing themselves and writing notes on hand-held notepads while several photographers were snapping shots of the school and the surrounding facilities.

People couldn't help but notice when Frank, Marie, John, and Katharyn entered the school grounds because Katharyn looked like a glamorous movie star. Some people started clapping, which caught the attention of the reporters and photographers who all rushed to see why the applause had started.

One reporter asked Katharyn if she was a movie star or a model, as the excited photographers snapped photos of her.

"No," Katharyn had said, shyly.

"Well, you should be," said one of the photographers.

He handed Katharyn his business card and said, "Call me."

At that moment, Walter Henley walked onto the stage and tapped one of the microphones, which got the attention of everyone there, including the photographers and reporters, who ran to get good vantage points near the front.

Katharyn looked at the business card in her hand, then looked at John and smiled.

Later that afternoon, back at Frank and Marie's place, they were joined by Raphael, Aniela, Samuel, and Laila who had all been at the opening of the new school as well.

Marie and Katharyn had made refreshments, while Frank, with the help of Raphael and Samuel, was busily cooking various sorts of meats on an outdoor grill, which was now all the rage according to him. A large table was set up in the back yard and all the ladies were sitting at it, sipping their drinks.

Katharyn looked over to where John had remained, standing alone since they'd come outside. He'd been acting strangely all afternoon, Katharyn had noticed, as had all the others.

Frank, spotting Katharyn looking at John, handed the cooking utensil he was using to Raphael and patted him on the shoulder before heading over to John.

"Everything okay, big guy?" Frank asked, seeing a pained expression on John's face.

John stood in silence, staring off into the distance, then he turned his head to look over at the table where Katharyn was seated. Frank followed John's gaze.

"I failed her," John said.

"Who?" Frank asked, "Katharyn?"

"No," John replied, looking down at the ground in front of him. "Medora."

Frank said nothing, understanding his friend was in immense internal pain and turmoil.

"And every one of them since," John added, almost in tears but holding them back. "I was lucky to survive when they came for Katharyn and her mother… Athena gave her life for me, Frank."

John was clearly at the edge, barely holding in his emotions, something a Guardian is not known to express or display. Frank knew his old friend well and could see that he was visibly struggling. Thankfully, they were far enough away from the table where the ladies were chatting and laughing.

But Katharyn had noticed.

"What do you mean, John?" Frank asked.

John looked off into the distance again, remembering the day the Corvidaens had taken the lives of his eternal partner Athena, and Katharyn's mother, Nakoma. Frank said nothing while he waited for John to decide if he was going to tell the story.

"You, Mariangela, and the others had gone into the rift… just as it was closing," John began, looking at Frank, who nodded but remained silent.

"The Corvidaens got through. Thousands of them this time…. We managed to kill a lot of them but there was just too many of them, Frank…. so many of them," he said, with the events of that day still painfully fresh in his mind…….

TELLUS

Jonathon watched from the ground as the ship carrying his friends flew into the rift and disappeared inside it.

"Safe journey, Francis," Jonathon whispered as he watched the rift slowly closing.

At that moment, a massive number of Corvidaens burst from the rift just before it closed. At first it looked like a big dark cloud, but Jonathon quickly realized, as the cloud separated and dispersed into swarms of screaming deadly creatures, that he was mistaken. The Tellus defense system sirens began wailing as Jonathon watched the Corvidaens circle and separate into smaller groups, most of which landed on the grounds in the city area.

But one small swarm remained in the air and headed for the mountain where Nakoma and Katharyn lived.

"Athena!" Jonathon roared, then turned and ran, with the lightning speed afforded to all immortal Guardians, in the direction the Corvidaens were heading.

Arriving at the outside terrace of Nakoma's home fortress, Jonathon saw Athena watching the Corvidaens coming towards them. Not seeing Katharyn or her mother anywhere, Jonathon began to panic.

"Where's Katharyn and Nakoma?" he called out, causing Athena to turn around.

"Nakoma is in the safe room," Athena replied, then looked behind Jonathon, and finding nobody, she said, "I thought Katharyn was with you."

Jonathon looked to the sky and figured the Corvidaens would be upon them within seconds.

Turning to head inside, Jonathon said, "Keep Nakoma safe. I'll find Katharyn."

He then disappeared in a flash to search for her.

Athena raced to the safe room and just got the heavy door closed in time before the Corvidaens arrived.

"We're trapped!" Katharyn's mother Nakoma yelled, holding the weapon Athena had given her, and pointing it towards the door of the safe room.

Outside, the Corvidaens were trying to break through, their piercing screams echoing throughout the building as they continued their efforts to force their way into the room. Athena was using all her strength to hold them off, trying to keep the door closed.

"Katharyn!" Nakoma yelled, realizing they were the only ones in the room. "Where's Katharyn?"

"Jonathon has gone to get her," Athena yelled above the din outside.

Unable to hold them off any longer, the Corvidaens broke through, and Athena was thrown across the room from the force of the door breaking from its hinges. Nakoma screamed and started firing her weapon at the Corvidaens now filling the room, killing some of them, but missing a lot. Athena rolled onto her back where she had landed and started firing her weapon also.

As both weapons found their targets, Corvidaens disappeared into nothing as they died, their death screams echoing around the room.

But Athena was not quick enough to kill them all, and something was wrong with Nakoma's weapon. It had stopped firing and several Corvidaens were closing in on her.

Nakoma screamed out, "Athena!"

Athena saw Nakoma was in danger and fired at the creatures, one of which now had Nakoma in its grasp. Athena killed it just as Jonathon entered the room, with Katharyn tucked closely behind him.

"Mother!" Katharyn exclaimed as she rushed over to where Nakoma was lying motionless on the floor, a burn mark now visible on her forehead.

Athena rose to her feet as she watched Katharyn kneel beside her mother.

Jonathon stood motionless just inside the room, and seeing Nakoma, dropped the weapon he was holding to the floor and lowered his head, realizing he had failed once again to protect a pure-born.

From out of nowhere, another Corvidaen, a much larger one, burst into the room behind Jonathon.

"Jonathon! Watch out!" Athena yelled, throwing herself between Jonathon and the creature.

Jonathon barely had time to react as the Corvidaen struck out at Athena with its razor-sharp talons, slicing into her chest and piercing her heart. Athena fell to the floor as Jonathon ducked under another swipe from the massive creature and then picked up the weapon he had dropped. He was just about to fire when the Corvidaen came at him, slashing at him with its talons. Jonathon fired several times into the creature as it attacked him again and managed to kill it, but not before he sustained a severe injury.

Bleeding profusely from a deep gash on his neck, Jonathon stumbled towards Athena, and fell to his knees next to her.

"Athena!" Jonathon cried out.

But it was too late because all the life was gone from her eyes.

....

Frank's backyard

Frank remained silent.

This was the first time he had heard this story and Jonathon was clearly still distressed about the events. Frank put a hand on John's shoulder.

"I'm sorry, Jonathon," Frank said, saying his proper name out of respect.

They both looked over at Katharyn, who was watching them.

"Katharyn has never spoken about that day," John said, locking eyes with Katharyn for a moment before looking away. "I'm sure she blames me."

TEN

It was late, almost midnight. Jonathon couldn't sleep because the memories of that fateful day on Tellus were still haunting him. The night air was cool and crisp, and Jonathon was leaning on the porch railing, staring up into the starry night sky, the weight of the world seemingly on his shoulders.

He hadn't noticed Katharyn was standing silently in the doorway watching him. She eased up behind him and put a hand on his shoulder, which startled him. He turned to see Katharyn looking at him worriedly.

"Katharyn," John said. "It's late. What are you doing up?"

"Couldn't sleep," Katharyn spoke softly. "Same as you, I'm guessing."

John said nothing.

He looked up into the night sky again. Katharyn moved next to him and did the same.

"Do you think she is up there watching over us?" Katharyn asked.

John glanced at Katharyn and asked, "Your mother?"

"No, Jonathon," Katharyn replied, turning to look at him. "Athena."

John looked away quickly trying to hide his surprised expression. He was suddenly overcome with emotions again and Katharyn noticed him struggling to keep them bottled up.

"I was watching you today, Jonathon," Kathryn said, breaking the silence between them, "when you and Francis were talking… I've seen that look before… the same look you have now."

Jonathon looked at her now but said nothing, and Katharyn knew she was right.

"I know you loved Athena. So did I…. and I know you blame yourself, but I don't, Jonathon," Katharyn said, touching his arm.

John's chest heaved and he sighed heavily, trying to hold himself together.

"If I'd got there quicker," he finally said.

"No," Katharyn replied. "I should've stayed at home with Mother as you had always told me to do whenever the rift opened… If anyone is to blame, it is me."

John said nothing because he didn't blame Katharyn at all.

He only blamed himself.

It was his job to protect her and her mother.

He thought he'd have enough time to say goodbye to Francis, Mariangela, and the others before they left. He'd watched their ship take off and fly into the depths of the rift. But he'd stood there far too long, he now knew, watching as the Corvidaens come through at the last moment before the rift closed.

Yes, in his mind, he was to blame, no one else.

"I should've gone with you," John eventually said.

Katharyn smiled and shook her head slightly.

"You wouldn't have let me go, Jonathon. That's why I snuck off… to the launch site," she said. "I was watching them, too. I wanted to know about the people who were leaving Tellus. I'd heard you and Athena discussing it one night… I was on my way back when you found me."

"You were there?" Jonathon asked, a confused look on his face.

Katharyn dropped her head and nodded.

"I saw you there. I watched you all say goodbye… And I watched them take off and go into the rift. That's when I headed back home," she explained, guilt in her voice.

John sighed and looked away, contemplating everything Katharyn had just told him. Eventually, he turned and faced her.

"Why didn't you ask me?" John asked.

"Athena said you would say no… *Would* you have let me go with you?" she asked.

John dropped his eyes momentarily, then said, "I don't know… probably not. No."

Katharyn responded with a shrug that implied, 'See, Athena was right.'

They both stood in silence for a while, gazing into the heavens. Katharyn glanced sideways at John, then again noticed the large scar on his neck. She knew this man, her immortal Guardian, would do anything to protect her, including sacrificing himself.

Jonathon didn't know that it had been Katharyn who'd saved his immortal life that day after he collapsed unconscious and bleeding to death. She had somehow managed to stem the blood flow and held firm pressure on the neck wound until the medical specialists arrived.

Jonathon had teetered on the edge of death for many days. No medical specialist had ever operated on a Guardian before, let alone an immortal, and Jonathon had lost a lot of blood, blood no person on Tellus possessed. Seven days later, Jonathon eventually came out of his near-death slumber to see Katharyn sitting by his side, holding his hand.

He never knew she had not left his bedside the entire time.

"Jonathon," Katharyn said, breaking the long silence on the porch, "Athena told me."

John looked at Katharyn.

"Told you what?" he asked.

"Everything… Everything you wouldn't," Katharyn said, then looked up into John's eyes. "I know you and Athena were the originals… the first two Guardians. The *only* Guardians."

....

A few nights later, John was standing on the bank of the lake watching the last remnants of moonlight disappear in an eclipse, a total lunar eclipse. It was late at night and, now with total darkness hiding his presence, it was the perfect time for what he was there to do. Frank had asked for several of the weapons John had brought from Tellus and the medical equipment case.

"Future technology could work miracles in this time," Frank had told him.

John touched the neck of his suit and the facemask appeared and enclosed his head. He turned and looked around to make sure nobody else was there, even in the dead of night, then certain he was alone, he entered the black water and started swimming for the underwater caves.

When he reached the ship, he went inside and waited while the lake water drained out of the transition chamber. Entering the ship's main area, John stood motionless for a few moments, listening to the quiet, before he touched the neck of his suit to retract his facemask. He then went about collecting the weapons Frank had requested and brought them to the flight control area of the spacecraft.

"Jonathon," a voice echoed from the shadows somewhere behind him.

Startled, John put the weapons down and turned slowly to where the voice had come from.

An entity emerged, surrounded by a mist, and engulfed in darkness, then slowly transformed into someone John knew of but had never seen. The dark figure stood several meters away, with an evil grin on its face, staring at John. The dark figure was tall, like John, and clearly menacing although his face was strikingly handsome, almost angelic.

"Athanasius," John gasped, standing tall and guarded but also not understanding how this evil being was now right there, inside the ship with him.

Athanasius moved slowly around the control room, keeping his distance from John but never taking his eyes off him.

"I see you are wondering how I'm here," Athanasius responded, opening his arms and looking around him. "… I'm not."

John glanced down at the weapons and Athanasius noticed.

Athanasius smiled and shook his head.

"Jonathon, Jonathon, Jonathon," he said, still slowly moving around the space between them. "Those things won't help you because I'm not really here."

Athanasius stopped moving around and looked straight at John.

"I almost had you in that wormhole, old friend," he said, with a devilish grin on his face.

"I'm not your friend," John snarled.

Athanasius shook his head.

"Come now, Jonathon. You and I have been battling since the beginning," he said. "Since Medora."

John inhaled a deep breath hearing Medora's name spoken; the memory of her death was still fresh in his mind as if it happened yesterday.

"So that makes us *very* old friends," Athanasius said.

"How?" John asked. "How are you here?"

Athanasius started moving around again and said, "I told you… I'm not really here."

He stopped and looked at John again.

"I'm still in The Darkness realm, unfortunately. But…"

"But what?" John asked.

"Every action has its consequences, Jonathon, and that stunt you pulled in the wormhole has given *me* a way of…" he paused, thinking of the right words, "reaching you again."

Athanasius subtly moved a little closer to John, and John noticed because he had not taken his eyes off Athanasius.

"Me?" John asked.

"Yes," Athanasius replied, "you, Jonathon."

Jonathon clearly did not understand, so Athanasius continued explaining.

"You thought it would be smart to destroy the wormhole so I couldn't use it anymore… And it worked," Athanasius said, nodding as if acknowledging a job well done. "But you're an immortal, old friend. You left an echo inside that thing, your *immortal* echo, and it reached The Darkness realm."

Athanasius moved around behind John.

"And now I can sense you again… even across time. I've done it before," he said, taunting John.

Athanasius moved around in front of John again.

"That was smart going back in time, Guardian. You made it almost impossible to find you, I will admit… almost," Athanasius said. "But I never give up because here I am, and I know that wherever you are, they are always close by, aren't they? The pure-borns."

John was getting nervous now.

If Athanasius could sense him, as he'd said, what did that now mean for keeping Katharyn safe?

Athanasius sighed.

"Your deception on Adamah worked well, Jonathon. Those useless creatures could never get the job done for me. You always managed to keep the pure-borns safe… until you didn't."

John still wanted to know how Athanasius was here, on Earth, inside his ship. He was supposed to be trapped in The Darkness for all eternity.

"How are you here, Athanasius?" John asked, still confused.

Athanasius shook his head.

"You don't listen. I told you. I'm not… I'm projecting myself here."

He moved a little closer again towards John. John stepped back and glanced at the weapons again.

"But it drains almost all of my powers, which means I can only do it for a very short time," Athanasius said.

John glanced at the weapons again, but Athanasius was on John in a flash, lifting him off the floor of the ship and holding him up by the throat.

"Your weapons are useless against me, Jonathon," Athanasius spat, now in a rage. "Where is she?"

"I've stopped those creatures before. I'll do it again," John said, in a choked gasp, due to the evil hand around his throat.

"I don't need them anymore, thanks to you," Athanasius snarled, tightening his grip.

Just then, Athanasius appeared to be fading.

He shook his head as if trying to clear his mind while still holding John up by the throat.

"Time for me to go, Jonathon," Athanasius said, his voice now sounding distant. "I know where you are now so don't bother hiding because I'll find you. I always do… I'm not going to kill you yet, but let's make it more interesting."

Athanasius then grabbed one of John's knees with his free hand. John screamed in pain as Athanasius' grip on his knee tightened and a searing heat burned right into the bones and down his leg.

"Let's see how good you are without your immortal speed," Athanasius said, then released his grip on John, who fell to the floor gasping and in agony.

"See you soon, *old friend*."

And with that said, Athanasius faded and vanished into nothing.

....

A few hours later, John was sitting in the lounge room of Frank's house.

It was just before dawn.

It had taken him ages to get the weapons and medical case back to the shore of the lake and into Frank's pick-up truck because he could barely walk, let alone swim. Thankfully, Frank's truck had an automatic transmission. John had thought so because his left knee and leg were now useless. He'd managed to drive home and was grateful Frank had been up and heard the vehicle pull into the driveway.

Frank helped John into the house then went back out to his truck and retrieved the weapons and medical case. He removed a small hand-held device from the medical case and waved it slowly over John's left knee and leg. A wide beam of blue light was coming from the device.

"This will heal the burns, John," Frank said, "but I don't think it will do much for the internal damage to the knee."

John grimaced at the pain when he tried moving his left leg.

"I thought immortals could heal themselves," Frank said, still using the device to heal the burns.

"Normally, we can. But wounds inflicted by another immortal, or immortal creatures, sometimes they never heal," John said, then touched the scar on his neck, "I was lucky with that one."

Frank nodded, agreeing John had indeed been fortunate.

Frank asked, "Athanasius said he can sense other immortals?"

"Yeah. He said he can sense me again," John replied nodding, "I'm guessing that's how he found us on Tellus."

"Can you?" Frank asked, turning off the healing device in his hand. "Can you sense another immortal?"

John looked at his left leg.

All the burns were healed, but the pain inside his knee was still there.

Thinking for a moment, John then replied, "I always knew where Athena was, come to think about it… So maybe."

"What about Athanasius? Can you sense him?" Frank asked, as he started to strap John's left knee.

John said nothing for a few moments while he looked inside himself to see if he could sense Athanasius.

"No," John replied, "Nothing… I didn't even know he was inside the ship."

"Who was inside the ship?" Katharyn asked, standing in the doorway of the lounge room.

Katharyn's sudden appearance made John and Frank whip their heads around.

Neither of them had heard her come downstairs.

……………………..

At breakfast, nobody spoke.

Katharyn hadn't said a word since John had told her and Marie, who'd woken to the downstairs commotion as well, exactly what had happened on the ship. The pain in his knee was excruciating but John was not going to let Katharyn see that, and thankfully the strapping Frank had applied allowed him to hobble around, albeit with some discomfort.

It's going to be a long hard day at work in this condition, John thought.

"You are not going to the mill today, John," Marie told him, "You can barely walk."

"I'll be fine, Marie," John said, the grimace on his face belying the truth as he sat down at the table.

Finally, Katharyn spoke.

"Marie is right, Jonathon. You need to rest," she said.

John realized Katharyn had been watching him and she had seen the pain on his face.

Marie got up from the table.

"I'll go ring the mill office," Marie said and headed into the other room to use the phone.

John looked at Frank who was nodding at him.

"Okay. Fine," John said, giving up.

Silence filled the kitchen.

Marie could be heard from the hallway talking on the phone and everyone was listening.

"Thank you, Gail… Yes, I will… Goodbye," she said, then appeared in the kitchen doorway. "All sorted, John. Gail said to take the rest of the week off."

Gail Henley, daughter of Walter Henley, ran the mill office for her father while he attended to his mayoral duties and other business interests. Gail was not married, and had a soft spot for John, and he sometimes felt uncomfortable in her presence because of it.

"Thank you, Marie," John said.

Katharyn got up and took her breakfast dishes to the sink. Something was on her mind, that was certain. Frank had noticed. John knew it as well. When Katharyn finished washing her dishes and wiped her hands, she turned around knowing John had been watching her every move. She looked him in the eyes and realized that he already sensed what was going to happen.

"I have to leave, Jonathon," Katharyn said.

Frank and Marie were stunned by the announcement, but John just nodded his head slightly, in acceptance of what Katharyn was saying.

"I know," John replied solemnly, averting his eyes from Katharyn so she wouldn't see the hurt in them. "You are not safe around me anymore… You need to get as far away from here… from me… as possible."

The emotion of the moment had gotten to Marie who burst into tears. She raced over to Katharyn and pulled her into a warm embrace, a motherly embrace.

"Katharyn," Marie sobbed, "where will you go?"

Katharyn had made up her mind.

She had been thinking about it since hearing what happened inside the ship hours earlier. Athanasius had found Jonathon and left him with a terrible injury, and Katharyn believed it was all her fault, being a pure-born. If Athanasius could sense Jonathon as he claimed, then Katharyn knew she had to leave for the sake of them both. She needed to get far away from Henleyville, far away from her beloved Guardian, and thanks to the photographer who'd given her his business card, she now had a plan.

"Capitol City," Katharyn replied.

ELEVEN

Capitol City – present day - Sunday October 1ˢᵗ

Katharyn had Lesley and Amy collected from the airport and driven to her apartment building in the city. She'd paid for their flights, insisted, even though she knew Lesley could afford it.

"Think of it as a late birthday gift," she told Lesley on the phone, much to her daughter's protest.

But Lesley gave in when she saw how excited Amy was about going to Capitol City to see her famous grandmother. Katharyn had become somewhat of a recluse in recent years, rarely stepping outside her apartment building without a hoard of security personnel in tow.

Lesley had grown up with her mother's paranoia and borderline obsession with security and never understood it. But she was annoyed that it was now affecting Amy.

Katharyn had only seen her granddaughter a handful of times since she was born and none of those times had been in her own home. And Amy was now experiencing the same security madness her mother had to put up with growing up here and she was finding it very confronting.

When Katharyn decided to leave Henleyville back in 1980 and travel to Capitol City, she followed through with her plan. She contacted the photographer who'd given her his business card and his bosses paid for Katharyn's flights and accommodation. Terrence Bailey had shown his bosses the photos he'd taken of Katharyn at the school opening in Henleyville and they'd been astounded by her natural beauty and had hoped she would contact them.

Katharyn quickly made a name for herself in the fashion arena of the eighties and nineties and graced the covers of all the best-known magazines. She became one of the country's highest paid supermodels and amassed a small fortune.

One thing that put Katharyn above the rest was that she appeared to never really age, and after many years in the headlines, she still looked like a young woman in her mid-twenties. It was a much talked about topic on television and in the print media during that time.

In one televised interview Katharyn did in the mid 1990's, she paid credit to her youthful looks to the beauty products she had been using, products derived from special formulas created by her silent business partners. After that interview aired, millions of people across the country, and indeed the world, wanted Katharyn's beauty products, and so her beauty empire 'Adanne by Katharyn' was launched and quickly became one of the highest selling beauty lines in the world.

But Katharyn had rarely been seen in public now for more than ten years and when she did venture outside her apartment building, she was always unrecognizable wearing large hats, dark glasses, and masks that cover much of her face.

Something must have happened to me in the wormhole, Katharyn concluded.

But Katharyn was wrong.

Although she is in her mid-sixties now, Katharyn looks and feels very much younger, at least twenty years younger in fact, and this is because she is a descendant of the immortal Aryanna, and a pure-born gifted with ageless beauty.

Yes, that is part of the reason but not entirely.

Katharyn's youthfulness is something that cannot be explained away using her beauty products even though her products have, and still do, produce remarkable results for their users.

In Katharyn's mind, Frank and Marie were her silent partners, and she owed an eternal debt of gratitude to them both. After all, it was they who had created the products Katharyn would eventually sell under her brand name 'Adanne by Katharyn'.

On Tellus, Francis and Mariangela were two of the world's top scientists specializing in many fields, and during their first years on Earth, they'd created various products for themselves to combat the different climatic conditions of the twentieth century.

Marie had given Katharyn some of their home-made ointments and lotions to take with her when she left Henleyville, products that would one day make her very wealthy.

She had also given Katharyn one very special product. Marie told her it was a one-use treatment to be administered on her twenty-fifth birthday.

This one-use treatment was the main reason Katharyn never seemed to age.

Lesley and Amy rode the service elevator to the penthouse apartment, along with three of Katharyn's many bodyguards. It felt all too familiar for Lesley who was accustomed to this level of security surrounding her, having grown up in this very building. But for Amy, it was a little intimidating, Lesley realized, when, on the way up, Amy reached out and held her mothers' hand tightly.

"Mother," Lesley protested upon entering the penthouse apartment, "Can we please have some normality?"

She gestured to the bodyguards.

"These gorillas are frightening your granddaughter."

"Amy dear, come here," Katharyn said, ignoring her daughter and opening her arms in welcome.

"Hi, G-ma," Amy replied, wrapping her arms around Katharyn, and hugging her tightly.

The 'gorillas' brought in Lesley's and Amy's travel cases and placed them in the foyer of the massive luxurious apartment. They looked at Katharyn, who nodded at them, then they left to take up their normal sentry positions outside.

Katharyn unfolded Amy from her hug and held her at arm's length.

"Look at you, my dear girl," Katharyn said, smiling with absolute joy at Amy. "You have grown so much."

Amy smiled at her grandmother.

"We haven't seen you for ages, G-ma," Amy said. "I'll be fourteen soon."

"Yes, I know," Katharyn replied with a smile, then looked at Lesley who was rubbing her forehead.

"Take your things to your room, Amy, then we'll figure out dinner," Katharyn said, kissing Amy on the cheek.

"Sure. Okay," Amy replied, then grabbed her travel case and headed off down the hallway.

Lesley had taken a seat on the plush lounge and was still rubbing her head. Katharyn made her way over to her daughter and sat down next to her, worry written across her face.

"Lesley, honey," Katharyn began, "Are you okay?"

Lesley looked at her mother, unable to hide her pain.

"No, mother," she replied. "I think I need to lie down for a while. My head is pounding and I'm a bit dizzy."

Katharyn put a hand on Lesley's thigh.

"Your room is set up… still," Katharyn said softly, "Go lie down. I'll bring your luggage in later."

"Thanks mom," Lesley said with a forced smile, then got up and went to her old room.

Katharyn sat in silence as she watched her daughter disappear down the hall. She knew there was something wrong, but Lesley hadn't told her mother that the tumor had returned with a vengeance this time, so Katharyn was left guessing.

Both mother and daughter had much to tell each other.

At that moment, a figure appeared in the doorway from the foyer and Katharyn looked up to see Joshua standing there.

"Thank you for making sure they got here safely, Joshua," Katharyn said, standing up.

Joshua came further into the lounge room.

"They didn't see me on the plane, Katharyn," Joshua replied. "And they were never in danger."

Katharyn nodded.

Joshua had watched over Lesley and Amy since they'd left home in Henleyville, completely unaware of his presence.

"Jonathon says hello," Joshua said, and Katharyn smiled sadly.

Amy finished unpacking her things and returned to the lounge room but stopped in the hallway entrance when she saw the strange man standing in the lounge room talking to Katharyn.

Amy heard everything that was said.

"Hello," Amy said, and both Katharyn and Joshua turned to see her standing there, staring at Joshua, with an odd expression on her face. "I've seen you before."

TWELVE

Henleyville – October 2nd, 1981

It was early evening, around seven pm. Daylight was a memory, and the stars were absent from the night sky because of the lingering rain clouds. Only the streetlights provided any guidance, but the man didn't need them. He knew where he was going. He pulled the collar up on his jacket as the rain started to get heavier and he quickened his pace, looking over his shoulder occasionally to see if he was being followed.

But nobody else was out in this weather and, for that, he was grateful. If anyone was to see him on the streets, it would complicate things even further. He slowed his pace when he got to Old Mill Road, and studied the lighted windows of the neighborhood houses to see if any of the occupants were looking out.

So far, so good, he thought.

He reached the house he was told about, the one with the letterbox on the big tree at the driveway entrance. He stood in the shadow of the big tree, its size hiding him from the view of anyone who might look out of the house.

He took out the handgun that was tucked behind him in the waist of his pants, removed a silencer from one of his jacket pockets and screwed it onto the gun barrel. He looked up and down the street again, taking in all the houses, and listened for the sounds of approaching vehicles. Satisfied nobody was around, he hustled up the driveway and onto the front porch of the house. He could hear the voices of several people inside, one of which he hoped belonged to the person he'd been sent to find.

"Your time has come," a voice had whispered to him a few days ago back home. "Find her."

He told his wife he had to go away on business for a few days and when he'd left, he somehow already knew where he was going.

The rain was coming down much harder now and the sound of it hitting the roof on the porch was drowning out the conversations from inside the house.

Samuel, Laila, Aniela, Frank, and Marie were all sitting around the dining room table and laughing at something funny Raphael had said. Frank and Marie had invited them all over for dinner to celebrate John's one year anniversary at the mill, but John was yet to grace them with his presence.

He was still at the mill.

Gail Henley was also having a small gathering after work for John, much to his embarrassment, but he couldn't exactly say no to the boss's daughter.

From the dining room, they all heard a loud knocking at the front door.

Samuel got up from his seat upon hearing it.

"That'll be John now," he said, "I'll get it."

Samuel headed to the front door and opened it.

Standing there in the open doorway was a tall man with dark skin holding a gun pointed straight at Samuel. With his eyes wide open in shock, Samuel had no time to react before the dark-skinned man pulled the trigger and shot him in the middle of his forehead, killing him instantly.

The sound of Samuel's body hitting the floor was muffled by the heavy rain on the roof, but Laila thought she heard something and rose out of her seat to investigate.

The dark-skinned man stepped over Samuel and entered the house just as Laila came out of the dining room. He shot her dead immediately, then moved to the dining room doorway and faced the others seated at the table, who all stared in silence at the gun aimed at them. The man knelt next to Laila, keeping his gun trained on the other people, and checked her neck on both sides and the back looking for something.

But he did not find it.

As he stood back up, he noticed a magazine on the hallstand next to the dining room doorway. On the front cover, was a picture of Katharyn, her head turned to the side slightly, her long hair draping over the front of her right shoulder, and in plain sight you could see the dove birthmark on her exposed neck just below her left ear.

The man picked up the magazine and held it up for the others to see, with the cover facing them.

"Where is she?" the dark-skinned man said.

At the mill, John looked at the wall clock and noticed the time was close to seven thirty pm. It was getting late, so he thanked Gail Henley for the gift and the party then headed out to his truck.

The rain had not eased, and the roads were dark and treacherous on the drive home. When John pulled into the driveway at Frank's place, he noticed the front door was wide open and a chill instantly went up his spine. He jumped out of his pickup truck and headed for the house as fast as his damaged left knee would allow him. Hobbling up the front stairs, he stopped when he saw Samuel lying motionless in the open doorway.

John reached down to check on him but saw that Samuel was dead. He stepped over Samuel and into the house, immediately spotting Laila lying on the floor near the dining room, eyes open but lifeless.

"No!" John exclaimed, distraught. "Frank! Marie?"

He reached the dining room doorway, looked in and saw why he'd heard no response from anyone. Raphael and Aniela were slumped forward in their chairs, dead from a gunshot wound to the back of their heads. Marie was seated facing the doorway, her head back, mouth open, and a small trickle of blood running from the bullet hole in the middle of her forehead. And Frank, his best friend of many years, was lying crumpled on the floor, dead. He'd been shot three times: one in the head and two in the chest.

....

The entire town was in shock when news spread of the murders at the Cooper house, and the news traveled fast. Reporters and numerous news vans flocked to Henleyville, and several days later the media circus still blocked much of Old Mill Road because the story had gone national.

The house was no longer declared a crime scene. Local law enforcement officers and dozens of forensic investigators had scoured every inch of Frank and Marie's house. John was questioned at length but had quickly been eliminated as a suspect thanks to Gail Henley backing up his story of being at the mill at the time of the murders.

Also, a neighbor a few doors down from the Cooper house, had told the police he'd been out on his front porch having a cigarette when he'd seen a man running down the street in the opposite direction of the Cooper house sometime around seven fifteen pm. John hadn't arrived home until around thirty minutes later.

And, anyway, John couldn't run because of his damaged left knee.

Katharyn was devastated when John had called her the night he'd found everyone dead and told her what happened. It was the second call he'd made after first calling the police. John told Katharyn to take extra precautions and to get additional security around her until he arrived in Capitol City. But Katharyn told him not to come. She told him to stay in Henleyville to take care of the funeral arrangements, and the Cooper house, and to safeguard the secrets they had brought with them from Tellus.

John argued with Katharyn that he needed to be there to protect her, but she insisted she was safe.

The building she was living in had several levels of security and to get to the top floor visitors had to be vetted first. Only those approved by Katharyn would then be allowed access to the lift. Even then, the elevator stopped on the floor below hers and the visitors had to get off and go through another security check before being allowed to access a different elevator which would take them to the top floor. Then, she advised John, three other security guards would double-check with Katharyn before the visitor would be allowed into her apartment, all while she watched every moment on a CCTV monitor.

John was stunned into silence when Katharyn told him all this. She said it had been a stipulation of hers written in her contract with the big fashion and beauty company that had wanted her signature. She'd told them she wouldn't sign with them unless they agreed to her requirements.

They did.

It was late in the evening now, five days after the shootings, and Old Mill Road was silent. Most of the news vans and reporters had left earlier in the day. Only a few stragglers remained, hopeful of getting an exclusive interview from the only survivor, John Miller.

Survivor?

He'd told every reporter who had harassed him that he hadn't been home at the time.

Would he have survived a bullet to the head?

He wasn't even sure if his immortal powers would protect him, and he hoped he never had to find out.

John stood silently in the lounge room, the horrific images of that fateful night flashing through his mind.

If I hadn't stayed at the mill after work, they'd still be alive, John thought.

"Did they have any enemies?" the responding Police officers, and the detectives who turned up later, asked John repeatedly.

"No," he replied, each time he was asked.

"Do you?" the detectives had asked.

John glanced at the detectives then quickly looked away.

"No," he eventually replied.

The detectives looked at one another silently at this delayed response from John.

"And you say nothing has been taken?" one detective asked.

"No," John replied, "… nothing is missing that I know of."

The detectives left a short time later, telling John they would be back in a few days to talk to him again. Maybe he would remember something by then, they'd said. They obviously felt he was hiding something.

And their suspicions were correct.

Something *was* missing, and John knew it because he had taken it the night he found his friends all dead. He'd seen it as soon as he had entered the dining room. In the center of the dining room table was a magazine with a picture of Katharyn on the front cover, and a large kitchen knife had been stabbed through the birthmark on Katharyn's neck, right through the magazine and into the table.

He didn't tell Katharyn, or the detectives.

It must've been Athanasius, John thought.

But why use a gun? He doesn't need any type of weapon.

Then something dawned on him.

He remembered what his neighbor had told the police about seeing someone running away down Old Mill Road and figured that Athanasius had found a new type of Corvidaen to do his dirty work, only this time in human form.

John went to the secret compartment hidden inside the wall of the storage space under the stairs and retrieved the weapons and the medical case.

I must protect her, he thought, *even if she doesn't want my help. It's my immortal duty as her Guardian*, he told himself.

He put the weapons and the medical case in the lounge room then went upstairs to his room and packed a few things for his journey to Capitol City. Not having his immortal speed anymore meant he had to get there by other means and his only options were driving or flying.

Having grabbed everything he needed, John came back downstairs and into the living then froze at the sight of a stranger standing there, almost naked except for something wrapped around his hips.

"Hello, Jonathon," the stranger said.

John noticed the stranger was tall, not as tall as him though, and well-built with shoulder-length brownish hair. He also noticed the man had piercing blue eyes which seemed to look right into John's soul.

"I am sorry about your friends," the stranger said.

John looked at the weapons on the lounge then back at the man.

"Who are you?" John asked, stepping further into the room.

The man smiled at John.

"My name is Joshua… Can I sit, please?" he asked, pointing to the lounge chairs, then moved to sit down without waiting for John to respond.

"I've been sent to help you, Jonathon," Joshua said, looking at the weapons as he sat down.

John moved around and picked up the weapons and the medical case and put them on the table in the dining room. He came back into the lounge room and stood in front of Joshua.

"Sent by who?" John demanded.

"The Creators," Joshua said calmly.

This surprised John, and Joshua saw it in his expression.

"So, you are a Guardian," John surmised.

"No, Jonathon," Joshua corrected him, "I am not a Guardian. I am from the Creators."

"From the Creators? What does that mean?" he asked, sitting down, and grimacing from the pain in his left knee.

Joshua gestured to John's knee.

"You obviously need help. And Athanasius has found a new way of…." he paused, looking for the right words, "deceiving us. The Creators know that, so I have come to assist you."

"Deceiving us? How?" John asked.

"I know you have figured it out for yourself, Jonathon," Joshua said.

"The man who killed my friends, he was sent by Athanasius?"

It was a statement rather than a question.

Joshua nodded.

"Yes. Athanasius redeemed this man and now he does his bidding. And he will stop at nothing till he finds Katharyn."

John glared at Joshua suspiciously.

"How do you know about Katharyn?" he asked.

"I am from the Creators, and of the Creators," Joshua replied. "We have watched from the beginning."

John seemed confused now.

"We?" he asked.

Joshua smiled and nodded.

"Yes... We."

"So, you... are..." John stumbled with his words but couldn't say what he was thinking.

"I am part of them, yes," Joshua confirmed. "They are part of me... like Aryanna."

"Aryanna?" John asked in shock.

"Yes, Jonathon. But I do not have The Pure," Joshua replied. "You do know about The Pure, don't you?"

John nodded yes.

Joshua continued, "Then you also know about the ancient laws and the prophecy."

"Prophecy?" John asked, getting more confused. "No, I don't."

"The prophecy foretells of the one who shall be gifted The Pure," Joshua explained, "when the child of the dove, the mother of life, takes no breath."

"What does that mean?" John asked.

"It means we cannot interfere with Nature, as is written in the ancient book of laws," Joshua said, "but we must protect the pure-child, Jonathon, and that is *my* job now."

John bristled at this revelation from Joshua.

"Katharyn is my life! I am her Guardian," John protested, angrily.

"Yet you are here, and she is not," Joshua said.

John stood up quickly, ignoring the pain in his knee. Joshua stood also and put his hands up to calm him.

"I am here to help, Jonathon. It is the will of the Creators," Joshua said. "You must stay here, guard your secrets, and wait for my return. I will go to Katharyn. The man who did this will not harm her. I assure you."

John walked away and opened the front door. He stood looking out for a while, saying nothing, trying to calm himself down. He had basically been relieved of his duty as Katharyn's Guardian by this newcomer who claimed to be like the Creators.

He turned to Joshua and stared at him.

"If you are a Creator, why not just fix it all now? Just…" he waved his hands around, gesturing, "put an end to it all: Athanasius, the guy who killed my friends, everything."

"I can't, Jonathon," Joshua replied, "I'm not a Creator here."

"You said you are *from* them, and *of* them," John insisted.

"Yes, but I only have limited gifts in this form," Joshua said, acknowledging his human form.

"Like what?" John asked.

"Same as you… before your injury," Joshua replied pointing to John's knee. "And I can *remove* a threat if needed."

"I see," John replied, knowing what Joshua meant.

"But here, in The Light realm, I can't give life... or save a life," Joshua said.

Both men said nothing for a while. Joshua knew John was trying to process these new revelations and he also knew John was probably skeptical of a random stranger turning up on his doorstep proclaiming to be something not of this world.

John came back and sat down on the lounge and rubbed his aching knee. Clearly, something else was on John's mind and Joshua sensed it.

"What is bothering you, Jonathon?" Joshua asked, sitting down next to John, and breaking the silence between them.

John looked into the piercing blue eyes of Joshua and saw that his concern was genuine.

"Why didn't the Creators stop all this madness in the beginning? Why did they let Athanasius carry out his threats and kill so many pure-borns?... And why couldn't I save Medora?" John said and put his head in his hands, clearly distraught.

Joshua reached out a put a hand on John's shoulder.

"It is the will of the Creators, Jonathon. We can't interfere with life in The Light realm. It is forbidden. And..." Joshua paused, taking his hand off John's shoulder, "we no longer have the power over The Darkness realm."

John looked at Joshua, not believing what he was hearing.

"You are joking, right?" John asked, sarcastically.

"Life can only be created in The Light realm... by Nature, Jonathon," Joshua began explaining, "and with any life, comes death. So, death can only happen in The Light also... If Athanasius stays in The Darkness realm nothing can harm him."

John thought of something.

"What happens if he comes here?" he asked. "Can you *remove* him?"

Joshua shook his head slightly.

"I don't know. He's immortal and very powerful now. I may be able to stop him, but I don't know if I can *end* him."

John nodded his head understanding what Joshua was saying. He looked at Joshua again who was now feeling a little awkward in his near-naked state. John noticed and felt the awkwardness as well of them both sitting next to each other.

"I have some clothes that should fit you," John said, getting up and heading for the stairs. "What size shoe are you?"

Joshua just shrugged his shoulders and shook his head.

John looked at Joshua's feet and then his own.

"I'll get some of Frank's," John said, noting that Joshua's feet were maybe a bit smaller than his.

And he was right.

Frank's shoes fit perfectly.

"Thanks Francis," John whispered to himself when Joshua finished dressing and put on the shoes.

Joshua looked different wearing clothes, normal almost, John realized, and for some strange reason he felt a strong bond with this newcomer.

Another immortal, just like me, John thought. *But better than me, though. Maybe he can succeed where I have always failed.*

A little while later, after Jonathon had given him Katharyn's details, Joshua opened the front door and stood in the doorway letting the cool night air wash over him. He looked up into the night sky and studied the stars for several moments then turned and faced Jonathon.

"Remember who you are, Jonathon," Joshua said, touching his own chest near his heart, "and where you came from… You are more powerful than you realize."

"I am just a Guardian," Jonathon replied.

Joshua smiled and shook his head.

"No, Jonathon," he said. "No, you are not."

Then, in the blink of an eye, Joshua was gone, leaving Jonathon wondering what he had meant.

THIRTEEN

Capitol City – Present day – October 2nd

The news channel was on, but Lenora Jackson wasn't taking much notice of it as she sat down and opened her laptop. She took some time going over the draft of her next column for the Capitol City Times making sure there were no mistakes, changing words and adding new lines. She picked up her coffee cup and took a sip while she re-read her corrections.

On the television, the news bulletin had switched to an "On This Day" segment which told viewers of events that happened in the past.

Lenora put her cup back down, having spotted another change that was needed in her column and started to amend it when the announcer on the television switched to an unsolved multiple shooting in Henleyville forty-two years ago.

This got Lenora's attention.

'…. Six residents of Henleyville were shot dead, execution style, in the early evening of October 2nd, 1981,' the reporter was saying.

Lenora watched as news footage of the house where the murders took place was shown, as well as some interviews of several locals, including a neighbor who said he saw a man running away from the scene.

'… Fortunately, John Miller, another resident of the house, wasn't home at the time otherwise there could have been seven victims…' the reporter continued as a video of a tall handsome man was shown with a tag at the bottom of the screen displaying "Survivor John Miller".

'… The brutal murders still remain unsolved to this day,' the reporter said, then the story ended.

Lenora quickly Googled the story.

There were dozens of articles and a few news videos of the 'Henleyville Tragedy', which one report had labelled it. But something bothered Lenora.

"Henleyville," she whispered. "Where have I heard that name before?"

A few hours later, Lenora had found out and was on the phone to her editor, Arnold Grey, even though it was almost nine pm.

"I'm telling you, Arnie, there is a connection there…… Yes, my column is almost done…… Look, I wanna go to this Henleyville place and check it out…. It's out of state, Arnie…. A few days, max, I promise…. Yes, okay. I'll finish my column tonight and email it to you…. I promise…. Okay…. Yeah, I'll keep you in the loop. Thanks Arnie," and the phone conversation ended.

Lenora booked flights, with a flexible return date, and a rental vehicle. She figured she would see how things panned out first before returning to Capitol City. The nearest airport to Henleyville was a couple of hours away, she realized, but she was able to book an early morning flight for the next day even at this late notice and, calculating for the two-hour drive from the airport, Lenora figured she could be in Henleyville by mid-morning. The only thing left to do now was finish her column and email it to Arnold Grey.

Tuesday 3rd October

The flight departed almost an hour late due to early morning fog and by the time Lenora arrived in Henleyville it was nearly midday.

This place is beautiful, Lenora thought as she drove slowly through the town center.

In fact, Lenora had been amazed by the lush countryside and mountain views on her drive from the airport. The air seemed crisper and cleaner here too, she noticed.

Lenora had written down agenda items late last night, with places and people she hoped to see and find. But first things first, Lenora needed coffee and something to eat. She couldn't remember the last time she had eaten, and her rumbling stomach was a constant reminder.

She noticed a diner on the other side of the main street as she drove down, so she did a U-turn and found a parking spot nearby.

Henleys Diner, Lenora noted. *That's on my list.*

Two birds, one stone.

Henleys Diner was busy, Lenora observed when she entered, but not full. There were still a couple of tables spare and one booth, so that's where Lenora headed.

This place is charming, Lenora thought, as she looked around, *and extremely clean and tidy.*

A few other patrons had seen Lenora come in and were gazing in her direction because everyone noticed an out-oftowner. Lenora smiled when she caught the eye of a young couple and they, in return, smiled back.

"Hi. What can I get you?" Jennifer Henley asked Lenora, who jumped when Jennifer appeared beside the booth table.

"Coffee, please. Long black" Lenora replied, picking up the menu off the table. "And… um… I'll have the BLT sandwich with grilled cheese, too. Thank you."

"No problem, hon," Jennifer replied, with a bright smile, then headed off towards the kitchen.

Lenora looked around the diner again.

There were two other wait staff attending tables and, from her vantage point, she could see an older lady behind the counter working the coffee machine. On the walls of the diner were photos of Henleyville from the early days, with one section devoted to what looked like a timber factory.

Must be the timber mill I read about last night, Lenora nodded to herself.

The couple who had seen Lenora and smiled at her, now got up from their table and headed to the door. The young woman looked over at Lenora and smiled again. Lenora did the same and gave a small wave. Jennifer Henley returned with Lenora's long black and had seen her wave at the young couple as they left the diner.

Jennifer put the coffee on the table.

"That's my daughter, Samantha, and her young man, Blake," she said. "I gave her the day off because Blake is only in town till tomorrow afternoon. He's on leave from the army."

Lenora looked at Jennifer Henley and noted her name tag said 'Jen'.

"Your daughter works here?" Lenora asked.

"Family diner, hon," Jennifer responded. "We all have to work here at some point."

A light bulb went on inside Lenora's mind.

"You're a Henley?"

"Since birth," Jennifer smiled. "Jennifer Henley. But just call me Jen."

"Lenora," Lenora said, holding out her hand to shake Jennifer's. "Lenora Jackson."

"Nice to meet you, Lenora Jackson," Jen said, shaking Lenora's hand.

A bell sounded at the kitchen counter.

"That's your BLT ready," she said and headed off to collect it.

About half an hour later, Lenora had finished her sandwich and was checking something on her phone when Jennifer Henley came back to her table and asked if there was anything else Lenora needed.

"Another long black would be great, please," she said.

Jennifer smiled then went over and grabbed the coffee pot, brought it back and refilled Lenora's cup.

"Thank you," Lenora said.

Jennifer was just about to leave when Lenora stopped her.

"Um… Can I ask you a question?"

Jennifer looked around the diner and saw that no one needed assistance at that moment.

"Sure," she replied.

Lenora grabbed her phone and tapped the screen a couple of times then turned it to show Jennifer Henley.

"Do you know this man?" she asked, watching Jennifer Henley closely. "His name is Haruto Tanaka."

Jennifer looked at the photo on the screen for several seconds then looked back at Lenora, sizing her up.

"I remember him, yes," Jennifer replied, cautiously. "Why?"

Lenora saw the guarded look on Jennifer Henley's face.

"I'm a reporter with the Capitol City Times," Lenora began. "My specialty is cold cases…"

Jennifer Henley cut her off.

"Yes, Ms. Jackson. I know who you are," she said.

This caught Lenora off guard.

Jennifer saw that Lenora was startled and a little confused, even for a famous reporter.

"I'm an online subscriber to your paper, Ms. Jackson," Jennifer explained.

"Oh… Um… Okay. Cool… Well, I'm working on another cold case, of sorts, and it involves this man," Lenora said, showing Jennifer the photo on her phone again. "He was last seen here in Henleyville… before he disappeared."

Jennifer nodded slowly.

"Like I said, I remember him," she claimed. "He was here."

"Here? As in, here in this diner?" Lenora asked.

Jennifer slid into the booth seat opposite Lenora and put the coffee pot on the table. She waved to someone at the service counter to get their attention then pointed to Lenora's cup.

"Time for my break anyway… and I need a coffee," Jennifer said.

One of the other waiters brought over a large mug, filled it from the coffee pot on the table then took the pot away. Jennifer took a large mouthful while Lenora sat watching.

"He sat right over there," Jennifer said, pointing to the table where her daughter had been sitting earlier. "It was mid-morning… around ten thirty. He was acting strange and mumbling to himself."

Jennifer kept staring at the empty table where Haruto Tanaka had sat, her mind thinking back to that day.

"Mumbling to himself?" Lenora repeated, trying to keep Jennifer talking.

"Yeah," Jennifer said as she turned back to look at Lenora. "It was weird. He kept saying 'my time has come,' whatever that meant."

Jennifer shook her head thinking about it.

"Are you sure it was this guy?" Lenora asked pointing to the photo on her phone which was now on the table.

"Yep. No doubt. We get that Capitol Enquirer magazine here, Ms. Jackson," she explained, "and some folks were still talking about that story when he showed up right here in town."

Jennifer took another long sip of her coffee.

"I actually spoke to him… well I had to because I served him. But I recognized him from his picture in the magazine… the same photo you have there on your phone," she said, nodding towards Lenora's phone.

"What did he want?" Lenora asked.

"I poured him some coffee and I said I was sorry for his loss - you know, his wife had died in the house fire - and he just stared at me with a sad expression on his face… It was like he had forgotten about her, and I had just reminded him. Poor man," she said, shaking her head again. "Anyway, he just started saying 'My time has come. I will find her.'"

"Find who?" Lenora asked.

Jennifer shrugged her shoulders and shook her head.

"No idea," she replied. "His dead wife, maybe. Who knows? But he kept mumbling the same thing, so I called Old John to come over because I just wanted this guy to leave. He was creeping me out."

"Old John? Who's Old John?" Lenora enquired, taking a drink of her coffee.

"John Miller. He owns the hardware store," Jennifer answered.

"John Miller?" Lenora spluttered, almost choking on her coffee.

John Miller was on Lenora's list of people to see, on top to be precise.

"You know him?" Jennifer asked, suspiciously.

Lenora had put her cup down and was dabbing her mouth with a napkin.

"No. His name came up while I was researching my article," she lied.

Jennifer could tell Lenora was hiding something, or not being quite truthful, so she got out of the booth, grabbed her now empty coffee mug, stood next to the table, and looked warily at Lenora.

"John came in and spoke to the man, Ms. Jackson. A few minutes later that Tanaka fellow left, and we never saw him again. Not in Henleyville, at least," Jennifer said then walked off towards the kitchen area.

A little while later, Lenora paid her bill and left Henleys Diner.

So, John Miller owns the hardware store, Lenora thought to herself.

She stood on the pavement outside the diner and looked up and down the street checking out the other businesses. Across the road and further down near the end of Main Street, Lenora saw the sign for Millers Hardware so that's where she headed.

The bell above the door jingled when Lenora opened it and went inside the hardware store.

"Be with you in a minute," a voice called from somewhere further inside the store.

The store was very neat and tidy, and the shelves were fully stocked with everything, and more, a home handyperson might need. Lenora noticed the store went further back as well so she headed down one aisle and into the rear of the store where most of the larger items for sale were displayed. She wandered back down another aisle and ended up in the front of the store again near the service counter.

A tall, broad-shouldered, muscular man was coming down one of the aisles. He had a slight limp, but Lenora didn't notice that because she was frozen in place staring at him as he went behind the service counter.

She recognized him, the face familiar.

No, not familiar, exactly the same, she realized.

Except he had the start of a beard, and his hair was a little different. It was longer now. Longer than in the videos she had watched the night before back in her apartment.

The news videos that were filmed in 1981.

"John Miller?" Lenora asked, clearly not believing her own eyes.

"Yes," John replied, in a friendly tone, "How can I help you?"

Lenora was still staring because, up close, the man was huge, approximately six foot five inches tall, she estimated.

"John… Miller?" she repeated, almost craning her neck to look up at him. "But… you… how?"

"Are you okay, miss?" John asked, hesitantly.

"Mr. Miller," Lenora began, "I'm… um… sorry, but you look exactly the same."

"Have we met?" John asked, now a little wary of the lady staring at him.

"No… Sorry," Lenora stumbled. "I'm a reporter, Mr. Miller. My name is Lenora Jackson and I work for the Capitol City Times…."

John cut her off.

"A reporter? I don't speak to reporters, Miss Jackson. You'll have to leave," he said, coming out from behind the counter and ushering Lenora towards the door.

Lenora now noticed his slight limp.

"Mr. Miller, please," she said, stopping at the door. "I'm trying to find out what happened to my husband, and I'm hoping you might be able to help me."

She took out her phone and showed John the photo of Haruto Tanaka.

"I think the same thing happened to this man, Mr. Miller," Lenora said.

John recoiled slightly when he was shown the photo and it had not gone unnoticed. Lenora regained her composure and began probing.

"1981, Mr. Miller," Lenora said, watching John closely.

John was visibly shaken at the mention of that year.

Yesterday was the forty-two-year anniversary of that fateful night and the memories remained fresh in his mind. John stared out through the front windows of his store as he tried to wrestle with the emotions that had suddenly filled him.

"Mr. Miller?" Lenora spoke softly and touched John's forearm.

John looked at Lenora Jackson.

"What is your husband's name?" he asked.

"Simon," Lenora responded. "Simon O'Reilly. He disappeared at work in October 2010."

John was nodding his head slightly.

"Where did he work?" he asked.

"Capitol City General Hospital," Lenora told him.

But John already knew that because he knew all their names and where they disappeared. He knew the name of every person he and Joshua had taken care of since 1981.

"I can't help you, Miss Jackson," John said, then headed off towards the back of the store.

"Can't… or won't, Mr. Miller?" Lenora asked, following him. "What did you say to Haruto Tanaka in the diner that morning that made him leave, Mr. Miller?"

John stopped and turned to face Lenora.

He remembered seeing the burn mark on Tanaka's right wrist, the symbol of the Corvus, and he remembered the evil grin Tanaka gave him when he saw John had seen it.

"Hello, Jonathon," Tanaka had whispered to him. "I know where they are."

John had recoiled hearing these words and left the diner in a hurry, Tanaka following him a minute later.

Lenora watched John Miller fighting internally with his memories.

"Mr. Miller… John," Lenora said, softly, "please help me."
John looked at Lenora.

"You won't find your answers here, Miss Jackson," he said then turned and headed further into the back of the store.

She watched him walk away, noticing his limp again.

There were more unanswered questions running through her mind now, top of that list being how can this man look like he has not aged a day in over forty years?

Lenora left the hardware store even more determined now. She took out her phone and searched for a motel. She found a charming one which was highly recommended by a travel advisor website, so she booked a room.

And charming it was.

The building itself had old world character but inside it was modern and fresh, and Lenora's room was large with a separate bathroom and lounge area.

The first thing Lenora did was email Arnold Grey to advise him she would be staying a few days. Next, she was determined to find out as much as she could about John Miller and the events of October 2nd, 1981, so opening the folder on her laptop that had all her Capitol City Times contacts, she began her research.

FOURTEEN

December 2016

Haruto Tanaka sat at his work bench inside his workshop, putting the finishing touches to another toy. This one was a wooden truck with a small wooden trailer that attached to a wooden hitch on the truck.

Making toys for children had been his passion for years. He had no children of his own because his wife had a genetic condition that caused premature ovarian failure, so he spent most of his spare time making toys and giving them to underprivileged kids.

Tanaka put down the wood carving tool he'd been using and looked at the little T-shaped piece in his other hand. He put the arm of the little wooden trailer on top of the hitch on the truck and inserted the t-piece.

It fit perfectly.

He moved the little truck, and it pulled the trailer with it.

This would make a little boy happy, Tanaka thought.

He got up and took the new toy over to another larger bench where there were dozens more toys, all made from wood, ready to be loaded up and taken to the school. Tanaka looked at his finished products and was pleased.

Above the bench on a small shelf was a photo of Tanaka and his wife. It was their wedding photo. They were both dressed in traditional Japanese clothing. Tanaka took the photo off the shelf and looked at it. His wife had been very happy that day, he remembered.

Beside him, Tanaka heard a voice whispering in his ear.

It sounded distant and echoed inside his head.

"Your time has come," the voice whispered.

Tanaka turned around but there was no one else there besides him.

"Your time has come," the voice told him again and the burn mark on Tanaka's right wrist started to heat up.

Tanaka dropped the photo from his hand and touched the burn mark on his wrist. His eyes flashed dark, and he stood tall with an odd expression on his face.

His eyes then cleared.

He felt different.

He had a new purpose now.

Stepping on the wedding photo he'd dropped, he walked out of his workshop and headed for his vehicle parked next to the crumbled remains of his house, the house that had caught fire and burnt down, killing his wife who had been trapped inside. Tanaka got into his vehicle, reversed out of his driveway, and drove away.

A couple of hours later, Haruto Tanaka drove slowly down Main Street in Henleyville looking for a place to park. He needed a plan because there were two pure-borns here and getting close enough to each of them without being seen would not be an easy task. One worked at the hospital and the other younger one would be in school now, he figured looking at the time on the clock in his vehicle. It was just after ten in the morning and Tanaka was in luck. A parking spot had become vacant, so he quickly eased his vehicle into it and parked.

He got out of his vehicle and looked up and down Main Street. There were people and cars everywhere, but this did not concern Tanaka. He still needed to figure out a plan, and spotting a diner further up the street, he headed in that direction. He hadn't had breakfast this morning and he was a little hungry. The diner would be the perfect place to sit and work through the details of what he was here to do.

Jennifer Henley noticed the man when he entered the diner. She noticed everyone when they came in. It was a habit she'd developed very early on in her career in the family business.

"Acknowledge everyone when they come in," her father had once told her. "Smile and make sure they are seated quickly."

Jennifer almost did a double take when the man came in and sat down at an empty table.

She knew this man.

Well, she didn't know him personally, but she'd seen his face before. It was on the front cover of a tabloid magazine she had read about a month ago. It was the man who'd lost his wife in a tragic house fire and then tried to kill himself by jumping off a bridge in his hometown a couple of hours away.

The same man who said an alien saved him.

A couple of other patrons in the diner must have recognized him from that very same magazine as well because there were hushed whispers and sly looks in his direction.

Jennifer watched as the man looked around and smiled at several of the people, who quickly looked away. She grabbed the coffee pot and a clean mug and went over to the table. As she got close, Jennifer thought she heard the man mumbling to himself.

"Good morning," Jennifer said to Tanaka. "Would you like some coffee?"

Tanaka looked up at Jennifer Henley.

His eyes look wild, Jennifer thought to herself.

"Yes," Tanaka replied then started nodding. "My time has come."

"Pardon?" Jennifer said as she poured his coffee.

"My time has come," he said again. "Yes. My time has come."

Jennifer left his table and retrieved a menu from the service counter. She brought it back to Tanaka's table and put it down. She noticed he was still mumbling quietly to himself, which was disturbing her a little.

"I'm very sorry about your wife," Jennifer said to Tanaka.

He stopped mumbling and looked up at her.

The expression on his face changed and Jennifer couldn't be certain, but she was sure his eyes went dark for a few seconds. Tanaka stared at Jennifer for several moments, expressionless, like he didn't know where he was or who he was.

"My time has come," Tanaka eventually said, softly, and smiled at Jennifer but not with his eyes. "I will find her."

Jennifer left his table and went behind the service counter, picked up the phone and dialed a number.

"John," Jennifer said into the phone, while watching Tanaka, "It's Jen. Can you come over?"

"What's wrong?" John Miller said, on the other end of the phone.

"There's a guy here… He's acting weird. I'm a bit scared, to be honest. Can you come over and talk to him?" Jennifer asked.

"Yeah. Okay. Let me lock the store and I'll be over," John told her.

A few minutes later, John Miller entered the diner and spotted Jennifer Henley who pointed at the Japanese man sitting alone at one of the tables. John looked to where Jennifer had indicated and went over to Tanaka's table. He heard the man mumbling to himself.

Tanaka stopped when John stood next to his table.

He looked up at John Miller.

"Hello, Jonathon," Tanaka said to him and smiled.

Jonathon hesitated.

Nobody in Henleyville calls him Jonathon, not since Francis and Mariangela. Katharyn still does but she lives in Capitol City.

"Who are you?" Jonathon demanded, his voice angry but barely above a whisper.

He didn't want to alarm the other customers.

"I know where they are," Tanaka said, and his eyes flashed dark.

Jonathon saw this and looked at Tanaka's right wrist and knew immediately that this man was infected by Athanasius' touch. He was a Corvidaen, and he was here to kill Lesley and Amy.

Jonathon leaned down close to Tanaka.

"You won't get near them," he said.

"Yes, I will, Jonathon. You can't protect them both," Tanaka replied.

Jonathon hurried out of the diner and headed back to the hardware store.

Tanaka took a sip of his coffee, put some money on the table then left the diner. He got back into his vehicle and drove away in the direction of Henleyville Hospital.

Jonathon watched Tanaka leave the diner and get into his vehicle. He knew where Tanaka was going and he now knew what vehicle he was driving, so he removed his ancient dagger from under the counter in his store and put it in the waist of his pants. He then left his store, locking it as he went, and jumped into his pick-up to follow Tanaka.

The older pure-born would be at the hospital now, Tanaka knew. It would be easy for anyone to walk in and out of the place without much fuss. It is a hospital after all. People come and go all the time, visiting patients or going there for medical appointments. Getting to her would be easy, he figured. Getting close to the young pure-born in the school would not.

He pulled into the hospital grounds, drove around the back, and parked near a loading dock area where service vehicles dropped off items and goods for the hospital.

Jonathon spotted Tanaka's vehicle going around the back of the hospital. He followed and saw him enter through the service dock and disappear inside. Jonathon needed to hurry. If Tanaka got to Lesley first, he would be too late to stop him. Jonathon parked near Tanaka's vehicle, got out then hurried into the hospital.

Tanaka went through the laundry facility and entered the main part of the hospital. He stopped to get his bearings. A sign on the wall pointed him to where he wanted to go, the hospital day clinic area. Tanaka wasn't bothered about the CCTV security cameras everywhere. Nobody would see him carry out his deadly task. He only needed to touch her, briefly, and his job would be done. He didn't know how he knew this; he just did. He'd known since the voice had whispered to him back in his workshop a few hours earlier.

Everything had become clear to him in that moment.

He knew where he had to go, who he was looking for, and what he needed to do.

"My time has come," Tanaka mumbled to himself when he spotted Lesley further down the hall going into another room.

Jonathon opened the service door and looked up and down the hallway. He knew where Lesley would usually be, so he headed in that direction. As he reached the hallway leading to the day clinic, he saw Tanaka further along. Jonathon was silently catching up to him when Lesley came out of a room and headed in the other direction. She hadn't seen either of them because she was looking at some paperwork in her hands.

Tanaka had stopped momentarily when Lesley had come out of the room, and this gave Jonathon enough time to come up behind him just as the man was about to go after her. Tanaka was a small man, so Jonathon grabbed him around the neck from behind and dragged him through a door into another room. It was a family room where visitors and family members could wait or have refreshments or even take a shower if they'd been staying overnight.

Fortunately, for Jonathon, the family room was empty. He didn't need witnesses for what was going to happen next.

Tanaka started to growl then morphed into a large Corvidaen, breaking free of Jonathon's strangle hold. The creature turned to face Jonathon, who had removed the dagger from his waist band and now stood with it ready to strike.

The creature smiled at Jonathon, bearing its deadly fangs.

"I'm going to enjoy this," the creature said, in its own unknown language.

"Not as much as I am," Jonathon replied.

A look of surprise registered on the face of the creature because it realized Jonathon understood what it said. Jonathon smiled at the creature and signaled a 'bring it on' gesture with his free hand. The Corvidaen growled angrily as it rushed at Jonathon, but he swiftly stepped to the side, a remarkable effort considering his bad knee, and slashed its throat as the creature lashed at him with its talons, slicing open Jonathon's right shoulder.

Momentarily stunned, the Corvidaen stood motionless, bleeding profusely from a deep neck wound. The creature put one of its taloned hands to the deep gash but there was no way to stop the bleeding. Then, from behind, Jonathon plunged his dagger deep into the middle of the creature's back and sliced upwards. The creature made a garbled screaming sound as it faded and then disappeared before Jonathon's eyes.

Jonathon went to the door of the family room, opened it slightly and looked out to see if anyone had heard the scream and was coming to investigate.

All was clear.

He looked back into the room and saw a vehicle remote on the floor. It was for Tanaka's vehicle, so Jonathon picked it up and left the family room, making sure he was not seen.

He went outside to his pick-up truck, grabbed his phone then got into Tanaka's vehicle, started it up and drove away. He had to get rid of the vehicle. If he left it in the hospital grounds, the security patrol would become suspicious of it and call the police.

And Jonathon didn't want the police getting involved or searching Henleyville for the vehicle's missing owner.

No.

He had to get this vehicle as far away from Henleyville as possible and, for that, he would need some help.

Jonathon grabbed his phone and made a call.

"I need your help," Jonathon said, when the call connected. "There's been another one… Meet me at the back of the hardware store."

Five minutes later, Jonathon parked Tanaka's vehicle behind his store then opened the glovebox and looked inside for registration papers or something with Tanaka's home address on it. He found what he needed and within a few minutes Joshua showed up. Having immortal speed meant traveling long distances in the blink of an eye took no time.

Jonathon got out and handed the vehicle's service book to Joshua.

"Take this vehicle to the address in there," Jonathon told Joshua, indicating the service book. "Leave it there. It'll look like he vanished from his home."

"Are you okay, Jonathon?" Joshua asked, noticing Jonathon's shredded shirt and the deep wounds.

"Yes. I'm fine," he replied. "Let Katharyn know Lesley and Amy are safe and unharmed. He went to the hospital first. Lesley never saw him. She never knew we were there."

Joshua nodded, got into Tanaka's vehicle then drove away.

FIFTEEN

Capitol City – October 3rd Present Day

Amy and Katharyn spent the day together shopping and dining out. It was a rare event for Katharyn, and determined not to upset her granddaughter, she ventured out without her various disguises. She still had her security chaperoning them everywhere but today she was not worried about anything except Amy's enjoyment.

And Amy loved every moment.

Katharyn was recognized almost everywhere they went. People were taking photos of her and asking for autographs and selfies, which Katharyn was obliging, much to the confusion of her security detail because she never did this.

Some of the focus was also on Amy, with many people asking if she and Katharyn were related and if Amy was a model too.

Lesley stayed in the penthouse apartment while her mother and daughter ventured out for the day. Actually, she was still sleeping when Katharyn and Amy left in the morning. She hadn't woken up since going to bed the night before not long after they had arrived.

Katharyn was worried about Lesley because she knew she was hiding something, but she was determined she wouldn't let Amy see how worried she was.

Joshua volunteered to remain in the apartment, having assured Katharyn it was safe to go out.

It was mid-afternoon when Lesley eventually woke up.

Groggy and with a sore head, she got up and showered in her ensuite bathroom. When she looked into the bathroom mirror, she didn't recognize the person she saw. Lesley looked worn out, fatigued, with dark circles under her eyes. Her head was heavy, and she still felt unsteady on her feet.

It's getting worse, she acknowledged, as she looked at her reflection again.

Lesley got dressed and tied her long hair back as she always did, a habit she maintained since starting her nursing career. It was her usual hairstyle. She looked at herself again in the mirror after applying a little make-up to hide the dark circles then left her room to find her mother and daughter.

But first she needed coffee so she headed to the kitchen where a full pot of aromatic hot coffee put a little smile on her face. Lesley grabbed one of the clean mugs next to the coffee pot, poured herself one then sat down at the large island counter in the middle of the huge kitchen.

She took a sip of her coffee as Joshua walked into the kitchen.

Lesley put her cup down and stared at the stranger in front of her, recognition spreading across her face.

"Hello," Joshua said, "I'm…"

But Lesley cut him off.

"Joe!" she said, pointing at him. "You're Joe… from the diner."

"Joshua," he replied with a smile that said you caught me.

"What are you doing here?" Lesley exclaimed. "Have you been following me… and Amy?"

Lesley then looked around.

"Where's Amy? Where's my mother?"

She was getting a little angry now, realizing that this man had possibly been following, or stalking, her and Amy.

But why was he here in her mother's apartment?

"Katharyn and your daughter went out for the day, Lesley," Joshua explained. "They are safe… And I… yes, that was me at the diner that day."

Lesley stood up, more determined.

"What is going on, Joe, Joshua, or whatever the hell your name is? And why are you here?"

Joshua held up his hands and remained calm.

"My name *is* Joshua, but everyone in your town, Henleyville, calls me Joe… That was Jonathon's idea," Joshua explained.

"Jonathon? Who's Jonathon, *Joe*?" Lesley asked, emphasising the name Joe.

Joshua smiled at this.

"First things first, Lesley, I'm not following you or Amy… I'm… watching over you… for Katharyn," he said.

"My mother?" Lesley said, confused, then started shaking her head. "It's her damn paranoia, isn't it? Well, I've had enough."

Lesley stormed off out of the kitchen.

Joshua followed her.

"It's not what you think, Lesley," he said, catching up to her in the lounge room. "There is much you don't know."

"What don't I know, Joe?" Lesley said, angrily, as she turned to face him. "That my mother is delusional? A paranoid nut job? And a hermit?... I've lived with it my whole life! So don't tell me I have no idea!"

Lesley started rubbing her forehead because her head was throbbing again, so she went and sat on the lounge. Joshua watched Lesley for a few moments then sat down next to her.

"There are things you don't yet know, Lesley," he said, softly, "and that's why Katharyn asked you to come."

"Why? To explain why she is a psycho?" Lesley snapped.

"No," Joshua replied calmly, which was annoying Lesley, "there is a reason why Katharyn has had to live this way…. And you as well."

"Family secrets, huh?" Lesley said, sarcastically.

Joshua ignored this, reached out and placed his hand on her forearm.

"It is not for me to tell you, Lesley. It must come from your mother," he told her.

Lesley felt a surge of warmth at his touch and, instantly, she felt calm. She looked into his piercing blue eyes and felt a sensation in her body she had never felt before. Her heart started beating a little faster. She looked down at his hand on her arm and he removed it slowly, aware that his touch might have made her nervous.

"What aren't you telling me?" she asked, looking into his eyes again, honest eyes, she realized.

She now noticed his face in more detail. He was rugged and handsome with a three-day growth, framed by his shoulder length brownish hair. Lesley felt the strange sensation surge through her body again.

"What haven't you told your mother?" he responded knowingly.

"What do you mean?" she asked.

"The tumor, Lesley," Joshua replied.

Lesley was shocked and stunned because only a handful of people knew about her condition.

"How?" she mumbled, unable to say anything.

"I felt it," Joshua said.

Lesley looked at her arm where his hand had touched her, and still felt the sensation.

"Who are you?" she asked.

"You have read the Book of Adamah…," Joshua began.

"Yes," she said, cutting him off. "How did you….?"

Joshua shook his head slowly.

"Tonight, your mother will explain," he said, and again touched her arm, "and *you* must tell her about the tumor… Amy too."

"Amy knows," Lesley said, dropping her head and looking down. "I had to tell her. Somehow, she already knew… guessed it, I think."

She paused then looked at Joshua with tears in her eyes.

"But I haven't told her it will kill me," she said, softly.

Joshua put his arms around Lesley, and she fell into him and cried.

This felt strange for Joshua but, for some reason, it also felt right. This stunningly beautiful woman, a pure-born he had helped to protect since her birth, now made him feel something he had never experienced since he came to be on Earth, and, in this moment, he understood how Jonathon felt about Athena.

Later that evening after dinner, and after Amy had spent over an hour regaling her mother of the day's events with her 'super-hot and famous G-ma', Katharyn, Lesley and Joshua were sitting outside on the open terrace of the penthouse apartment. The view was spectacular and overlooked the entire city and its surroundings.

Katharyn loved it out here, high up above the city.

It reminded her of her home on Tellus, the place where she grew up, a place she still loved and dreamed about returning to one day.

Lesley noticed her mother staring off into the night sky, lost in her thoughts. She had never seen her mother this calm and relaxed before, and she caught Joshua looking at her as well. They exchanged knowing glances and a smile then Lesley nodded at her mother.

Joshua nodded back.

"Mother," Lesley said, breaking the silence. "There is something I need to tell you."

"I know, my love," Katharyn responded, still looking at the sky.

She then closed her eyes and sighed.

"Amy told me."

Lesley gasped.

"It's okay," Katharyn said, looking at her daughter. "Don't blame her. I think I already knew anyway… or suspected it, at least."

Lesley was lost for words and felt ashamed now because she had kept this from her mother.

"A mother knows. And I've seen you like this before… Only, not this bad," she said, suddenly overcome with grief.

There was silence for a while.

Lesley stared at her hands, lost in thought.

"How bad is it, Lesley?" Katharyn asked softly, her voice breaking with emotion.

Lesley looked at her mother, the sadness and resignation on her face answer enough so Katharyn nodded and looked away, not wanting her daughter to see her tears.

"Katharyn," Joshua said, breaking the silence. "It is time."

"Yes," Katharyn acknowledged, wiping her eyes, "yes, it is."

Lesley had been waiting for this since earlier this afternoon, and eager to find out the secrets her mother had been keeping all her life, she decided to go first.

"Mother, why did you give me that old book?" she asked. "You told me to read it then you would tell me everything."

Katharyn was nodding.

"What is there to tell?" Lesley asked.

Katharyn got up and went over to the balcony rail and again looked up into the night sky, trying to find the constellation she used to see from her mountain home on Tellus. But the lights of the city made it almost impossible to see anything except only the brightest of stars and the moon.

"Do you remember what I told you about your father?" Katharyn said, still looking into the sky.

Lesley looked at Joshua, briefly.

"You told me he traveled a lot and disappeared one day before I was born," she replied.

Katharyn turned and faced her daughter.

"I made that up," she told her.

Lesley was taken aback.

She got up and went over to her mother.

Joshua also stood up.

"Made what up?" Lesley asked. "I don't understand."

"Everything," she replied, looking at her daughter. "You don't have a father, Lesley. You are a pure-born. So am I... So is Amy."

Confused, Lesley said, "Amy? Wait. What?"

"Steven is not her father. He can't be. You said it yourself, and it's true," Katharyn told her.

"No mother, you're wrong," Lesley said, shaking her head.

"Lesley, look at me… When you figured out the timing, and I know you did, Steven would've been out of town, on business as he'd told you, but we both know he was with *her,*" Katharyn said, almost spitting out the last word.

Lesley opened her mouth to protest but she knew her mother was right. She had done the math herself numerous times, but never believed it.

"He is not her father. He can't be. Amy is a pure-born, born of no man… Just like you… Just like me," Katharyn said.

Lesley remembered those words from the Book of Adamah, 'born of no man.'

"I have no father?" Lesley mumbled in shock, then looked at her mother. "And neither do you?"

"None of us do my love. We are all born of no man, since the very beginning," Katharyn told her.

Lesley walked away shaking her head trying to process all this new information but finding it hard to even comprehend, let alone believe.

"How?" Lesley asked, turning back to her mother. "How is this possible?"

Katharyn walked over to Lesley.

"We have the power to create life inside us. It happens in our twenty-sixth year… Lesley, look at me… I have never been with a man," Katharyn stated.

Lesley was shocked.

"Never?" she asked, bewildered.

Katharyn shook her head.

"No. Never."

Lesley looked at her mother, slowly understanding what she was inferring.

"Never?" Lesley repeated, the implications of this revelation now dawned on her.

Katharyn nodded her head.

"Wow. That's…" Lesley started saying.

But she couldn't finish that statement because yes, it was crazy, but also true. She stood still for a few moments processing this new information.

"So," Lesley continued, "the story in that book you gave me for my birthday…"

Joshua shook his head.

"It's not a story, Lesley," he said, his voice melodic.

Lesley's eyes widened as she turned and looked at Joshua, the melody of his voice somehow familiar.

She had a sudden flash of a memory from years ago when she was in the hospital after her surgery. His face, those eyes, the other person in the room, the intense flash of light then nobody was there.

She thought she had dreamed it all.

"You were there," Lesley said, pointing at Joshua. "You said, 'you are safe.' I wasn't dreaming, was I? It was you!"

She glared at Joshua then at her mother.

"Yes," Joshua replied.

"That man…" Lesley said, "He was one of the nurses. I remember… He had a burn mark on one of his wrists… Why do I remember that now?"

"He was going to kill you, Lesley. Athanasius had touched him… It had to be done to protect you," Katharyn said.

"Athanasius?... From the story?" Lesley asked.

"It is not a story, Lesley," Joshua reiterated. "Jonathon has been protecting pure-borns since the beginning and I… I have been here since before you were born for the same reason."

"Jonathon," Lesley repeated, "Jonathon. Who is this Jonathon person you keep mentioning?"

"He is a Guardian. One of the original Guardians, from the beginning," Joshua explained.

"One of?" Lesley said. "So, there are more?"

"There were only ever two," Katharyn said, "Jonathon and Athena."

"Were?" Lesley asked, picking up on her mother's use of the past tense.

"Yes," Katharyn said, sitting down again. "Athena died protecting my mother, your grandmother, when we lived on Tellus."

"Tellus?" Lesley said, looking at them both.

"I was born there, Lesley. I wasn't born here on Earth," her mother told her.

Lesley started laughing at the craziness she was hearing.

"Okay. We've gone from fantasy into science fiction now. Is that it?" Lesley sarcastically asked.

"We escaped Tellus through a time rift Athanasius opened," Katharyn said, ignoring Lesley's remark, "and landed here on Earth in 1980."

"Time rift? Delusional," Lesley said, throwing up her hands and looking at Joshua. "Didn't I say that?"

"We landed just outside Henleyville, Lesley," Katharyn said, still ignoring the hurtful remarks.

"Henleyville?" Lesley said, astonished.

"Actually, the lake, to be precise," Katharyn stated then turned to look straight at Lesley who had suddenly lost her voice. "Ask Jonathon to show you the ship."

"Jonathon? The Guardian Jonathon?" Lesley asked. "I don't know any *Jonathon*."

Katharyn turned away from Lesley and said, "You know him as John Miller."

Lesley's mouth dropped open at this revelation.

She had well and truly lost her voice now.

Inside the penthouse, out of sight of the others on the terrace, but close enough to have heard the entire conversation, Amy wept silently.

SIXTEEN

Henleyville – Friday 6th October

There had been more revelations after Tuesday night on the penthouse terrace and, now back home, Lesley was still trying to process everything her mother and Joshua had told her. But she still didn't want to believe any of it.

Lesley stood in her bathroom looking at her reflection in the mirror. She had always looked much younger than her years, as did her mother, but could her youthful looks really be because it is her ancient birth right?

"Ageless beauty," Joshua had said. "A gift from the Creators."

It's nonsense, Lesley thought, staring at her tired face in the mirror.

Her eyes still had dark circles under them, and her head was sore again this morning. It was a constant thing now, the soreness in her head, like a dull headache that never goes away. It made her tired all the time and she was sure she could feel life draining from her.

I do look every one of my forty years this morning, Lesley thought, as she washed her face and tied back her messy long hair, the same as she always did.

Lesley checked herself in the mirror one last time then turned her head to the left and touched the back of her neck just below the hairline behind her right ear. In her reflection, she could just see part of her birth mark. She never knew she had a birth mark until her brain surgery thirteen years ago.

When Lesley had been able to get up after the surgery and walk around, she had used a hand-held mirror to look at the back of her shaved head. She wanted to see the scars from the surgery. She hadn't expected to find a very distinct mark as well.

"It's just your birth mark," Katharyn had told Lesley, a little dismissively, at the time.

But, unlike her daughter, Katharyn had known its significance because Joshua had told her what it meant when Lesley was born. Neither of them had revealed any of this to Lesley during her and Amy's stay at the penthouse apartment.

Amy was still sleeping.

They had arrived home late last night, both tired from the flight and the two-hour drive from the airport, and Lesley knew teenagers always seemed to need lots of sleep.

Lesley went downstairs and made coffee for herself then took her cup into the lounge room where she plonked down on the sofa and put her feet up on the coffee table. The house was silent but the town of Henleyville was most certainly awake because Lesley could hear the muffled voices of children walking down Old Mill Road heading for the high school.

I promised Amy she could skip school today, Lesley thought, as she got up and headed outside with her coffee to the porch.

It was a beautiful crisp, clear day.

Her neighbors, the Morgans, from several doors down were out walking their dog and waved to Lesley when she came outside. She smiled and waved back and watched them as they went about their morning ritual.

Paul and Brenda Morgan had been trying to have children for more than three years now with no success, and it was on Lesley's advice that they both had tests to see if either of them had fertility issues. The results determined that Paul Morgan has a very low sperm count with poor motility, so they'd been undergoing IVF treatment at a clinic in the larger regional hospital four hours' drive away. Lesley knew they would be driving there over the weekend for their fifth treatment on Monday, the last four attempts having been unsuccessful.

"One last time," Brenda had told Lesley last week when they met for lunch, "If it doesn't work this time then we will think about adopting."

Lesley shook her head slowly, the smile gone, as she watched Paul and Brenda disappear from her view.

They are such lovely people, Lesley thought. *Brenda is one of my best friends. How can they fail so many times to conceive a child, yet I can apparently make one all by myself, with no help from anyone, not even a man? It doesn't make sense.*

But there were several things Lesley couldn't explain, which made her think otherwise.

When she was pregnant with Amy, the scans and ultrasounds had all confirmed a probable date of conception, and it coincided with the time when Steven had been out of town for eight weeks. Additionally, the estimation of Amy's birthdate was almost to the day.

She was born a week earlier than her due date but, even allowing for this, Lesley knew Steven could not be the father. They hadn't been intimate before he went out of town, and after he came back, Steven seemed distant and not interested in sex. This was the week before she found out she was pregnant.

And there was the fact that Steven was infertile.

Lesley sat down on her favorite chair on the porch, thinking about all of this, about Paul and Brenda Morgan, about everything her mother had told her the other night, about being a pure-born, about some place called Tellus, and about a spaceship.

Spaceship.

Lesley stopped in her mind at this thought.

Mother said, "Get Jonathon to show you the ship!"

Jonathon... John Miller?

Old John Miller?

A Guardian?

An Immortal?

Lesley shook her head then sipped her coffee.

....

Lenora Jackson sat in her rental vehicle about fifty meters down the street from 147 Old Mill Road.

Being an investigative journalist had its perks and Lenora had used many of them to find out all she could about 147 Old Mill Road, its original owners, Frank and Marie Cooper, and its current owner, none other than John Miller himself.

Apparently, John Miller was the beneficiary of the Coopers' will and he inherited the house, its contents, and a business in town when the Coopers were murdered back in 1981.

John Miller had turned the business, which has a small flat above the shop, into a hardware store when the timber mill shut down in early 1992. She also found out that John Miller had lived above the store since he inherited it. And the Cooper house, as the locals still call it, remained empty till almost fourteen years ago when its current occupants moved to Henleyville.

But there was another mystery here as well, Lenora had discovered, or not discovered, whichever way you look at it. She could find no evidence of John Miller's existence before 1980, and when she dug even deeper, there were no records of Frank and Marie Cooper before 1970.

The other people found dead in the house on the night of October 2, 1981, were never named so Lenora had no information on them other than there were another two male and two female victims. But her gut instinct told her that they, too, may have had unknown pasts.

Her first thought was maybe Frank and Marie Cooper were in witness protection and their past had caught up with them, with the other four people being collateral damage. But then John Miller showed up in Henleyville ten years after the Coopers, with no records and no history either.

Another person in witness protection? she wondered.

Possibly, she considered. *But why put a new person into a house with existing people in witness protection?*

No, this didn't make sense to Lenora.

She'd never heard of this happening before and one of her federal 'friends' had confirmed that for her.

People can live 'off the grid' and 'off the record.' Lenora knew that, but three people in the same town having no documented history before showing up in Henleyville ten years apart seemed far too coincidental for Lenora's liking.

Maybe he was an undercover law enforcement officer, she thought next.

Possibly, Lenora surmised.

But she knew undercover agents always had a back story that could be 'verified.'

So why did John Miller stick around in Henleyville after the murders if he was an undercover law enforcement officer?

Lenora dismissed this idea almost as quickly as she thought of it because why would the Coopers leave everything to John Miller if he was an undercover agent, or a cop, or even in witness protection himself?

No, none of these theories made sense to Lenora.

There was something else going on here in Henleyville and Lenora was determined to get to the bottom of it, which is what she was telling Arnold Grey on the phone in her rental vehicle.

"I will… Gotta go, Arnie," Lenora said, ending the call, as the lady at 147 Old Mill Road came out onto her front porch.

Lenora picked up her notebook and read the name again she had written down last night.

"Lesley Jones," Lenora said, putting the notebook back on the passenger seat. "Good morning, Miss Jones."

She watched as Lesley Jones waved at a couple walking their dog then stood watching them for a few moments before sitting down on her porch.

In her research, Lenora had found out that Lesley Jones is the daughter of fashion and beauty mogul Katharyn Jones, owner, and CEO of 'Adanne by Katharyn,' another person who she could find no record of before late 1980. Lenora had been shocked by this finding because she uses some of Katharyn's skin care products.

During her latest update with her editor Arnold Grey, she urged him, "Get me an interview with the highly reclusive Katharyn Jones at any cost, Arnie."

"I'll try," he told her. "But no promises."

About half an hour later, Lenora saw Lesley get up and go back inside her house. It was almost eight am, Lenora saw when she checked her phone. She knew that John Miller would be opening his store any minute now, so she started her vehicle, did a U-turn, and headed for Main Street.

Henleys Diner was open, so Lenora parked further up Main Street, closer to Millers Hardware, then walked back to get a large, long black coffee. This would be her first of the day and she had been craving it since spotting Lesley Jones with her own coffee on her front porch.

When she entered the diner, Lenora immediately felt hungry as well. Deciding to have some breakfast, she took a window seat at the front so she could watch the comings and goings at Millers Hardware.

"Long black, Ms. Jackson?" Jennifer Henley asked, appearing beside Lenora's table.

Lenora smiled up at her.

"Good morning, Jennifer. Large, please," she replied. "And please call me Lenora."

"Sure," Jennifer said. "Are you having breakfast this morning?"

"Yes," Lenora said, nodding, then pointed at the specials board. "I'll have the Friday breakfast special, please."

"Eggs Royale it is, Ms. Jackson," Jennifer said and headed off to the kitchen.

Lenora shook her head and smiled as Jennifer Henley walked away.

Further down the street, John Miller was putting out an a-frame sign on the footpath in front of his store and Lenora spotted him from her window seat vantage point. She watched as he went back inside the store then reappeared moments later with a broom and began sweeping the footpath.

She also noticed the limp again.

Jennifer returned to Lenora's table, put down the long black coffee, looked out the window following Lenora's gaze and saw she was watching John Miller.

"He's a good man, Lenora," Jennifer said, startling Lenora.

Lenora looked at her coffee and then at Jennifer.

"Yes. Yes, he is… I spoke with him the other day," Lenora said, picking up her coffee and taking a sip.

The coffee was hot and tasted wonderful.

"Was he able to help you with your investigation?" Jennifer enquired as they both again watched John Miller through the window.

Lenora took another sip of her coffee, not taking her eyes off John Miller still sweeping the footpath.

"He's thinking about it," Lenora lied.

Jennifer nodded then went over to serve a couple who had come in a few minutes earlier.

About an hour later, Lenora was sitting in her rental vehicle with another large, long black coffee, takeaway this time. She was getting addicted to the Henleys Diner coffee. It was the best Lenora had ever tasted, and she had been to Italy and France, but none compared to the delicious hot beverage in her hand right now.

Main Street was getting busier, and she was glad she'd come earlier otherwise there would've been nowhere to park because the street was now full and every time a spot opened another vehicle pulled in almost immediately.

The hardware store was busy, too. There had been a nonstop procession of customers since it had opened.

It must be doing very well, Lenora figured.

Lenora finished her coffee and was deciding whether to leave or not when a familiar vehicle drove slowly past her. She'd seen that exact same vehicle this morning in the driveway of 147 Old Mill Road. The vehicle was doing the 'parking spot crawl' as Lenora had labelled it in her mind after seeing dozens of locals doing the same thing.

Lenora smiled and nodded when, as if by magic, a vehicle pulled out of a spot right in front of Millers Hardware and Lesley Jones quickly parked in the empty space.

When Lesley got out of her vehicle, Lenora noted that she was wearing a nurse's uniform, then remembered from her research that Lesley Jones worked at Henleyville Hospital as the head nurse.

Lenora had found this a little strange and wondered why Lesley Jones didn't work in her mother's company. After all, it's practically a global empire and Katharyn Jones is how old now?

Nobody knows for sure that Lenora could find out, and Katharyn Jones has never publicly disclosed her age.

The only thing Lenora knew was Katharyn was a young woman when she was discovered back in 1980 and she had not been seen in public for more than ten years, until Tuesday, when the Twitter-verse exploded with photos of the reclusive Katharyn Jones and her stunning granddaughter, Amy.

Lenora couldn't believe it when her Twitter account went crazy with people tagging her into the dozens of photos and selfies. The woman looked far too young to be Katharyn Jones, so Lenora had Googled her and found photos of Katharyn from her early years as a fashion model, plus several television interviews recorded in the 1990's.

The thing that amazed Lenora, and everyone else now it seems, is that Katharyn Jones has barely aged in almost thirty years.

There was something else the Internet was currently going crazy about since the reclusive Katharyn Jones' recent appearance: Who is Katharyn's granddaughter?

The answer to that question Lenora hoped to discover for herself.

She watched as Lesley Jones entered Millers Hardware.

....

The bell jingled as Lesley opened the door to Millers Hardware and went inside. She always smiled when she heard this sound. It was old-fashioned but she loved it.

 Most of the other shops and businesses on Main Street had changed to automatic doors which opened when you got close and an infra-red beam would sound a buzzer inside when you crossed its path, letting the owners know a customer had entered.

But not Millers Hardware.

Not John Miller.

 He had kept the same front door and bell that Frank and Marie had when it was their business. John liked the sound of the bell jingling too. It reminded him of his friends, and it was an homage to a time long past.

John Miller looked up from behind the counter when the bell jingled and smiled when he saw Lesley Jones come in. She smiled back but not with her eyes, he noticed, as she walked over to the counter.

"Hello, Lesley," John said.

Lesley just stood there looking at him intensely, with a strange curiosity on her face. She looked at his eyes, his face, his hair, and then John saw her look at the scar on his neck.

Her silence was making him a little nervous.

"Everything okay?" he asked.

Lesley sighed and looked him straight in the eyes.

"You tell me… *Jonathon!*" she said.

John's eyes widened a little and he opened his mouth slightly to say something but didn't, and Lesley saw the truth in his expressions.

"So, it's true," Lesley said, with a little sadness. "You *are* a Guardian."

John looked around the store but nobody else was inside.

"Katharyn told you?" John said, guilt written on his face.

"My mother… Yes," Lesley snapped.

John took a step back even though there was a counter between them, and Lesley saw this.

"I'm sorry, John," Lesley apologized, changing her tone and shaking her head. "It's been an eventful week."

"Yes," John acknowledged, "Your mother is making headlines again… as is Amy, apparently."

"Oh yeah," Lesley agreed. "Amy is beside herself. It's all she talks about. Her phone has been going crazy since Tuesday night."

Lesley looked at John again and saw concern in his eyes.

And he had good reason to be concerned.

With all the new publicity about Katharyn, and now Amy, John feared that if Athanasius had recruited more of the many assassins he had created over the past forty-plus years, then this new-found fame would make Amy a target.

John had been on high alert since Tuesday, even more so than he already was. Athanasius's foot soldiers had not stopped coming since the first one in 1981, and John was certain they would be coming again.

John knew Katharyn was safe with Joshua protecting her, but with Lesley and Amy it was harder. Lesley worked at the hospital and Amy was in school, and after school she would hang out with her friends. And it was only when Lesley had day shifts that they were both home in the evenings at the same time.

A Guardian's job is hard enough, but without his immortal speed, it was stretching John to his limits.

"Is it all true... what my mother told me?" Lesley asked.

"I don't know what Katharyn has told you, Lesley," John replied then looked around the store again, "But here... and now... is not the place to be having this conversation."

Lesley looked at her nurse's watch pinned to her uniform and saw the time.

"Yes. You're right. My shift starts in ten minutes," she said and looked at John again, an idea coming to her.

"Come over tonight... for dinner. I get off at seven pm... I have so many questions. Please, John."

John thought about her request then nodded and said, "Yes... And please call me Jonathon."

....

Lenora watched as Lesley, then John Miller, came out of the store. Lesley turned and hugged John Miller warmly and Lenora saw John Miller return the gesture. She raised her camera and managed to snap a few photos of them both embracing.

SEVENTEEN

Around seven-thirty that evening, Jonathon pulled into the driveway of 147 Old Mill Road and switched off the engine of his pick-up. He sat for a few minutes just staring at the house, the Cooper house, a place he had only returned to a couple of times since 1981.

The last time was to fix the leaking kitchen tap for the new tenant. Up until Lesley and her new baby had moved in, the house had sat empty. But when Jonathon heard that Lesley had applied for the vacant head nurse position, he offered the house rent free to the hospital, on the provision they kept its history and current owner a secret.

Jonathon took a deep breath, exhaled slowly, then got out of his vehicle and headed for the front door.

....

More than forty years had passed since Jonathon last sat at the dining room table in Frank and Marie's house, as he still considered it to be even though his name was now on the title deed. Memories never go away for an immortal, not for anyone really, and the memories of this house and his long-gone friends were still very fresh in his mind. He had not told Lesley about the history of the place and unless someone else had told her, he was sure she still didn't know.

And that's the way Jonathon hoped it would stay.

Lesley noticed Jonathon was very quiet during dinner.

Amy was fascinated by him.

She knew him as old John Miller from the hardware store, but he'd insisted she, too, call him Jonathon.

"Very formal," Amy said but not in a nasty way.

In fact, she liked it better than Mr. Miller or just John, and sitting at the table looking at him, Amy decided that the formal version of his name suited him much more. He has a presence about him, Amy realized, a formality, and she liked it as did her mother.

Lesley started clearing the table and Jonathon saw the deep scar on the table where the knife had been stabbed into it on that fateful night. It was deep and, looking closer at it, he was sure he could see a small piece of the magazine still jammed down inside it.

Amy's phone started ringing and she picked it up as she rose from the table.

"Dinner was great, Ma," Amy said then came over to Jonathon and kissed him on the cheek, much to his surprise, and her mother's.

Jonathon watched as Amy hurried out and went upstairs to her room.

"Seems like you've made an impression," Lesley said, shocked by her daughter's display of affection.

"Does she know?" Jonathon asked.

"No. Yes. I don't know," Lesley replied. "I don't know what mother has told her… or what she heard at the penthouse. But she always seems to know what is going on."

Lesley looked around the room.

"I wouldn't be surprised if she has listening devices everywhere connected to her phone," she joked.

Jonathon smiled.

"She's smart… and very perceptive," he said.

Lesley sat down at the table across from Jonathon, eager to ask the questions burning in her mind.

"Are you really immortal?" she asked.

"Yes," he replied.

"How old are you?"

"I've been around since the beginning," Jonathon told her, "Since Medora… Me and Athena."

Lesley nodded her head.

"Yes. Mother told me about Athena," she said. "I'm sorry, Jonathon."

Jonathon nodded slowly as he looked down at the table and the knife scar.

"So… you can heal yourself, too?"

Jonathon took his eyes off the knife scar and looked at Lesley.

"Yes. We can only die if mortally wounded by another immortal," he told her then turned his head so she could see the scar on his neck.

Touching it, he said, "I got this when Athena died… We were protecting your mother and Nakoma, your grandmother, from the Corvidaens. Athena jumped between me and one of the creatures, but she was mortally wounded… and it almost killed me, too, if not for Katharyn."

"Mother?" Lesley asked, amazed, because she had not heard this version.

"Yes… Athena was down, and I was too slow. The creature slashed at me and sliced open my neck… badly… but I managed to kill it," he explained. "… I collapsed after that and if not for your mother stemming the blood loss from my neck, I would be dead."

Lesley put her hand to her mouth while listening to this.

Katharyn had not told her daughter the grizzly details about the events of that day.

"Kathryn was only Amy's age," Jonathon continued. "She saved my life… but her mother lost hers. Athena, too… I had failed… again."

Lesley reached out and grabbed one of Jonathan's hands.

"No, Jonathon. If it wasn't for you, my mother, me, and Amy would not be here."

Jonathon was shaking his head.

"No, Lesley," he said, removing his hand from Lesley's grasp. "If I had died, none of you would be here… Your mother saved me, and in doing so, she saved herself and you and Amy."

Lesley sat up straighter.

"Rubbish, big man!" she said, which took Jonathon by surprise. "She may have kept you alive until you healed, but it was you who protected her before that, and ever since. And if it wasn't for you getting mother off that planet then none of us would be here."

Jonathon looked at her and saw the steely resolve in her eyes, that same look Katharyn had given him many times.

"Three generations of us, Jonathon," she said. "Three generations you have kept safe."

"I've had some help since we've been here," he said.

"Yes. I've met Joshua, or Joe, as he is known around here. I remembered him from when I was in hospital… and he was here a few weeks ago eating in the diner, stalking me it seems, at my mother's request," she said then smiled when she saw the horrified look on Jonathan's face.

"I can't move like I used to," he said, as a form of explanation.

Lesley nodded.

"Mother told me how you got your knee injury," she said, "which brings me to my next question… Where is the spaceship?"

....

Sunday afternoon, the sun was setting, and it was getting dark quickly. Nobody was at the lake now and Jonathon was certain they hadn't been followed from town. He had done this many times over the years, checking on the ship and sometimes sleeping inside it.

It was where he had escaped to after Frank, Marie, and the others had been killed. He couldn't stay in the house because it was a crime scene and the authorities had blocked all access.

Standing on the bank now as night was quickly pushing the daylight away, Jonathon felt calm. He looked at Lesley standing next to him wearing the same suit her mother had worn on their journey through the rift.

It fit her perfectly, he noticed.

Like mother, like daughter, he thought.

Amy was at home face-timing friends from school who couldn't get enough of their now semi-famous classmate. Lesley had asked Jonathon not to mention the spaceship to Amy just yet, and he had agreed it was a wise decision.

"I look good in this," Lesley said, noticing Jonathon looking at her.

Jonathon smiled.

"Yes," he said then showed her where to touch the neck of the suit to engage the face mask.

"Press just here and the mask will come out and cover your face, like this."

He demonstrated by pressing his own suit, which made his mask cover his face. He pressed it again and the mask retracted into the neck of his suit.

"Now you press yours and see how it fits," he advised.

Lesley pressed the neck of her suit, and the face mask covered her face. She looked around and moved her head up and down with the mask on.

"Can you breathe?" Jonathon asked.

Lesley nodded.

"Yes."

"Okay. Turn your suit lights on… here," he said, pressing the suit on the left side of his chest, "and let's go."

He watched as Lesley did as he requested then he engaged his own face mask again then they walked into the lake and disappeared below its surface.

As they arrived at the entrance to the water cave, Lesley's eyes widened in amazement at what she was seeing inside. The spaceship wasn't resting on the floor of the massive lake cave. It was hovering in place, illuminating the space it was occupying and everything around it.

It seems to be alive, Lesley thought, *and it's huge.*

Jonathon reached the entry hatch first and pressed a panel to open it. They both went inside then Jonathon closed the hatch and the water drained out of the transition chamber. He pressed his suit to retract his face mask and Lesley did the same, then he pressed a panel on a wall of the chamber and a door opened to access the inside of the ship.

Lesley was in awe and speechless as they went inside.

It looks like something out of a science fiction movie, she thought to herself.

She stood there taking in the surroundings and listening to the sounds of the ship but the silence inside was eerie.

Jonathon was about to speak when he felt something inside him, a gut feeling, an instinct, like the awareness he once had about Athena, the same awareness he now has about Joshua.

But this feeling he had now?

This feeling made him very uneasy.

Jonathon stood silent for a few moments, waiting, and listening, but the feeling persisted.

"This way," he eventually said, and Lesley followed.

He took her to the flight control center of the ship then went to a control panel and touched a button. A shield outside the ship opened, uncovering a massive forward window, and revealing the underwater view of the lake in front of them.

"This is amazing," Lesley said, looking out into the illuminated waters and shaking her head in wonder.

Jonathon smiled.

"Yes. It is."

Lesley turned and looked around the flight control center.

"How big is this thing?" she asked.

"Fifty meters long, thirty-five meters wide and ten meters high at its tallest point," Jonathon told her.

"Wow," she replied as she sat in the same control chair her mother had more than forty years ago.

As Jonathon watched her, he was thinking about Katharyn and how scared she had been but also how brave she was.

"There's actually two down here," he said, touching another button on the control panel which turned on all the lights in the command center of the ship.

"Two?" Lesley repeated, looking at him.

"Two of these," he replied, indicating the ship. "Two ships… The other one is a bit older but almost the same. It's behind us."

Lesley instinctively looked behind her not realizing how silly that was.

"I didn't see it," she said, turning back to Jonathon.

"You won't. It's in sleep mode sitting on the bottom of the cave," he said.

Lesley nodded her head.

"The one Francis and Mariangela came in," she said.

Jonathon was startled a little hearing his friends' proper names spoken, and Lesley noticed his reaction.

"Mother told me," she said. "She told me everything… I'm sorry, Jonathon."

Jonathon dropped his head and looked down.

"Katharyn told you what happened? In the house?" he asked.

Lesley got up and went over to him.

"Yes," she replied.

"And you're not bothered that six of my friends were killed there?" he asked.

"No… Mother said they were good people," Lesley replied.

She wandered around for a few moments touching things before coming back to him.

"Sometimes, in the house when I'm alone, I feel a presence… but it doesn't scare me. It comforts me," Lesley told him.

Jonathon was looking at her with a deep concern on his face. The mood had changed. Her mood had changed, and he felt it.

She touched his arm then started walking around the command center again, taking in the futuristic environment.

"Death doesn't scare me, Jonathon," she continued. "I've dealt with it my entire career. I've nursed people through the end stages of their lives, and I was there when most of them passed… Death comes to all of us… at some point."

She stopped talking and absentmindedly touched the back of her head for a moment or two, emotions now welling up inside her.

"It's the people we leave behind, Jonathon… Family, and friends, left to grieve. That's what scares me," she said, looking at him with tears in her eyes now.

Jonathon walked over to Lesley.

"What's wrong, Lesley?" he asked, deeply concerned now.

Lesley fell into him, wrapped her arms around him and started crying into his chest.

"I'm dying, Jonathon," she mumbled as she cried.

"Dying?" he repeated as he unfolded her from her hug.

He held her away from him slightly so he could look into her eyes.

"What do you mean?"

Lesley used one of her hands to wipe her face and eyes, regaining some of her composure.

"The brain tumor… it's killing me. I don't have much time left," she said starting to cry again. "I don't want to leave Amy."

Jonathon pulled her into his arms, and she cried hard into his chest again. He didn't understand how this could be happening.

No pure-born had ever died from an illness that wasn't caused by Athanasius. His death touch had taken many over the millennia, drained of their life within a day or two and left as gruesome hollowed shells of their former selves with a burn mark on their foreheads.

But this wasn't caused by Athanasius, and Jonathon realized he had no idea how to deal with a brain tumor.

"You had it removed, though," he said.

"It grew back," she said, removing herself from their hug and wiping her eyes, "bigger and badder… It can't be removed this time."

"There's nothing they can do?" he asked, and Lesley shook her head indicating no.

Jonathon ran his hands through his hair in frustration and started pacing around.

"How much time do you have?" he asked.

"Six months… at the most," she told him.

....

It was almost nine pm by the time Jonathon dropped Lesley back home. They said their goodbyes and Lesley waved from her porch as Jonathon reversed his pick-up out onto Old Mill Road and slowly drove away.

He passed a vehicle parked a few houses down and knew someone was sitting inside it. Jonathon had noticed he'd been followed from the lake all the way to Old Mill Road and now he knew who it was.

He was annoyed that he'd been careless.

If he and Lesley had been seen coming out of the lake, the ramifications could have dire consequences, especially if the ships were discovered.

This was not good.

He would have to put a stop to this before anyone else found out because he knew Lenora Jackson would stop at nothing to find the answers she so desperately wanted.

....

Lenora's phone rang just as she was watching John Miller reverse out of Lesley Jones' driveway.

The caller ID told her it was her editor.

"Arnie," Lenora answered, still watching the pick-up as it came slowly towards her, "What's up?"

"You need to get back to Capitol City asap, Lenora," Arnold Grey blurted out.

"Why?" she asked as John Miller drove past her vehicle.

"It seems you have friends in high places. Katharyn Jones has agreed to an interview… with you," he told her.

"Shit!" Lenora said, loudly, "No way. Really?"

"Yep," Arnold said, "An exclusive."

"Wow… That's great, Arnie," Lenora said. "When?"

"Tomorrow, Lenora. So, get your butt back here. Now!" Arnold Grey said then hung up not waiting for a response.

EIGHTEEN

The Darkness Realm

Athanasius stood with his eyes closed, an evil smile on his face. Rows of fires, seemingly burning from nothing, illuminated The Darkness around him. Dozens of Corvidaens, the death dealing creatures Athanasius had once used to carry out his evil deeds, stood anxiously in the shadows waiting for their master's next commands.

Athanasius raised a hand to silence them then opened his eyes.

"Well, that is interesting," Athanasius said, then turned to face the horrendous creatures. "Katharyn's daughter is dying."

The creatures started to talk amongst themselves enthusiastically but in an unknown language only Athanasius understood.

"You," Athanasius said, pointing to the largest creature who was standing silently. "How long till the next cycle?"

"It is almost upon us, master," the Corvidaen answered in its own language.

"Good," Athanasius said. "Prepare for my projection. You are coming with me this time. Gather some of your best… I have a new plan."

Athanasius had been listening to the conversation between Jonathon and Lesley on the ship, something he'd always been able to do since the Creators had banished him to The Darkness realm.

Every immortal has an echo.

And every immortal possesses the ability to locate other immortals anywhere in the universe.

It had been easy for Athanasius when they were on Adamah because Jonathon and Athena had apparently lost this ability and Athanasius had used this to his advantage, easily homing in on their location then sending his creatures to exact his revenge.

Initially, Jonathon and Athena managed to stave off every attack from the Corvidaens and this had frustrated Athanasius for a long time until he discovered he could project himself from The Darkness.

Armed with this new ability, he decided he would send the Corvidaens to keep Jonathon and Athena distracted, then project himself and hide in the shadows until a pure-born was unguarded, at which time he would emerge and carry out his deadly vengeance without being seen.

However, with all pure-borns now being mortal, their echo had vanished leaving Athanasius with no means to locate them. He assumed they would be residing in the same location along with their Guardians, but projecting himself drained most of Athanasius' power which meant he could only do it for a short time.

When Medora died after one of the attacks, Jonathon guessed that whenever the Corvidaens came, one of the creatures must have hidden in the shadows waiting for the opportunity to strike and kill the pure-borns.

He didn't realize it was, in fact, Athanasius himself.

So, Jonathon and Athena hatched a plan which required the help of the old Guardians, who were now mortals. Whenever the Corvidaens came, the remaining pure-borns, Medora's daughter and granddaughter, would be taken by the old Guardians and hidden in the homes of others far away. In their place, Jonathon and Athena used the bodies of the recently departed, displayed as if they were sleeping, resting, or sitting.

This plan had succeeded many times over the following years until one day when Medora's daughter, Tahira, refused to leave her home when the Corvidaens came. The old Guardians secretly whisked away her fourteen-year-old daughter to safety while Tahira argued with Athena and Jonathon.

Her defiant stance ultimately ended with her death from Athanasius' touch.

With Tahira gone, Athanasius knew there was now only one remaining pure-born standing in the way of him receiving The Pure and escaping The Darkness.

But recovering from projecting himself took time, even for a powerful immortal, and taking Tahira's life had drained more of Athanasius' power than he realized. That is when he figured out that Jonathon and Athena had been deceiving him for many years.

In The Darkness, it took twelve of Adamah's years for Athanasius to regain his full immortal powers after taking the life of a pure-born. But in between the deaths of Medora and Tahira, it had taken much less time for Athanasius to recover from each projection because he wasn't actually taking the lives of pure-borns.

He realized he had been killing the already dead.

Twelve Adamah years had passed since he'd taken Tahira's life. Athanasius had regained all his immortal powers and after watching the Corvidaens fail time and time again, he was determined to end the life of the last remaining pure-born himself, obtain The Pure, then exact his revenge on the Creators for banishing him.

....

ADAMAH
120,000 years ago

The news spread quickly throughout the village.

Helena, the granddaughter of Medora, had given birth and a celebration would take place on the shore of the lake where the newborn pure-child would be cleansed then named, as was the tradition. The old Guardians believed the essence of Aryanna lived in the sacred waters of Adamah and that the bathing of each new pure-child in the life blood of the lands added new life to it.

Jonathon and Athena were on high alert because it had been a difficult birth for Helena. The baby was not the right way around inside and it had taken the birth maid, herself an old Guardian, much time and effort to turn the baby before delivery. Helena was weak from exhaustion after the birth and Athena suggested to her that she stay behind and rest while the newborn was taken to the lake.

"No," Helena said, getting up slowly from the birthing cot, "I must cleanse her myself. It cannot be done by another."

People had come from everywhere to witness the ritual, even from the village far on the other side of the mountain which overlooked the valley near the lake.

Jonathon was up there now, keeping watch for Corvidaens, while Athena and the old Guardians were at the shore of the lake with Helena. The new pure-born child, born with the mark of the dove, was cleansed in the sacred waters by her mother, and she named her Nakoma, meaning warrior spirit for surviving her troubled birth.

Helena was still very weak, and from his high vantage point Jonathon saw her hand over the pure-child to one of the old Guardians, then collapse to the ground. In an instant, he was down there kneeling by her side, as was Athena.

Helena was losing blood, hemorrhaging from the complications of the difficult birth. Athena picked her up then raced her back to the village. The birth maid, and several other old Guardians with medical experience, arrived shortly after to attend to Helena.

A few hours later, Helena was sleeping but she was pale and very weak from severe blood loss.

"Helena cannot nurse the baby," the birth maid told Jonathon and Athena. "She is too weak, and her milk has not yet come."

Athena looked into the eyes of the pure-child in her arms and baby Nakoma stared fiercely back at her.

Warrior spirit indeed, Athena thought to herself and smiled at little Nakoma.

"There is a new mother in the village on the other side of the mountain. I have already sent word. Take the child there. You are expected," the birth maid told them.

Athena looked at Jonathon.

"I'll go," she said.

Jonathon nodded and Athena left immediately.

"There is nothing for you to do here, Guardian," the birth maid said to him. "She is asleep, and we can keep watch. Get some rest yourself."

Jonathon looked at the two other old Guardians in Helena's room and they nodded, agreeing with what the birth maid had said, so Jonathon left and went down to the shore of the lake.

He sat down and looked out over the sacred waters for a while, then closed his eyes and listened to the waves washing up onto the shore as the afternoon sun warmed his face.

Jonathon was startled awake when a massive thunderclap echoed throughout the valley. He had fallen asleep on the shore, and he realized from the setting sun that he had slept for several hours. He looked to the sky when lightning started flashing across the lake. It seemed to be emanating from one point high above the center of the now still waters.

Jonathon quickly got to his feet.

Lightning flashed continuously, striking the water and the shore around him, and from where it was emanating, the sky began to split apart.

Jonathon moved back away from the edge of the lake then saw something emerge from within the lightning storm. It was large, and shiny and was moving silently through the air. Jonathon watched as the huge flying object circled high above him and the valley, and then flew out over the lake before coming back and landing on the shore.

Dozens of villagers had gathered at the tree lines when the lightning storm had started and now, they stood fixated on the strange large object that had come from the sky.

A few minutes after the flying vessel landed, six people emerged from inside and stood in front of it. A man, maybe a little older than the others, stepped forward.

He was holding something in one of his hands.

Jonathon thought it looked familiar and stepped closer as the man, holding up his other hand as a gesture of peace, approached him.

"Hello," the man said to Jonathon, "I'm looking for the owner of this."

The man lifted the object he was holding, and recognition spread across Jonathon's face.

It was old, very old, far older than Jonathon knew it to be, but he knew what it was just the same.

The man held in his hand the ancient Book of Adamah.

"Where did you get that?" Jonathon demanded. "And who are you?"

The man came closer to Jonathon.

"My name is Francis. I found this in a hidden cave deep inside that mountain," he said, pointing.

The villagers who were watching from the tree lines moved down closer to get a better look at the newcomers and the giant vessel they had come in. The other five people who had arrived with Francis now moved up behind him to look closely at Jonathon, who didn't get any sense of danger from them.

The man called Francis turned the ancient book over and showed Jonathon the back cover. There was an unusual marking on it, one that Francis had also found on other objects he'd discovered inside the mountain cave, and one that was clearly displayed on the battle vest the huge man in front of him was wearing.

"Is this your mark?" Francis asked, looking at Jonathon's vest.

"Yes," Jonathon said.

Francis turned to the others behind him, smiled, and they all nodded.

"What is your name, friend?" Francis asked Jonathon.

"Jonathon," he replied. "I am a ..."

Francis cut him off.

"A Guardian. Yes. We know."

Jonathon became wary.

"How did you know that?"

"We deciphered the inscriptions etched around the borders on this book," Francis said, indicating the old book. "as well as some writings inside it. That's how we were able to find you."

Jonathon looked suspiciously at Francis and the other newcomers standing behind him. There were indeed ancient inscriptions on both covers of the book, etched by Jonathon himself, plus other writings he'd recorded on the pages, but he didn't know their meanings. All he knew was that he was propelled to transcribe them.

Francis saw the wariness of Jonathon's face.

"There is much to tell, Jonathon, but first let me introduce you to my companions," Francis said.

The others came forward to greet Jonathon.

"This is Mariangela, my wife. And this is Raphael, Samuel, Aniela, and Laila," Francis said, introducing each of them, who, in turn, shook hands warmly with Jonathon.

Seeing Jonathon greet these strange newcomers, the villagers came down closer and started interacting with them as well, introducing themselves and marveling at the large vessel resting on the shore of the lake. It was almost dark now but the lights on the vessel illuminated the surrounding area brightly, reflecting off the tree lines and making the lake waters glisten.

Suddenly, one of the old Guardians burst through the trees and ran down to Jonathon and the rest of the crowd.

"Jonathon!" he yelled, "Come quick. It's Helena."

Jonathon turned quickly hearing this then was gone in a flash.

The old Guardian looked at Francis and the others, then at the large vessel resting on the shore of the lake.

"Follow me," he said to them.

At Helena's house, Jonathon burst into the sleeping room and stopped. The birth maid was leaning over Helena and looked up when he came in. The other men in the room looked at Jonathon then lowered their eyes and shook their heads indicating there was nothing they could do.

"She has been touched, Jonathon," the birth maid said.

Jonathon went over to the cot Helena was lying on and saw the mark burned on her forehead. An evil laugh echoed all around them and throughout the house. Jonathon swiftly removed his battle sword from its sheath and spun around ready to strike. He looked around and quickly realized that Athanasius, himself, must have been there.

Jonathon yelled loudly in rage, the sound of his agonizing cry echoing throughout the entire village and beyond. The birth maid and the old Guardians recoiled, scared of what Jonathon may do.

But his rage was not directed at them.

He was angry with himself for falling asleep on the shore of the lake.

"Why wasn't I summoned when the creatures came?" Jonathon yelled at the old Guardians.

"There were no creatures," one of them replied.

"We were always just outside the room, Guardian," the birth maid said, trembling with fear.

At that moment, Athena appeared in the doorway, brandishing her battle sword.

"What has happened?" she asked. "I heard your rage."

Jonathon ignored her and nobody else dared speak a word.

But Athena didn't need an answer because she had already spotted the burn mark on Helena. She closed her eyes, knowing what this meant, then looked at Jonathon.

"Where is the pure-child?" Jonathon asked, angrily.

Athena sheathed her battle sword.

"She is with the new mother, Jonathon. She is safe," Athena told him, trying to calm his rage.

"There were no creatures this time, Athena," Jonathon said.

"Then how…" Athena began to ask.

"It was Athanasius," Jonathon told her.

"Athanasius came here?" Athena asked, incredulously.

"Did you see any creatures on the other side of the mountain?" he asked.

"No, Jonathon," Athena replied. "Everything is quiet there… What are you thinking?"

"I don't know. But Athanasius was definitely here," Jonathon said, then looked at Helena again, Athena following his gaze.

The old Guardian who had summoned Jonathon, arrived at the house with Francis and Mariangela. The other four newcomers had remained behind with their vessel.

Jonathon heard them enter the house and come to the doorway of Helena's room. He looked at them for a few moments, thoughts rolling around inside his head, then looked back at Helena lying on the cot, and watched her life slowly draining from her.

Athanasius' death touch is merciless, Jonathon thought.

He looked at Athena, who was thinking the same thought, then walked over to Francis.

"You said my journal helped you find this place," Jonathon enquired, and Francis nodded.

"Yes. It did," he told him.

Jonathon thought for a few moments, toiling with a decision.

"Can it help you get back to where you came from?" he asked.

Francis smiled warmly and touched Jonathon on the arm.

"Yes, my friend," Francis replied. "Yes, it can."

A few hours later, Helena died.

The traumatic birth and the hemorrhaging had already severely weakened her body and Athanasius' deadly touch had rapidly drained what little life she had left.

"We can take her with us, Jonathon," Francis told him. "We can bury her there so the child will always have a place to visit her mother."

Jonathon agreed, so a little while later Raphael and Aniela had Helena placed in a stasis pod ready for the journey.

"How many people can this thing take?" Jonathon asked, standing inside the large cargo area of the flying vessel, and looking at the pod housing Helena.

Inside the pod, even though Helena's face was shallow and drained of life, Jonathon saw a small smile on her lips.

Maybe even in death, she is happy that her daughter will he safe, he thought.

Francis looked to Raphael and Aniela for an answer.

"We can take probably thirty at the most," Aniela guessed.

The next morning, they discovered that only a few of the villagers wanted to leave Adamah. A dozen of the old Guardians chose to go, and a handful of young couples decided to leave as well, but everyone else wanted to stay.

So, Athena gathered some of her things to take with her while Jonathon went to his hidden cave deep inside the mountain.

He went over to a table he had crafted out of an old tree trunk and picked up the ancient Book of Adamah, which looked so much newer than the one Francis had brought with him. Jonathon ran his hand over the leathery covers and touched the symbol on the back, then looked at the intricate inscriptions he had carved around the borders of both covers.

Something came to his mind, a distant memory perhaps, and it was vague, but it was also a thought which made no sense. He felt it had some significance, though, so he placed the book down then carefully cut a small section of the stitching along one edge of the back cover, opening a pocket between the layers. He found his scribe and wrote something down on a piece of bark paper then folded it up and inserted it into the pocket, pushing it deep inside, then stitched the cover back together.

Leaving the book there, Jonathon stood for a few moments at the entrance to the cave looking back inside his secret sanctuary, then went up the mountain above the cave entrance and pushed several large boulders down causing a minor avalanche which filled the opening to the cave, hiding its existence.

On the shore of the lake, the villagers were saying their goodbyes to those who were leaving. Athena, with Nakoma in her arms, stood with Francis and Mariangela waiting for Jonathon to show up.

It was early morning.

The day had only just begun, and Francis was keen to leave.

Jonathon turned up just as the dust was settling on a lower part of the mountain, the remnants of the avalanche. Jonathon noticed the others were looking at the mountain, obviously having heard the rumble of the falling rocks a few moments ago.

"The ship is ready," Francis told him.

"Alright. Let's go," Jonathon said.

Athena looked at Jonathon for a moment, knowing he had been the cause of the rumbling noise and the dust cloud, then they all followed Francis and Mariangela to the entrance hatch and entered the ship.

Athena was carefully strapped into one of the spare seats in the command center then another safety harness was placed over her to hold baby Nakoma securely to her chest. Jonathon was next and Raphael made sure he was safely strapped into the other spare seat, before joining Aniela at the front of the command center. Taking his seat at the flight control, Raphael touched a panel on the console in front of him and the shield that covered the forward window opened, revealing the view they would all see from their seats.

Francis looked over his shoulder and smiled at Jonathon and Athena.

"We'll be there in no time," Francis said to them, and Jonathon noticed the very old book on his lap.

The ship lifted off the shore then flew up over the mountain, circled back over the valley then headed towards the lake, the sacred waters of Adamah. Aniela touched several panels on her console then lightning started flashing everywhere from a point in the sky out in front of the ship.

Jonathon and Athena looked out the forward window and watched as the sky began to split apart, just as Jonathon had seen it do the evening before.

"Hang on," Raphael said, "It's going to get a little bumpy."

He pushed the speed control of the ship, and in a flash, it was inside the rift they had created.

The ship was traveling at lightning speed through the rift, with a kaleidoscope of colors and lightning flashing across the front of the ship and thunder booming outside all around them.

The forces inside the rift were shaking the ship violently and Nakoma was crying loudly with fear.

Then, as quickly as it all had started, everything went quiet, and the ship emerged from the rift into bright sunshine and clear skies.

Raphael steered the ship over a valley with many magnificent structures and elaborate buildings seemingly reaching for the heavens, then flew up and over a mountain which looked familiar to both Athena and Jonathon.

Through the forward window, Jonathon could see a body of water in the distance, small but still substantial.

"That's our water supply," Francis said, pointing to the body of water. "The rains are due soon and it will triple in size from the runoff."

Jonathon and Athena looked at each other as the ship banked and headed for a large flat area with red flashing lights surrounding it. Athena looked down at Nakoma who had settled and was now sleeping.

Raphael landed the ship next to a squadron of smaller galactic fighter ships, shut down the drive engines then turned to Jonathon and Athena.

"Welcome to Tellus," he said.

NINETEEN

TELLUS

The villagers and old guardians who travelled from Adamah were settled into new living quarters and welcomed with open arms by everyone they met.

Francis and Mariangela took Jonathon, Athena, and Nakoma to a magnificent residence with an open terrace. It was built high up on a mountain with a view that looked out over the valley below it, the surrounding hills and forests, and the body of water in the distance.

The sun was setting, and the last rays of its light painted the sky, and horizon, in spectacular shades of orange and red. Thousands of lights switched on, illuminating the city in the valley below and as far as the eye could see.

Jonathon stood on the terrace surveying the highly advanced futuristic world before him and strangely felt at home high above the people of Tellus.

Athena came out onto the terrace and stood next to him.

She studied the visage before them, the magnificent city in the valley below, the forest and hills on its borders, and had a feeling they'd done this many times before.

"Incredible, isn't it," she said.

"Yes. Yes, it is," Jonathon replied, watching the colors fade from the sky as night rolled in.

"Where is Nakoma?" he asked, glancing at Athena.

"She is with a wet nurse," Athena replied, then noticed a confused look on his face. "Same as a new mother, Jonathon."

"Okay," he said, nodding.

From behind them, Mariangela called out, "Athena, Jonathon. Come eat."

"This will be your residence, for Nakoma," Francis explained to Athena and Jonathon during the meal. "I thought it would be ideal, considering you love this mountain so much."

"How did you find my cave?" Jonathon asked, between mouthfuls of food.

"It was discovered during the construction of this place," Francis began explaining. "We needed to install a lift inside the mountain for easy access to this top section. The cave was found during that process. Construction was halted and they contacted us to investigate."

Jonathon and Athena listened intently as they ate their meals. The food was amazing and plentiful, just how Guardians liked it.

"I recognized its significance immediately, Jonathon," Francis was saying. "And don't worry. The cave has been preserved just as you left it. We found a new spot for the lift."

"It's still there?" Jonathon asked, incredulously.

Francis nodded.

"Yes. Everything was catalogued and photographed, but nothing has been removed. Oh, except for the book. Sorry."

"Can I see it?" Jonathon asked.

"The book?" Francis enquired.

Jonathon said, "No. The cave."

Francis nodded.

"Sure. We'll go tomorrow."

"How did you find us?" Athena asked. "And how did you make that thing appear in the sky?"

"All in good time," Mariangela said. "Eat, then rest tonight. Tomorrow we will explain everything."

Francis nodded, agreeing with his wife.

The following morning, Francis took Jonathon to the cave while Mariangela stayed with Athena and the wet nurse. Mariangela had summoned one of Tellus' top medical specialists to check on the health of baby Nakoma, and after a thorough examination, she was given a clean bill of health.

"She has a strong and healthy heart," the doctor advised them. "How is her appetite? Is she feeding?"

The wet nurse nodded her head.

"Oh yeah. Like a warrior," she replied, and they all laughed.

When Francis and Jonathon reached the cave, the outside looked totally different to the last time Jonathon had seen it, which in his mind was just yesterday. It now had an ornate stone and metal façade covering much of the mountain around it as well as a large solid metal door closing off the entrance.

Francis held the electronic device on his wrist against a small panel on the left side of the façade, and the door slid open and into the mountain revealing the inside of the cave.

Jonathon stood there looking inside.

He had done the same thing only the day before on Adamah but, in reality, it was thousands and thousands of years ago.

"How long ago was I here?" Jonathon asked Francis. "It wasn't yesterday, was it?"

"No, my friend," Francis replied. "That avalanche you caused happened about a hundred and twenty thousand years ago."

Jonathon shook his head in astonishment then entered the cave and Francis followed just behind him.

Everything looked exactly as he had left it on Adamah. He went over to the wooden table he'd carved from a tree trunk and ran his fingers along its surface. His scribe was where he had left it, as was the bark paper he'd used for his journal. He looked at the mark he had carved into the wall of the cave, the same mark he'd carved into the back cover of the Book of Adamah, the same mark that was on his battle vest.

Francis came up beside him and looked at the carving on the wall as well.

"What does that mean?" he asked.

"I don't know," Jonathon replied. "But sometimes I have visions, dreams really, and that symbol is everywhere in them."

Francis nodded and began thinking.

"The inscriptions on the old book... how did you come up with them?"

"They are just random symbols and markings I remembered from my dreams," Jonathon told him. "You said you deciphered them. What do they mean?"

Francis studied Jonathon for a few moments.

"The inscriptions on the front cover tell of time travel and wormholes," Francis told him.

"Wormholes?" Jonathon repeated.

"Yes. The thing we created in the sky and flew into... We call it the rift," he said. "But it's actually a wormhole."

Jonathon nodded but didn't really understand.

"What about on the back cover? What do those mean?" he asked.

Francis looked straight into Jonathon's eyes.

"Exact space-time coordinates to find Adamah… and you."

Later that morning, up in the mountain residence, Francis and Samuel were telling Jonathon and Athena they had been invited to meet with the governing council members and the commander of the armed forces on Tellus.

But first they were told they needed to shower and change their clothing.

"Shower?" Athena queried.

"Same as bathing, only standing up," Jonathon quipped, grinning at her.

Athena punched his arm.

"I know that," she said. "Why do we need to shower?"

Jonathon leaned in close and sniffed her.

"I think because you smell," he told her.

Athena thumped him again, this time in his mid-section and much harder. Jonathon and the others laughed loudly.

After showering, Jonathon emerged wearing the clean long dark pants and new boots that had been left in his room for him. He had also neatly trimmed his beard, and his wet hair was now pulled back into a ponytail which hung just above his shoulders.

He was still warm from the hot shower, something he had never experienced before, so he went out onto the terrace without his battle vest on. It, too, needed cleaning and Mariangela had snuck it and his soiled clothing out of his room while he was in the shower. A silky white linen pullover shirt had been left on his bed along with the pants and new boots.

Standing on the terrace, Jonathon held the shirt in his hand by his side and looked down into the valley below where thousands of people were going about their daily routines.

Francis came out onto the terrace.

"We are due to meet the council members soon, Jonathon."

Jonathon turned around and Francis saw the mark on Jonathon's muscular chest, the same mark as on his battle vest, the same mark carved into the wall of the cave. Jonathon looked down at his chest, at the mark Francis was staring at, then put the shirt on covering his bare torso.

"I don't know what it means, Francis," he snapped, then went back inside.

Francis and Mariangela took Jonathon and Athena to meet with the governing council members where both Guardians were officially welcomed to Tellus.

Athena looked radiant.

Jonathon had barely taken his eyes off her since she had emerged from her shower wearing the new clothes she'd been given. She'd thumped him so many times after catching him staring at her, that his arm was now starting to hurt.

During the meeting, they both noticed that Francis and Mariangela were held in the highest regard on Tellus and wielded a lot of influence with the council members.

This could be a useful situation, Jonathon thought.

At the meeting with the commander of the armed forces, Jonathon and Athena learned that Samuel and Laila were high-ranking officers and highly skilled battle soldiers with years of fighter pilot experience, which impressed them immensely. The commander explained that the armed forces of Tellus encompassed substantial ground and air battalions, but the main focus was the galactic defense system, which had its massive base of operations on the moon.

"The moon?" both Jonathon and Athena asked, incredulously.

"Yes," the commander said, then drew their attention to numerous large screen monitors on the wall, which showed various views of the operations base on the moon, views from satellites in the outer regions of the solar system, plus a view of Tellus in all its magnificent glory.

They watched as several extremely large spacecraft, much bigger than the one they had arrived in, took off from the moon and began circling Tellus.

"We have satellites from here to the edge of our solar system, monitoring anything and everything that moves in outer space," the commander advised them. "If one of them signals an alert, we can mobilise our global defense system within seconds."

With their heads still spinning from what they'd seen and learned in the command center, Jonathon and Athena were taken to the armory where they were shown all kinds of weapons, some of which Samuel and Laila operated to demonstrate their firepower.

The Guardians had never seen anything like these weapons before. Their own weapons were basic and primitive in comparison.

In the evening, after the meal was over, Jonathon asked Francis about the various weapons he had been shown, and whether he and Athena could get some of them. He also requested a safe room be built in the residence, with reinforced walls, no windows, and a thick solid metal door that locked from the inside. Jonathon explained he would take no chances and no risks with Nakoma's life because she was the last of the pure-borns, so Francis agreed to these requests without hesitation.

His final request was for Helena to have a resting place so Nakoma could visit the mother she would never know. Mariangela said she would see to this request herself.

A little later, they were all sitting outside on the terrace.

The wet nurse had fed Nakoma, and she now lay asleep in a crib between Jonathon and Athena.

Francis watched Jonathon and Athena looking up at the moon, obviously still trying to comprehend all they had learned today, then glanced up at it himself.

"It's a lot to take in, isn't it?" he asked.

"Yes," Athena responded.

Jonathon remained silent.

Something was bothering him and had been since they'd arrived home.

"Why are there no old people here?" Jonathon asked, looking at Francis and Mariangela.

Mariangela and Francis looked at each other.

"There are many here, Jonathon," Mariangela told him.

"Yeah. I didn't see any either," Athena said.

"Everyone here looks younger than we do," Jonathon said.

"How old *are* you, Jonathon?" Francis asked.

"I'm immortal, Francis. I don't know," he replied, a little abruptly.

"We don't age," Athena told them. "We look the same as we did when we were put on Adamah."

"When was that?" Francis enquired.

Jonathon replied, "Well, according to you, more than a hundred and twenty thousand years ago."

Athena shook her head at Jonathon's petulance.

"It was when her great grandmother was born," she said, indicating Nakoma, then leaned down to check on her.

"Can you remember anything before then, Athena?" Mariangela asked her.

Jonathon looked at Athena who didn't answer immediately. Francis too was watching her closely, eager to hear her response.

"Sometimes, I think I do," Athena said, then shook her head. "I don't know… I get visions that flash through my mind. Brief ones. There and gone in an instant… They don't make sense really, but…"

Jonathon was very interested now.

"But what?" he asked.

Athena looked directly at him.

"The symbol on your battle vest," she said, "I see it in my visions… in my dreams, too. It's like I should know what it means. I recognize it but can't remember why."

Jonathon noticed Francis was watching him closely, for any reaction to what Athena had divulged, so kept his expressions neutral.

"You haven't answered my question, Francis," Jonathon said, steering the conversation back to the subject he wanted answers to.

"Ah, yes… Well, Mariangela is right. There are many older people here, us included," Francis said.

"We are in our nineties," Mariangela added.

"But you both look so young," Athena said, staring at them.

"DNA genetic modification," Francis declared.

Jonathon and Athena just stared blankly at him.

Francis chuckled at their reaction.

"We played around with an idea when we were just young scientists," he told them, referring to himself and Mariangela. "Genetic engineering has been around since long before us…

but we discovered a way of telling the genes to basically stop the aging process."

"We don't actually get younger," Mariangela added, "if that's what you are thinking. No. We do grow older. Just extremely slow. Francis and I are in our nineties as I said, but physically and genetically, we are only about forty years old."

"Wow," Athena said. "So, everyone on Tellus is much older than what they look like."

"Yes," Francis said. "Except the very young. They don't receive the DNA modification treatment until they have reached full maturity at the age of twenty-five."

"Do people die here?" Athena asked.

"Eventually, yes, from natural causes. And from accidents, too. Those can't be avoided," Francis said. "But not from disease or violence. We have none of that here on Tellus."

"When people reach the age of one hundred, they can choose to have another DNA treatment or forego it. If they choose the latter, then they start to age quicker because their genes begin returning to normal," Mariangela explained, "and within a few years they pass away."

Both Jonathon and Athena nodded, understanding.

"What if they choose option one?" Jonathon asked.

"Well, you saw for yourself today, my friend. No one here looks older than about fifty," Francis replied.

The conversation dried up for a while.

Mariangela refilled the drinks on the table between her and Francis and offered to do the same for Athena, but she declined.

Jonathon got up and went to the edge of the terrace, leaned on the barrier railing, and looked down into the bustling metropolis below, still very much alive this late into the evening.

Athena rose and picked up the crib with the sleeping Nakoma.

"I'm going to take her inside. It's getting cool out here," she said, then went inside, Mariangela following her.

Francis picked up his drink and went over to where Jonathon was standing.

It was a clear night and the moon had moved a little higher into the sky making it appear smaller. The cool night air brought the aromas of the distant forests to Jonathon's nose, aromas he had always loved, and they made him think of Adamah and the people they'd left behind.

He wondered if they were safe and he wondered what they were doing, and if they missed their Guardians. And then he thought of Athanasius and what he might do when he realized Nakoma was no longer on Adamah.

"How many people are on Tellus?" Jonathon asked, breaking the long silence.

"Approximately five million," Francis said, "scattered all over the world… But not everywhere is habitable, Jonathon."

"Why not?" he asked.

Francis looked up at the moon for a few moments to collect his thoughts before he answered.

"In another time, long ago, there was a great war, a world war," Francis began. "It was a different place back then… A different planet really. Inhabited by billions."

Francis took a swig from his drink, turned around and leaned against the terrace railing.

"War was common," he continued. "So were weapons of mass destruction. It was at a time when several powerful countries wanted to establish space operations on the moon. The world's richest people basically ran everything, but several jealous dictator-type empires decided they should instead… Money, power, and greed, Jonathon. That's what it was all about."

"What happened?" Jonathon asked, wanting to hear the end of the story.

Francis looked at Jonathon then finished his drink in one go.

"The dictators joined forces and launched their weapons of mass destruction against the rest of the world," he said. "You can imagine what happened next."

Jonathon nodded his head slowly, understanding what Francis meant.

"Retaliation," Jonathon said.

"Yes. The other major countries launched their own WMD's. The world was destroyed. Populations were wiped out. Cities, countries, obliterated. And the fallout from the bombs wiped out much of what was left, fauna, flora, everything," Francis said.

"Did anything survive? Did *anyone*?" Jonathon asked.

"That's the crazy thing about it. The rich people did. The billionaires who ran everything, they had contingency plans for exactly what happened. They'd built huge, highly sophisticated, underground bunkers hidden in specific countries in case of a world war. Yes, the rich survived, as did many of the people who worked closely with them… But the world population went from billions down to a few thousand in a matter of days… The people above ground who survived the initial bombings died not long after from radiation poisoning. That's what wiped out almost everything else, too."

Jonathon shook his head after hearing all this.

He couldn't imagine a world where these things could happen. He knew natural disasters could devastate the lands and animals, and even some of the people, but what Francis had told him was not a natural disaster by any means.

Humans had done this to themselves.

"After about five hundred years, it was safe enough for people to return to the surface… But, to this day, there are still lands around the world that are desolate and uninhabitable, Jonathon, even after three thousand years," Francis told him.

TWENTY

TELLUS - Ten years later

Life was good on Tellus.

Francis and Mariangela had chosen to have their next DNA modification treatment, having both celebrated their one hundredth birthdays the previous year. Jonathon and Athena found it remarkable because Francis and Mariangela looked basically no older than when they'd first met them and after their next treatment, they would age even slower.

Nakoma had grown into a beautiful, and feisty, young girl.

At ten years of age, she displayed all of the warriors' spirit her name implied. She followed Athena everywhere and was fascinated by all Athena taught her, but she was especially intrigued by Athena's battle suit. Nakoma would often sit on Athena's lap, touch her battle vest, and tell her she wanted to be a Guardian just like Athena when she grew up.

And that's what Nakoma was doing now as they sat on the terrace after having lunch.

Suddenly, high in the sky over the city, lightning started flashing everywhere but there were no storm clouds anywhere. The tentacles of lightning struck the tall buildings of the city in the valley below, and the side of the mountain near the terrace. Then the lightning stopped briefly as the sky began to split apart.

Athena's eyes widened as a dark cloud burst out of the rift into the sky and began spreading. Knowing exactly what it was, Athena stood, put Nakoma down and looked directly into her eyes.

"Remember what I taught you," she said, and Nakoma nodded. "Go."

Nakoma ran inside the house and disappeared out of sight.

Down in the city, the defense system alarms bellowed out their warning sounds which put the armed forces of Tellus on active alert. Athena watched as numerous galactic fighter star ships took off and started firing into the dark cloud that was still coming out of the rift.

In a flash, Jonathon was at her side, observing the mayhem in the sky.

"Where were you?" she asked him, but Jonathon didn't answer.

"Is Nakoma in the safe room?" he asked, watching the cloud come a little closer to the mountain.

"Yes," Athena replied.

"I'll get the weapons," Jonathon said, then raced inside.

First, he checked on Nakoma, making sure the safe room door was securely closed and locked, and satisfied it was, he took the weapons from a cabinet behind a false wall.

Back out on the terrace in a flash, he handed one of the weapons to Athena and she checked it was fully charged, loaded, and ready to fire.

"The Corvidaens," she said, "how did they find us?"

"No idea," Jonathon said, "but here they come."

They both aimed and started firing their weapons at the approaching Corvidaens.

There were thousands of them circling in a massive swarm, their deathly screams echoing across the valley. Dozens of the Tellus defense force fighter ships were now in the air, flying in and out of the swarm, firing their advanced weapons at the creatures while the battalions of soldiers on the ground defended the city from the onslaught.

The large weapons the Guardians held were long and heavy requiring both hands to operate and fire them, and when they hit their targets, Jonathon and Athena saw that the Corvidaens evaporated and disappeared into nothing.

They both looked at each other for a moment after their first kills.

"Cool," Athena said, and Jonathon nodded.

The swarm separated when the Corvidaens spotted Jonathon and Athena firing at them from high up on the mountain side. One swarm headed straight for them while the rest of the swarm split into two and came at them from both sides.

The battle raged on for what seemed like an eternity. The Tellus ground forces sustained heavy casualties and numerous fighter ships were taken down by Corvidaens that landed on them in the air, ripped them open, and killed the pilots.

Jonathon and Athena fired continuously at the swarms, glad for the capabilities of their advanced weapons. But some Corvidaens managed to evade the weapon fire and land on the terrace, so Jonathon and Athena retreated to the doorway to block entry to the residence while they continued firing at the creatures, but there were just too many.

A group of very large, and very angry, Corvidaens launched themselves at Jonathon and Athena causing them to drop the weapons. Removing their battle swords from the scabbards on their backs, they both began fighting the old way and managed to kill several large Corvidaens just as two Tellus fighter ships appeared, hovered near the terrace, and began firing at the rest of the Corvidaens that had landed there.

It was Samuel and Laila.

They managed to kill every one of the creatures on the terrace just as an enormous galactic star ship came down from high up in the atmosphere and fired a large device into the rift. Whatever the device was, it exploded inside the rift causing a wave of blue energy to expand outwards killing the rest of the Corvidaens instantly.

Jonathon and Athena stopped and watched them all disappear as the rift closed. They both looked at fighter ships still hovering above the mountain residence and waved to Samuel and Laila, acknowledging their help.

Athena raced inside to the safe room.

It was still secure.

Nakoma unlocked and opened the door hearing Athena's voice then jumped into her arms and hugged her.

Jonathon put his battle sword back into its scabbard, picked up the weapons and went inside to find Athena.

"Is she okay?" Jonathon asked, outside the safe room.

"Yes," Athena said, still holding Nakoma in her arms, "she is a brave young warrior."

Nakoma's face beamed hearing Athena say this.

Athena saw the anger on Jonathan's face and knew why.

"How did they find us?" she said. "And who opened the rift?"

"That is what I want to find out," Jonathon said, then was gone in a flash.

He arrived at the command center within seconds.

"Commander," he said, announcing his presence to all in the room. "How many did you lose?"

"A dozen fighter ships and as many pilots," the commander responded, looking at Jonathon. "What the hell were those things?"

Jonathon looked at him and the others in the command center who also wanted an answer.

"That is hard to explain," Jonathon said.

"Give it a try," the commander demanded, so Jonathon told him the story of Adamah, Athanasius and his creatures from The Darkness, the Corvidaens.

After listening intently and not saying a word, the commander finally said, "I know about your book. I just never believed it."

Everyone in the command center was fixated on Jonathon after hearing the detailed story he'd just told them.

"Immortal, you say," the commander said. "Can you die?"

"Not from anything you could do to me," Jonathon said, understanding what the commander was thinking.

The commander nodded at Jonathon wondering if this was true, while thinking he'd like to try.

"Who opened the rift?" Jonathon asked, forcefully.

"It wasn't us, Guardian," the commander retorted. "Only certain ships have the technology to create a time rift, and none of those were flying today. In fact, none are functional in their present state."

"What do you mean?" Jonathon asked.

"The ship you came in ten years ago, and the others in the fleet like it, are undergoing upgrades. We're installing the latest technology and fitting the new drive engines we have developed," the commander told him. "So again… it wasn't us!"

The commander turned his back to Jonathon indicating he was done with the questioning, so Jonathon left and returned home to the mountain residence.

When he got there, he was greeted by Samuel and Laila who he thanked sincerely for their help earlier. Francis and Mariangela showed up not long after Jonathon got back. Nakoma greeted them both with huge hugs which they lapped up. She thought of them as her aunt and uncle.

"Jonathon, Athena, we were in the treatment facility when the defense alarms sounded. We couldn't leave," Francis told them.

"Are you both okay?" Jonathon asked.

"Yes, yes. We're fine, Jonathon," Mariangela replied. "But we were worried about you both, and little Nakoma."

"Thanks to Samuel and Laila showing up when they did, all is well," Athena said, smiling at both fighter pilots.

"Those flying things," Laila said, "What were they? They seemed determined to kill you two."

"They are Corvidaens. Creatures from The Darkness. Immortal creatures. Which, I don't understand," Jonathon said, turning to look at Francis. "How *did* they find us? The commander said he didn't create the rift."

Francis thought for a few moments before giving his opinion.

"I can only surmise that the rift stayed open on Adamah," Francis said. "We closed it when we arrived back here but… maybe it has remained open at the other end."

"That was ten years ago," Athena reminded them all and Jonathon nodded, agreeing with her.

"But," Francis said, raising a finger to help him make his point, "don't forget we traveled a very long way into the future."

"So, if the rift stayed open when we left Adamah, you're thinking it's taken ten years for Athanasius to find us a hundred and twenty thousand years in the future?" Jonathon asked, not quite believing what he was saying.

"How much do you know about Athanasius? How powerful is he?" Francis enquired.

Jonathon and Athena looked at each other for answers.

"We don't really know," Jonathon answered. "We know he is immortal and can reach out from within The Darkness and take life with his touch. And he created those creatures, so he is powerful."

"Hmm, maybe," Francis said, thinking.

"Well, however he found us, we now have to be on high alert," Athena said, and everyone agreed.

"That large ship that came down and fired something into the rift killing all the Corvidaens… what was it?" Jonathon asked.

"That was one of our WMD's, a weapon of mass destruction," Samuel told them all.

....

Similar battles happened every few years for the next thirty years. Athanasius had indeed found a way of using the rift above Adamah to his advantage at will.

Fortunately, Nakoma and later her daughter, Katharyn, were always unharmed during the battles. And sometimes the massive blue energy explosives didn't always kill every Corvidaen. The creatures had learnt, after numerous lost battles, to take to the ground as soon as they emerged from the rift instead of remaining in the air.

The Tellus ground defenses protected the mountain residence from below, and the fighter ships, along with Jonathon and Athena, always managed to stave off the swarming air attacks but it was getting harder. The Corvidaen numbers had increased to tens of thousands and the battles were taking longer and longer, with the Tellus armed forces suffering many losses each time.

The pressure on Jonathon and Athena was increasing.

The council members and the commander of the Tellus armed forces were demanding the Guardians take Nakoma and Katharyn and leave. If it wasn't for Francis and Mariangela defending them, they would've been exiled years ago, but Mariangela made a point of reminding the council members of the value of the knowledge they possessed thanks to Jonathon's book. The rifts had made it possible for them to travel through time.

Additionally, Francis had reminded the governing council members that with their approval, the commander had used the rifts to travel forward in time and bring back more highly advanced technology and weaponry. This new technology had enabled their engineers to modify the fleet of spacecraft for interstellar space travel, crossing vast distances in space within a few moments of launching from the lunar base.

Jonathon studied the surly faces of the council members as they talked among themselves.

"It doesn't matter. They're right," Jonathon told Francis. "Too many people have lost their lives because of us. We need to find a new home."

"Where?" Francis asked.

"Not where… when," Jonathon replied.

"When?... Jonathon..." Francis began saying.

"Where is the book?" Jonathon asked, cutting him off. "My book. The Book of Adamah?"

"It's in the cave. Why?" Francis asked.

"Let's go," Jonathon said, then headed out of the great hall.

At the cave, Francis opened the door and they both went inside. Jonathon went over to the table and picked up the ancient book.

"The morning we left Adamah, I came here," Jonathon said, "... to look at my things and say goodbye, I guess. And my book was here too. It's not really old like this one, but... anyway, I picked it up and was looking at the covers and the inscriptions. Then I had one of my visions, just thoughts I guess, so I wrote them down and put them inside the back cover of the book."

"Wait. Inside *your* book?" Francis asked, then touched the book in Jonathon's hands. "You mean *this* book?"

Jonathon nodded.

"Show me," Francis said.

Jonathon picked up the very old knife from where he'd left it that morning on Adamah and cut the stitching on the back cover, in the same place he had the first time, and then carefully removed the piece of bark paper from inside. He handed it to Francis who noted it was very well preserved.

Francis slowly unfolded the paper then studied the writings on it. There were three lines of symbols on the paper, some of which were similar to the symbols on the covers of the old book, but the rest Francis had never seen before.

"Do you know what these writings mean?" Francis asked him.

"No. But I have a feeling they might help us," Jonathon said.

He repaired the stitching on the cover of the old book and put it back in its place. Then they both left the cave.

....

It took a few days for Francis and Mariangela to decipher some of the writings. Two of the lines of symbols were possibly space-time coordinates to another planet but the third line of symbols, a group really, was proving more difficult to translate. None of these symbols made sense to any of the scientists and scholars on Tellus.

"We'll go to this place first, Jonathon," Francis said, after revealing their findings about Jonathan's writings on the paper and what it all meant.

He was with Raphael, Aniela, Samuel, and Laila, the same flight crew from forty years ago.

"We'll make sure it's a safe environment, then return and collect you all," Francis added.

"I'm coming too," Mariangela told them.

Francis was about to protest but he saw the determined look on his wife's face and decided not to argue.

"Sure. Okay," he said, giving in.

"Another planet?" Jonathon asked. "Are you sure that's what it says?"

"Well, to be honest, we're not sure," Francis told everyone. "We have no reference material on Tellus for some of the symbols, especially the third line of writing."

"Then how can you be certain?" Jonathon enquired.

"The symbols for the space-time coordinates were relatively easy to decipher. They are like the symbols on the covers of the book. We've checked the coordinates with our navigation technology, and they seem to be valid. It's the name of the planet we're not sure of or if it's real," Francis said.

"Why?" Athena asked.

"We have no records in our archives of its existence," Mariangela replied, "So, we are uncertain of the translation."

"What is it called?" Athena asked.

"We think it is called Gaea," Francis said.

Jonathon stood tall hearing the word spoken aloud.

For some reason he didn't yet understand, he knew this place. A brief vision flashed through his mind, of a time when large creatures inhabited the lands, seas, and skies.

"It is real," he announced to the others, who all turned to look at him.

TWENTY-ONE

Capitol City – Monday October 9th, 2023

Lenora Jackson stood in the foyer of the building where Katharyn Jones apparently lived in the penthouse apartment. She was fifteen minutes early for her seven pm appointment, a stipulation made by the reclusive Katharyn herself.

Lenora was forewarned of the strict levels of security she would encounter: no cameras, no phones, no recording devices, no handbags, no bags of any kind. She was only allowed a notepad and a writing implement and these, she was told, would be provided when she arrived.

Lenora was searched and scanned by the security officers in the foyer. Her bag and phone were taken from her and placed in a locked cabinet. Satisfied she had no hidden electronic devices, one of the security guards led Lenora to the lifts and swiped an electronic card on a reading device which opened the lift door. He motioned for Lenora to step inside with him, which she did, then he pressed a button on the panel inside the lift.

It stopped at what Lenora assumed was the top floor, but she was mistaken. When the lift door opened, she was ushered over to two more security personnel who, again, searched and scanned her.

"Are you kidding me?" Lenora protested, but none of the guards answered or acknowledged her.

They walked her to another lift and one of them tapped a card to a reader, the lift door opened, and they gestured for Lenora to go in. When she entered the lift, she noticed there was no panel of buttons to select a floor. She was just about to say something to the security guards when the door closed.

Lenora looked around the lift then noticed a small camera in the corner of the ceiling panel. She looked straight into the camera, its red light blinking back at her.

Watching from a room inside her apartment, Katharyn studied the face of Lenora Jackson for a few moments then pressed a button which made the lift rise to the penthouse floor.

"Bring her to the sitting room then come get me. I'll be on the terrace," Katharyn said to Joshua, who had been watching Lenora Jackson on the monitor as well.

Lenora exited the lift and was confronted with two more security personnel, large men with no necks and very tight uniforms, standing in front of a set of double doors. As Lenora approached, one of the large men touched an electronic device on his right ear, listened, then opened one of the double doors.

Lenora entered the large foyer of the penthouse apartment and was greeted by Joshua.

"Ms. Jackson, thank you for coming," Joshua said. "Our apologies for the security measures, but it is necessary."

Lenora said nothing.

She was just staring at the man in front of her, his piercing blue eyes mesmerizing her.

"Please, come this way," Joshua said, gesturing for Lenora to follow him.

He led her to the sitting room, a large expensively decorated room with a fireplace and several seating lounges. On an antique coffee table in front of one of the lounges was a notebook covered in a leather binding, a gold pen set next to it, and a tray of refreshments.

"Have a seat, Ms. Jackson. I'll let Katharyn know you are here," Joshua said, then disappeared out of the room.

"Oh, I think she already knows I'm here," Lenora mumbled to herself.

Katharyn. He called her Katharyn.

Hmm... Husband? Boyfriend? Lover?

Personal assistant probably, Lenora thought, as she walked slowly around the room looking at all the antique ornaments and artwork.

A few minutes later, Katharyn entered the sitting room.

"Ms. Jackson," Katharyn said, announcing her presence.

Lenora turned and saw Katharyn Jones standing just inside the room, dressed in a thigh length sheer black dress that hugged her svelte figure, and her long, richly colored hair pulled around to drape over her right breast.

Lenora was awestruck and couldn't help but stare at Katharyn. The woman looked incredible, a natural beauty, and Lenora guessed not a day over forty.

That's not possible, Lenora thought. *Katharyn Jones was a young woman in the early 1980's. She must be in her mid-sixties now, at least.*

Lenora blinked her eyes rapidly.

"Ms. Jones... I'm sorry for staring, but you look amazing. I think I'm in love," Lenora said, jokingly, then smiled.

Katharyn blushed and smiled.

"Please, call me Katharyn," she replied as she walked over to Lenora Jackson and shook her hand softly.

"Thank you for inviting me here, Katharyn. It's a privilege to meet you. I know you don't give interviews anymore," Lenora said. "Why now, may I ask?"

Katharyn gestured to Lenora to sit on one of the plush lounges, which she did. Katharyn took a seat in the only single armchair in the room and crossed her legs elegantly.

It was only then that Lenora noticed Katharyn was barefoot, and she couldn't help staring again.

"I never wear shoes inside," Katharyn said, following Lenora's gaze.

Lenora looked up quickly and smiled an apology, then regained her composure. Katharyn was making Lenora's heart race for some reason and Lenora never got nervous doing an interview, at least not until now.

"You asked for me specifically," Lenora said, both a statement and a question.

"I have followed your work for a long time now, Ms. Jackson," Katharyn said.

"Lenora. Please, call me Lenora," she requested.

Katharyn nodded once and smiled.

"Lenora..." she said, "I, too, am interested in unsolved mysteries... 'cold cases' as you call them."

This was not entirely true but wasn't technically a lie either.

Katharyn, Jonathon, and Joshua had kept abreast of all news articles relating to people who had mysteriously disappeared since late 1981, when the man who killed all their friends vanished without a trace.

They knew what had happened to him, and to every one of them since then.

They just didn't want anyone else to find out or to start investigating any of the disappearances, of which there were many, more than two dozen in the past twenty years alone.

But nobody else knew this.

Jonathon had called Katharyn immediately after Lenora Jackson had confronted him in his hardware store asking questions about Haruto Tanaka and her husband, Simon O'Reilly.

"I don't think she will give up, Katharyn," Jonathon told her during the phone call.

Katharyn had friends in high places too, much higher, and more powerful than Lenora Jackson's contacts, and personally requesting the award-winning investigative journalist to do her interview served two purposes for Katharyn.

Firstly, it got Lenora out of Henleyville, although, after what Jonathon told her when he called late last night, it might have been too late.

And second, Katharyn and Joshua wanted to find how much Lenora Jackson knew.

But this would not be easy.

Lenora Jackson had a reputation for being cagey and a bulldog.

"Yes, those are my specialty, Katharyn, but…" Lenora said, then stopped.

"But what, Lenora?" Katharyn pressed.

Lenora liked the way Katharyn said her name.

"I'm working on something different at the moment," she replied, "A missing person case."

"Yes," Katharyn agreed, "Your husband, Simon."

This got Lenora's journalistic hackles up immediately.

"How did you know about that?" she asked, then nodded her head as she made the connection. "Ah yes. John Miller. He told you, didn't he?"

"I've known for a long time Ms. Jackson. It must be... what..." Katharyn said, then turned to look at Joshua who was standing near the doorway, "thirteen years now?"

Joshua nodded yes.

This knowledge threw Lenora a little, but she did note that Katharyn didn't dispute knowing John Miller.

She hadn't exactly confirmed it either.

She had ignored Lenora's remark about him, and now Katharyn had stopped calling her by her first name. Lenora realized the dynamic had shifted. It was not her doing the interview, it was Katharyn Jones in the driving seat.

"How could you possibly know that?" Lenora asked, staring straight at Katharyn.

Katharyn stared right back.

"You filed a missing person's report, did you not?" she said.

"Yes," Lenora admitted.

"Yes," Katharyn parroted, "I have connections, too, Lenora, and nobody gets in here without a thorough background check."

Okay. She's back to calling me Lenora, Lenora thought to herself. *Good. Maybe I can save this interview.*

"Why am I really here?" Lenora asked.

Katharyn and Joshua exchanged looks.

He moved and sat down on the plush lounge opposite Lenora.

"I'm hoping we can help each other, Ms. Jackson," Joshua said.

Lenora looked at Joshua warily.

"Who are you?" she asked him.

Katharyn replied instead, "Joshua is my… advisor."

"Joshua," Lenora repeated, still looking at him. "Do you have a last name, Joshua?"

Joshua smiled.

"No."

Lenora nodded at him, unconvinced.

"Lenora," Katharyn said, drawing Lenora's attention away from Joshua. "How many missing persons are on your list?"

Lenora didn't answer straight away.

She needed time to figure out what their game plan was, and now that they wanted to know how many she was investigating, Lenora realized they had to be all connected somehow, with Henleyville the possible starting point.

In Lenora's experience, if you give a little you get a little, and she figured Katharyn Jones probably had more than just a little to give.

"Six," Lenora eventually replied. "No. Seven," she corrected, "One of them is a couple. So… seven."

Joshua sat forward on the lounge and looked at Katharyn.

"Lenora," Katharyn said, her voice filled with warmth again, "There are many more than seven."

Lenora was now confused and a little shocked.

"More than seven?" she asked, looking at them both.

Katharyn pointed to the expensive leather-bound notebook on the table.

"Inside that is a list of names of people who have… disappeared since October 1981," Katharyn said, glancing at Joshua.

Lenora was dumbfounded, and her expression showed it.

She leaned forward, reached for the notebook on the coffee table, picked it up and opened it.

Inside it, she did find a list, a very long list, of names and dates. She looked at the list and saw Simon's name and the date he disappeared. She also found the names of the other people on her list, with dates noted next to each of them as well.

Lenora looked at Katharyn.

"What is this? How…?"

Katharyn ignored this.

"We need your help, Lenora," Katharyn urged.

"My help? How?" Lenora asked, still shocked at the size of the list.

Katharyn got straight to the point.

"Simon had a burn mark on his right wrist, didn't he?" she asked.

"Yes," Lenora replied, hesitantly, "How did you know that?"

"So did every one of the people on that list," Katharyn told her. "We know how they all got the mark."

She glanced at Joshua then looked back at Lenora.

"We need to know when."

Lenora was shaking her head.

"All of these people had that same mark on their right wrist," Joshua said. "We know how they got it. They all had… an encounter."

Lenora gasped.

"The shadow person," she said, making the connection.

"Yes," Katharyn admitted, "but we just don't know when. Something connects all the people on the list: a time, a place, an event. We just can't figure out what it is, Lenora. That's why we need your help."

"If you can't figure it out, with all your resources, then how do you expect me to?" Lenora asked.

"I don't have your instincts, Lenora," Katharyn told her. "You think outside the box. You find clues and evidence where nobody else ever thought to look… You've helped solve numerous cold cases and won awards for it. That is why I need you, Lenora."

Lenora could tell that Katharyn was being genuine, and her heart was racing again because she liked the idea of being needed by Katharyn Jones.

Why am I feeling like this? Am I Starstruck? Maybe, she thought.

"Why is this so important to you?" Lenora asked.

Katharyn got up and started pacing around the room, contemplating whether to tell Lenora or not, then she sat down next to Lenora.

"Because my family is in constant danger, Lenora… We have been since we came here and I'm tired of it," Katharyn said, clearly distraught.

She looked into Lenora's eyes.

"That list, they all encountered your 'shadow person'… that's how they got the burn mark. What I need to know is *when* he comes."

"He?" Lenora asked.

"Yes," Katharyn said, nodding, "He… He is dangerous, and will stop at nothing until me, my daughter, and my granddaughter are all dead."

"Katharyn," Lenora said, softly, "Why not go to the police with all this?"

"This is far beyond the capabilities of the authorities here," Katharyn replied.

"Who is this guy?" Lenora asked, looking at Katharyn then at Joshua but neither of them offered an answer.

Lenora sat quietly for a few moments processing everything she had learned. She looked at the list again and a thought came to mind, with several pieces starting to fall into place for her.

"October 1981," she said, then tapped the list. "The first one went missing in October 1981, and in my investigation, Henleyville keeps popping up."

She was looking directly at Katharyn then.

"It has something to do with the murders there in October that year, doesn't it?"

Katharyn nodded.

Lenora breathed in deeply, exhaled slowly, then stood up.

"Okay. I'll help you," Lenora said, closing the leather-bound notebook and holding it to her chest. "But I want to be there when this guy gets taken down."

Joshua stood up, and Katharyn rose as well and picked up the pen set from the coffee table.

"Here," Katharyn said, handing Lenora the pen set. "Take this. It's a gift."

Lenora accepted the offer.

"Thank you," she replied.

They all headed for the foyer.

"I will pay you for your time, Lenora," Katharyn said, handing her a business card. "Email me your bank details."

Lenora looked at the business card in her hand and turned it over. It had Katharyn's private number on it.

"My direct number," Katharyn said, reading Lenora's mind.

Joshua opened one of the large front doors to the penthouse apartment and the two security guards outside turned and stepped aside to allow Lenora to leave. Lenora stepped into the open doorway then stopped and turned around to face Katharyn.

"What's at the bottom of that lake, Katharyn?" Lenora asked.

Katharyn looked at Lenora for a few moments before answering.

"Stop harassing John Miller and I'll show you," Katharyn told her.

. . . .

About an hour later, Lenora entered her apartment, went to the kitchen where she removed a very small object from the vintage hair clip that had been holding her hair up at the back and plugged in into a USB port in her laptop. She pressed a few keys on the laptop then heard Katharyn's voice loud and clear.

Lenora smiled to herself.

The device had recorded everything.

TWENTY-TWO

Henleyville – Saturday 14th October 2023

It was Amy's birthday, and she'd been up since the first rays of sunlight had peaked over the eastern horizon. It was nearly eleven am and her mother was still not up. Katharyn had called Amy earlier to wish her happy birthday and to tell her she had put 'a little something' in her bank account for this special occasion, her 'age of awareness' Katharyn had called it.

"What does that mean, G-Ma?" Amy had asked her on the phone.

"I'll tell you everything next time I see you," Katharyn had said.

After the call, Amy had gone online to check her bank account and was amazed at how much her grandmother had given her. She'd gone to tell her mother but found Lesley still sleeping, so she didn't disturb her.

But now it was getting late.

Lesley had promised to take Amy to the lake for a birthday lunch and to celebrate with her friends. Also, a solar eclipse was happening today, and she wanted to be there to witness it.

Amy knocked on her mother's bedroom door, but Lesley didn't answer so Amy opened it, went over to the bed, and sat down on it carefully.

"Ma?" Amy whispered, "Are you getting up? We're going to the lake. Remember?"

Lesley opened her eyes, and Amy saw the pain in them.

"I can't, honey. I can't even sit up," she told a worried Amy. "Call Jonathon. He'll take you… I'm sorry, Amy."

"It's okay, Ma," Amy said, softly caressing Lesley's arm. "G-Ma called me this morning."

"Did she?" Lesley replied softly and tried to smile. "That's nice."

Amy looked at her mother who had closed her eyes again, then got up and headed for the door.

"Amy," her mother said, and Amy stopped and turned around. "Happy Birthday."

But it wasn't.

Not for Amy.

Without her mother with her at the lake, it wasn't going to be a happy birthday at all.

She quietly closed her mother's bedroom door, went downstairs, and called Jonathon.

At the lake, Jonathon sat quietly watching Amy and her friends having fun, celebrating her fourteenth birthday. There was lots of food on the table for them at the public recreational area. Lesley had planned ahead for this day, arranging everything that was needed for the party with Jennifer Henley. Jonathon had gone by the diner and collected it all before picking up Amy.

One of Amy's friends had brought a portable stereo system, and it was belting out tunes Jonathon had never heard before.

Teenager music, he figured, not liking it much.

Everyone seemed to be having fun, he observed, but occasionally he saw Amy just standing alone watching everyone else, with a worried look on her face, and he knew she was thinking about her mother.

As another vehicle pulled into the lake car park, Jonathon looked up to the sky and noticed the eclipse had begun. It was going to be an annular solar eclipse, the news reports had said, which meant there wouldn't be total darkness, but it would be very close. At the full eclipse point, a ring of red would be all that could be seen surrounding the moon as it blocked out the sun and would last only a few minutes at the most.

Lenora Jackson found a spot with a good view of the recreational area and the lake beyond it, so she pulled in and shut down the engine of her rental vehicle. She'd been watching John Miller since he'd closed his store earlier than normal today. He'd then gone to Henleys Diner and collected several boxes of what Lenora presumed was food and drinks. From there, she followed him to 147 Old Mill Road where he picked up Lesley Jones' daughter, Amy, and took her out to the lake.

Lenora had a different camera with her today.

A better camera than just her phone.

It had a telephoto lens with a special filter that would allow her to take photos of the eclipse as it happened, but it also meant that Lenora could easily watch John Miller up close without leaving her vehicle.

He looks different today, Lenora thought, looking through the camera at him.

She pressed the button a few times, taking several digital shots. Lenora looked at the small screen on the camera, checking each photo for focus. Satisfied, she looked up at the sky and took several photos of the eclipse as the moon moved a little more across the sun.

She saw John Miller stand up and turn around to look in her direction, so she slunk down in her seat. She held up the camera and looked through the lens at him and saw that he wasn't looking at her, but at another vehicle that was pulling into the car park. Lenora looked around searching for the vehicle and watched it park on the other side of the car park.

She knew the vehicle and so did John Miller because he was walking towards the car park.

Lenora continued watching as Lesley Jones got out of the vehicle. She had on a large hat and dark sunglasses, and she seemed to be walking very slowly. John Miller rushed over to her as best he could with his bad knee, held one of her arms and assisted her to the recreational area.

Lenora took lots of photos.

She watched as Lesley's daughter, Amy, ran over to her mother, obviously excited to see her, and kissed her. Then she saw Amy Jones turn down the music which had been blaring loudly since Lenora arrived.

It was nearing one pm and daylight was disappearing a little quicker now. The total annular eclipse was only a few minutes away, so Lenora took several more photos of the event, then checked she had enough memory left in the camera and switched it to video mode.

The sky was almost dark now.

Lenora looked over to where the party was happening, but it was too dark to really see anything, so she lifted the camera and focused on the eclipse which was only moments away.

As the moon moved in front of the sun, fully blocking it out, Lenora held her finger on the camera button, capturing the amazing astrological spectacle in real time.

In The Darkness, Athanasius closed his eyes and cleared his mind, concentrating his power to project himself.

"We are ready," the largest Corvidaen told Athanasius in their unknown language.

"Change to your original form," he commanded them. "You have your instructions."

The fires that constantly burned in The Darkness extinguished as Athanasius began his projection, taking the selected creatures with him.

Arriving at his destination, Athanasius spotted the Guardian and two of the pure-borns in the distance, then he looked to the sky knowing he had only a minute or two this time.

Athanasius had selected only four Corvidaens to come with him, the largest one, and three of the ones the creature had selected, and they now stood with him in the temporary darkness of the eclipse. They were in human form, their original form, and dispersed when Athanasius signaled them to leave.

Athanasius spotted someone sitting in a vehicle in the car park, and seeing who it was, an evil grin spread across his face as he moved towards her.

"Lenora," an echoing voice said from beside her in the vehicle.

She stopped filming the eclipse and looked to where the voice came from, and saw a shadowy figure surrounded by mist sitting in the passenger seat. She gasped in horror and dropped the camera as the shadow person reached out and grabbed her arm around the wrist.

"Simon says hello," Athanasius taunted her.

"You're… the shadow person," Lenora exclaimed, now terrified.

She tried to scream out for help, but no sound came from her.

"We don't have much time, Lenora," Athanasius said, gripping her wrist tighter.

Lenora felt a burning heat travel from her wrist through her entire body, and she started feeling different. She felt like she was changing inside. Her head became foggy, and her eyes started glazing over.

Athanasius leaned close to Lenora.

"Be ready," Athanasius whispered in her ear, "Your time will come."

Lenora collapsed unconscious just as the eclipse ended and the moon began moving again revealing a tiny sliver of the sun. At the same time, Athanasius vanished from inside her vehicle and returned to The Darkness, very pleased with himself.

It was dark when Lenora regained consciousness.

She looked up to the sky searching for the eclipse then realized everything was dark because it was nighttime. Looking out through the windows of her vehicle, she saw the car park was empty.

She checked her phone for the time.

It was past eight pm.

What happened? she wondered, trying to remember.

She kicked something on the floor and, looking down, she saw it was the camera. As she picked up the camera, she noticed the burn mark on her wrist and dropped the camera again as she suddenly remembered her encounter.

She recognized the mark.

It was the same burn mark Simon had on his wrist after his accident. Lenora quickly looked at the passenger seat where the shadow person had been, but no one was there.

"Simon!" she gasped, realizing everything he had told her was true.

Lenora looked at the burn mark on her wrist again and felt nauseous. She hurried out of the vehicle and expelled everything that was in her stomach, which wasn't much.

Her head was pounding, and she felt very weak.

She picked up the camera off the floor of the vehicle, threw it on the passenger seat, then got in and headed back to town.

At 147 Old Mill Road, Jonathon was on the phone with Katharyn telling her about Lesley and her sudden decline in health. Amy had come back downstairs in tears after helping her mother into bed.

"Please stay," Amy had begged him, before phoning her grandmother and asking her to tell him.

Katharyn agreed with her granddaughter.

"Yes. It's a good idea. Stay with them, please, Jonathon," Katharyn almost pleaded, "until we can get there early next week. I have an important meeting here on Monday that could prove vital to all of us."

"Vital how?" Jonathon asked, somewhat intrigued, but currently more worried about Lesley and Amy.

"I don't know yet. I'll talk to you on Tuesday when we get there," she told him.

"Okay," he said.

"You know Amy is at the age of awareness now," Katharyn said.

Jonathon was looking at Amy, who was sitting on the lounge, pretending to not listen.

"Yes, I know Katharyn."

"Don't say anything till I am there, Jonathon," Katharyn said. "Can you put her back on, please?"

Jonathon handed Amy's phone back to her.

She went off up to her room, talking to her grandmother all the way there.

Jonathon went outside, sat on the front porch, and looked up into the night sky but there were no stars. Heavy storm clouds had moved in just before sunset and after an initial onslaught, it was now just raining lightly.

There was no moon tonight either.

It had made its appearance about eight hours earlier and had been the star of all the news bulletins across the country.

Still looking at the sky, he thought of everyone who had been taken from him, from Medora to Nakoma, his long-time friends who had been killed in this very house, and Athena, his eternal partner.

Now Lesley was dying too, and he was powerless to stop it.

Out of the corner of his eye, Jonathon noticed something moving behind the big tree at the end of the driveway. Jonathon stood and instinctively reached behind him to remove his battle sword from its scabbard.

But it wasn't there.

It was safely locked away in the flat above his store.

The rain started to get a little heavier.

Someone *had* been hiding behind the big tree because the person came out from behind it and stood at the end of the driveway.

It was a man, Jonathon realized.

A tall man with dark skin and a bald head.

Jonathon looked around the porch for anything he could use as a weapon but found nothing. The tall dark-skinned man started walking up the driveway towards the house. Jonathon saw he was grinning, an evil grin, and he had something in one of his hands.

Jonathon moved to the stairs as the man got closer.

The dark-skinned man reached into his pocket and took out a small object which he started screwing onto the end of the object in his other hand. Jonathon realized it was a handgun and the man was attaching a silencer.

Jonathon stared at the man, who was now standing on the path at the bottom of the stairs.

How could this be? Jonathon thought. *Joshua said he took care of this one.*

"I can guess what you are thinking, Guardian," the dark-skinned man said, his voice deep and with a West-African accent. "I am supposed to be dead."

The man raised the handgun and aimed it at Jonathon.

"I'm not," said the man, "and we've come to finish the job."

He fired twice, hitting Jonathon in the chest.

Jonathon rocked back with the impact of the bullets then tumbled forward and fell down the four stairs, landing at the feet of the dark-skinned man.

The man went to step over Jonathon, thinking he was dead, but Jonathon opened his eyes, grabbed one of the man's legs and hurled him across the front yard and into the big tree at the end of the driveway. The man hit the tree hard, dislodging the metal letterbox, and he lay motionless for a moment before getting to his feet.

Jonathon stood up, too.

"Your friends died quickly, Jonathon," the man said, taunting him. "You, I will take my time with."

The dark-skinned man morphed into a very large Corvidaen and Jonathan's eyes widened as the massive creature bounded towards him, screaming its horrendous battle cry.

Jonathon tried to evade it but without his immortal speed he couldn't, so the creature was on him in a flash, slashing at him with its large razor-sharp talons and trying to bite him with its fangs. Jonathon grabbed both of its arms and held them away from him then headbutted the creature as hard as he could. The creature was stunned momentarily so Jonathon took the opportunity to swing it around and fling it across the yard again, this time hitting the side of his pick-up truck head-first.

Jonathon knew his only chance was to kill the Corvidaen but, to do that, he needed a weapon. He quickly scanned the yard as the creature rose to its feet again and moved its head from side to side, cracking the bones in its neck.

Jonathon spotted the letterbox on the ground near the big tree. The lid had come off and was lying a few feet further away.

The creature saw what Jonathon was looking at and started running for it at the same time as Jonathon.

The Corvidaen was quicker because it didn't have a bad knee, but just as it was about to pick up the lid, Jonathon barreled into its side and they both tumbled across the ground. Jonathon looked around for the letterbox lid, but the creature kicked out at him and sent Jonathon flying backwards, landing on his back several meters away.

The creature was on top of Jonathon in a flash, slashing at him with both talons. Jonathon grabbed both of its arms and mustering all his strength, snapped them causing the Corvidaen to reel back screaming in pain.

Jonathon stood up and started walking towards the creature. Its arms were now useless, hanging limp by its sides, but it still came at Jonathon, trying to kill him by snapping at him with its mighty jaw and large sharp teeth. Jonathon punched the creature hard, making it stumble backwards but it came at him again. So, Jonathon punched it again, much harder this time, sending it thumping into the big tree at the end of the driveway.

Jonathon picked up the letterbox lid as he strode towards the creature then, with all his immortal strength, he shoved the lid so hard into the creature's chest, it split its heart in two, came out of its back and lodged deep into the tree trunk.

He backed away and watched as the Corvidaen died and morphed back into the dark-skinned man. As he turned around to head into the house, Jonathon looked up and saw a light was on in one of the bedrooms.

Standing at the window, staring down at him, was Amy.

She had seen, and filmed, the whole thing.

TWENTY-THREE

Amy watched Jonathon put the body of the dark-skinned man in the back of his pick-up and drive away.

About an hour later, after disposing of the dead man, Jonathon returned and now he stood in the bathroom down the hall from his old room. He'd removed his shirt and was looking in the mirror at the bullet wounds in his chest. One bullet had gone right through the center of the mark on his chest, the mark he still had no idea of its meaning, and barely missed his heart. The other bullet had pierced his left lung.

Neither had killed him.

His internal organs had healed instantly.

He is immortal, after all.

No Earthly weapons have any effect on him, nor can they hurt him. Stun him, yes, but only momentarily.

Jonathon watched as the bullet wounds healed and disappeared. However, the scratches and gashes from the talons of the Corvidaen would take longer to heal, and some would leave scars.

Jonathon knew the only way an immortal could die was by the hand of another immortal piercing the heart, which got him thinking. Joshua had supposedly killed that same dark-skinned man more than forty years ago. And on Tellus, the Corvidaens disappeared when they were struck with weapon fire or when the galactic defense starships used their blue energy wave weapons.

Jonathon knew that Athena died because a Corvidaen had slashed open her chest and ripped her heart apart.

Then it dawned on him.

We've been killing the same ones over and over again.

"The Corvidaens never die," he said to himself in the mirror.

Then another startling thought came to him.

"We… The man said *we are coming to finish the job*."

Jonathon turned around quickly to leave the bathroom but stopped immediately because Amy was standing in the doorway staring at him.

She looked at the gashes on Jonathan's arms and torso and noticed the strange symbol on his chest over his heart. She stared at it for a few moments then looked up at Jonathon.

"Who *are* you?" Amy said, softly.

Jonathon pushed past her.

"Not now, Amy. I need to call Joshua."

Jonathon went out to his truck, found his phone, and called Katharyn. She answered almost immediately, and Jonathon asked to speak with Joshua. Jonathon told Joshua everything that had happened earlier and what he'd figured out about the Corvidaens.

There was something else Jonathon realized too while he was talking to Joshua.

"I think when Athanasius touches them and burns that mark on their wrist, he's turning them into Corvidaens," Jonathon said, wandering around the front yard while talking on the phone. "They are no longer human."

"And you think when they disappear, they don't actually die, they go back to The Darkness to fight another day?" Joshua said.

"Yes. I'm sure of it. And I think there's more of them out there. So be careful. Trust no one. And remember, the only way to kill them is to pierce the heart."

Jonathon ended the call and went back inside to find Amy.

Lesley was up.

She was in the kitchen making herself a coffee and Jonathon stopped in the doorway when he saw Amy sitting at the kitchen table. Lesley smiled at him and asked if he would like a hot drink.

"I'll make it, Ma," Amy said, getting up. "You sit down."

Lesley looked worse, Jonathon noticed, as she sat down.

Her face is drawn, her eyes are heavy, the dark circles under them seem to be getting darker and deeper, and it looks like she is hunched over, he thought to himself.

Jonathon sat down at the table as Amy placed a cup of hot coffee down in front of him. He looked at her and smiled but she just glared at him.

"Thank you, Amy," Jonathon said.

"There's a cake in the fridge. It's for your birthday. I was going to do it at the lake, but I forgot to take it," Lesley said to Amy.

"It's okay, Ma," Amy said, sitting down at the table with a hot chocolate. "I'm not hungry."

Jonathon picked up his coffee and took a sip, all the time looking at Amy who was watching him like a hawk. Lesley, even in her poor state, picked up that something was not right.

"What's going on?" she asked them both.

"Nothing, Ma," Amy replied, smiling at her mother but not with her eyes. "Mr. Miller was telling me before where he comes from."

"Really?" Lesley said, looking at Jonathon and raising her eyebrows. "And what did Mr. Miller tell you?"

Jonathon shook his head slightly, letting Lesley know he had said nothing.

"Well, he was just getting to the interesting part… about how he can kill monsters with his bare hands!" Amy snapped.

"Amy!" Lesley scolded.

"I saw you!" Amy said, her voice getting louder as she stood up. "I saw everything!"

Amy ran out of the kitchen and went up to her room, slamming the door closed.

Lesley looked at Jonathon.

"What the hell, Jonathon?"

So, he told her everything, and that Amy had witnessed it all from her bedroom window. He also told her what he'd figured out, and what he'd told Joshua on the phone.

"This is still all new to me, too, Jonathon. I can't imagine what is going through Amy's mind after seeing that, here at the house, in our own front yard!"

They sat in silence while Lesley replayed in her mind everything Jonathon had just told her.

"How much danger are we in?" Lesley asked.

When Jonathan didn't respond she looked at him and saw the answer in his eyes. It was not the answer she wanted.

"That much, hey," she said, then breathed in and out deeply.

"I think you both should go stay with Katharyn," Jonathon said. "The security there is impenetrable."

Lesley shook her head.

"I'm too sick to fly, Jonathon. The cabin pressure would play havoc with my head. And I don't think Doctor Mac would give me a medical clearance anyway."

"Drive then. I'll drive you both."

"No," she said, smiling sadly at him. "I can barely walk around my own home without passing out. There's no way I'm sitting in a car for twelve hours."

Jonathon said nothing for a few moments while he thought of options. A plan formed in his mind.

"Okay," he said, "I'll stay here with you both. I'll get somebody to look after the shop… or I'll just close it. I don't know. I can decide that later. But there are a few things we must do first."

"Such as?" Lesley asked.

"Amy is at the age of awareness. We must tell her everything. Katharyn told me to wait till she gets here on Tuesday but after what she saw tonight, I don't think we can hold off till then," he explained.

Lesley nodded slowly in agreeance.

"Okay," she said. "What next?"

"There are some weapons hidden in the house. I need to show you both how to use them," he said.

"Weapons? In the house?" Lesley repeated, taken aback.

"Yes. Sorry. I should've told you," Jonathon said, apologetically.

Lesley was not happy that this piece of information had been kept from her.

"I've been over every inch of this place since we've been here, and I haven't found any weapons. Where are they?" Lesley asked.

"There's a hidden storage compartment," Jonathon told her.

"Where?" she demanded.

Amy appeared in the doorway at that moment.

She'd been listening to everything since running out of the kitchen. She'd run upstairs, slammed her bedroom door then snuck back down and hid around the corner from the kitchen.

"Under the stairs," she announced to incredulous stares from her mother and Jonathon.

"Amy! How long have you been listening?" her mother demanded.

Amy just smiled and sat down at the table.

"Nice performance," Jonathon said, looking at Amy who grinned at him. "How many times have you done that?"

Amy shrugged her shoulders.

"I'm *aware*," she said, emphasising the word, "of more than you think, Mr. Miller."

"Amy! Stop that, please," Lesley said. "Sorry, Jonathon. I don't know why she's behaving like this."

Jonathon just smiled and shook his head.

"What?" Lesley said to Jonathon.

"Your mother was exactly the same at her age," he said, still smiling a little.

"Sorry, Ma… Sorry, Jonathon," Amy said, sincerely. "G-ma told me a few things when we were out shopping… and I was listening when you were all outside on the terrace that night."

"And I'm guessing you were eavesdropping last Friday night, too," Lesley stated, realizing her daughter's deception.

Amy dropped her eyes, having been caught out.

Lesley shook her head, unhappy with Amy's behavior.

"It's best that everything is out in the open now, Lesley. I don't like keeping secrets," Jonathon said.

He turned his attention to Amy.

"The question is what *don't* you know?"

Amy looked at Jonathon. He felt her eyes penetrate deep inside him.

"Well, I still don't know where you came from," she replied.

TWENTY-FOUR

Capitol City – Monday October 16

Lenora stood in the foyer of Katharyn's apartment building. It was almost ten am. Lenora hated Mondays because her boss was always on her case about her next column which was due each Wednesday by five pm to make the Friday edition.

And today was no different.

Arnold Grey had already rung her and emailed her numerous times since six o'clock this morning, reminding her about the deadline. Lenora had rung Katharyn on Friday to arrange the appointment, after she had arrived in Henleyville for another stealth mission to monitor the comings and goings of John Miller. She'd told Katharyn Jones that she had discovered some unusual coincidences with a few of the people on the list that may have some significance.

Lenora showed the security people the notebook and pen set, the gifts from Katharyn. Lenora had told Katharyn she would be bringing them with her. Lenora handed over her bag and was searched and scanned the same as the last time, while one of the security people checked the notebook and pen set.

With a nod from the head security officer, Lenora was taken to the lift. Ten minutes later, she was standing in the sitting room of the penthouse apartment waiting for Katharyn to appear.

On the table, like her previous visit, was a tray with refreshments. This time it was tea, coffee, and an assortment of breakfast buns and fruit.

"Lenora," Katharyn said, coming into the room. "It's nice to see you again."

"Good morning, Ms. Jones," Lenora said.

Katharyn was in casual attire this morning, Lenora noted. Denim shorts and a loose-fitting white blouse that was not buttoned up all the way. Her hair was tied up at the back, and as always inside her apartment, her feet were bare.

"Please, take a seat. There's tea and coffee if you like. Are you hungry?" Katharyn asked as she sat down in the armchair.

Lenora couldn't help but notice that Katharyn wasn't wearing anything under the blouse.

"No, thank you, Katharyn," Lenora said, once again entranced by Katharyn. "I'm not feeling well today."

"Perhaps you are tired from all your travels recently," Katharyn said, smiling.

"Yes," Lenora said, knowing full well Katharyn probably knew she had been in Henleyville since Friday and only got back late yesterday.

"So, you said you have some information," Katharyn said, wanting to get to the point of this meeting.

"I do. Well, I think I do," she said, opening the notebook to where she had made some entries.

Katharyn got up, came over and sat down on the four-seater lounge next to Lenora.

"What did you find?" Katharyn asked, leaning closer so she could see what Lenora had written in the notebook.

Lenora's heart was racing because Katharyn was sitting so close to her. She could smell her perfume, just a hint of it, not overpowering at all, and Lenora wondered what brand it was. *It's probably Adanne,* she figured.

Lenora started feeling light-headed and a little nauseous. She took a few moments to compose herself then removed the long gold-plated pen from the pen set and started showing Katharyn her notes and what they meant.

"It may be a really big coincidence, like I said on the phone, but in my experience, I'd say not," Lenora said.

"How did you discover this connection?" Katharyn asked.

"It was actually my boss who did. I told him I was going out of town for the weekend," she said, then looked at Katharyn who knew she meant Henleyville. "Anyway, he told me to get some good shots of the solar eclipse, then he said to me, 'didn't your husband have an accident during an eclipse?' and that's how I made the connection. I checked a lot of the names on the list and there was either a solar eclipse or a lunar eclipse on, or just before, the dates you say they went missing."

"An eclipse," Katharyn said, sitting back in the lounge. "That's excellent work. And we have your boss to thank for it."

Lenora said, "Well, yes, him and Simon."

Simon, Lenora thought, and her hand gripped the long gold-plated pen a little tighter as the mark on her right wrist started to burn and turn red.

"Now is your time," a voice whispered in Lenora's ear causing her to drop the pen.

Lenora's eyes glazed over then flashed black and she started to rock back and forth.

"Lenora, what's wrong?" Katharyn said, startled by Lenora's sudden change in demeanour.

But Lenora didn't hear her.

She launched herself onto Katharyn, straddling her where she sat and held her down with her left hand. Then she placed her right hand over Katharyn's heart, and the burning heat from the mark on her wrist traveled through her hand and into Katharyn's breast.

Katharyn screamed and Joshua appeared in an instant throwing Lenora across the room and into the wall. Lenora stood up and shook her head then morphed into a large Corvidaen.

Joshua picked up the long gold-plated pen and in a split second he was thrusting the pen deep into the heart of the scowling creature.

The creature looked at the gold-plated pen sticking out of its chest and pulled it out. It took a step towards Joshua then collapsed to the floor. Joshua watched as the Corvidaen changed back into its human form and took its last breath.

He rushed over to Katharyn who was struggling to breathe, and he saw she had quickly aged in the few moments since she was attacked. He also saw the mark now on her forehead, the mark of the Ouroboros.

He picked up Katharyn's phone off the table and called Jonathon who yelled angrily when he was told the fateful news.

"How quickly can you get her here?" Jonathon asked, still overcome with rage.

"Ten, fifteen minutes," Joshua told him.

"Make it quicker, immortal, and meet me at the lake," Jonathon snapped back then hung up.

Lesley, having heard Jonathon yell, got out of bed and went downstairs to find out why.

"Jonathon, what's wrong?" she asked.

"Your mother. She's been attacked," he said.

Lesley gasped in horror.

"No!"

"We have to go, Lesley. Now!" he said and headed out to his truck.

"Amy! What about Amy?" Lesley cried as she got into the pickup.

"There's no time," he said, reversing out of the driveway and speeding off. "She'll be safe at school."

They arrived at the lake in record time.

Luckily there had been no police patrols.

Jonathon put on his spacesuit and went into the lake. About ten minutes later he returned carrying one of the stasis pods from the ship. He put it down just as Joshua arrived carrying a lifeless Katharyn.

"Mother!" Lesley screamed when she saw her, and the mark burned on her forehead.

Katharyn's face was hollow, her breathing was shallow and sparse, and she had aged rapidly. Lesley grabbed her mother's wrist, checking for a pulse, but couldn't find one, so she felt her neck.

"Are we too late?" Joshua asked Jonathon.

"I don't know," Jonathon said, opening the pod.

"She still has a pulse," Lesley said between sobs, "but it's very weak."

"Put her in. Quickly," Jonathon urged.

Joshua placed Katharyn in the stasis pod and Jonathon closed it, then pressed several buttons on the control panel which started the cryogenic suspended animation sequence. They all watched as the small window frosted up on the inside.

"What do we do now?" Lesley asked, tears still running down her face.

"We take her to the ship," Jonathon said.

"I'm coming, too," Lesley said.

Jonathon looked at Lesley.

There is no way she is strong enough to swim down to the cave in her weakened condition, he thought.

Joshua was watching Jonathon and obviously read his mind.

"I will take her down, Jonathon. Lesley, you just hold onto me. I'll do the swimming for the both of us," he told her.

Jonathon nodded, sensing there was no point arguing about it.

"I have extra suits," he told them.

Down on the ship, Jonathon locked the stasis pod into its cradle and connected it to the ship's main control systems, even though all of Katharyn's biological functions had been temporarily stopped. Jonathon wasn't taking any chances. If something went wrong with the pod, the main control system would detect the malfunction, take control, and keep Katharyn in suspended animation for as long as needed.

Lesley was sobbing, standing next to the pod, looking at the face of her mother through the little window, a face she now didn't recognize. Joshua put his arms around her, and she turned and cried into his chest.

Jonathon looked at the other pods in the stasis chamber, knowing what they carried inside them.

Lesley eventually stopped crying and wiped her eyes. She looked into Joshua's eyes and smiled warmly at him. They went over to where Jonathon was standing, looking into one of the other pods.

Lesley saw a man inside, his eyes closed, and a small hole in the middle of his forehead.

He looks peaceful, she thought.

She wandered around and looked at the faces of the people in the other pods, then glanced at Jonathon who was still visibly distraught and angry.

"Are they your friends?" Lesley asked, politely.

"Yes," Jonathon said, then looked at Lesley. "I'm going to take them home."

"Home?" she repeated.

"To Tellus," he said.

Lesley looked at the six pods, then at her mother's.

"And you want to take mother there?" Lesley asked.

"It is her home, too. She was born there… And I think they can save her," he told her.

TWENTY-FIVE

"I told you to trust no one," Jonathon said to Joshua.

They were back at 147 Old Mill Road, the Cooper house.

Jonathon had collected Amy from school and Lesley was upstairs in her room telling her what had happened to Katharyn. Jonathon was angrily pacing around the living room and could hear Amy's anguished cries which only made him angrier.

"Yes. I was careless," Joshua admitted.

"So were your security clowns," Jonathon said. "You knew about the burn mark on the right wrist. Why didn't you inform them what to look for?"

"I am sorry, Jonathon. I have no excuse," he said.

"Where were you? Why was that woman alone with Katharyn?" Jonathon demanded.

Joshua looked at Jonathon, not sure how to answer his question.

"I was away… temporarily," he said.

Jonathon stopped pacing and stared at Joshua.

"You are really starting to annoy me, immortal. Away where?"

"Please, Jonathon, with respect I had no choice. I was summoned," Joshua told him.

Jonathon continued to stare at Joshua.

"You mean by them?" he asked, pointing his right index finger towards the ceiling.

Joshua nodded.

"The Creators, yes."

"You? Why? Why not summon me?" Jonathon asked, spreading his arms wide.

"You cannot be summoned, Jonathon. It is forbidden," he said.

Jonathon bristled with anger hearing those words.

He walked over and stood in front of Joshua.

"Forbidden?" he repeated, parroting Joshua. "Forbidden!!"

Joshua put up his hands, palms out, trying to calm Jonathon.

"With respect, it is not I who wrote the ancient laws."

Jonathon looked him in the eyes for a few moments then walked away.

"I have a message for you, Jonathon, from… from them," he said.

"Really?... I can't wait to hear it," Jonathon said, sarcastically.

"It is a message with two parts," Joshua began. "First… remember who you are."

"You've said that to me before, Joshua, a long time ago and yet, here I am, hearing the same thing again," Jonathon said.

When Joshua didn't say anymore, Jonathon prompted him.

"What's the second part of the message?"

"The child can help you," he said.

Jonathon turned and looked at Joshua.

"The child? What child? The only child I know is Amy, but she's not actually a child anymore. Is that who they meant?"

"I believe it is, yes," he said, then paused as Jonathon sat down on the lounge. "Jonathon, there is something else I learned when I was summoned back."

Jonathon had his elbows on his knees and his head in his hands, not looking at Joshua.

"Yeah? And what is that?" he mumbled.

"A true immortal never dies."

Jonathon looked up and stared hard at Joshua, contemplating this revelation.

....

A few days later, Jonathon, Lesley, and Amy were in a secluded area on the other side of the mountain near the lake. It was a small clearing inside a pocket of thick forest. A dirt track led to the clearing and was normally only accessible by four-wheel-drive vehicles, but Lesley's all-wheel-drive SUV made the trek without any issues.

Jonathon had brought them all the way out there, in the middle of nowhere, to show them how to use the weapons he'd retrieved from the hidden compartment under the stairs in the Cooper house.

Amy was fascinated by them.

The weapons were larger than any automatic or semi-automatic rifle she had seen on television, and now holding one she realized just how heavy they really were. But being strong and athletic for her age, she managed to hold the weapon correctly without much effort.

Lesley, however, was finding it difficult to keep the weapon up. She had no strength in her arms anymore. It was too heavy for her because she was getting sicker and weaker by the day.

Doctor Mac had put her on permanent sick leave from the hospital after talking with Jonathon and making a house call on Tuesday morning, when Lesley could not get out of bed. Amy was pretending everything was okay, but Lesley could tell that her daughter knew the reality of what was happening: the tumor was killing her mother. Lesley didn't have long to live.

She returned to her vehicle, unable to stand up any longer and she sat watching Jonathon and Amy together laughing and joking with each other. Amy was having a ball firing the futuristic gun.

She's a natural, Lesley thought and smiled to herself.

Amy ran over to the car holding the weapon facing down as Jonathon had instructed.

"Ma, this thing is so cool. I could eliminate a lot of people with this," she said, beaming at her mother.

"Amy!" her mother chastised.

"Kidding, Ma. Jonathon said I can keep this," she said, then ran back to him.

....

Later that evening, Lesley was in bed exhausted from the day.

She hadn't eaten anything at dinner and her failing health was now a major concern for Jonathon. He went upstairs and knocked lightly on her bedroom door.

"Yes," Lesley answered, her voice barely more than a whisper.

Jonathon poked his head inside the door.

"Can I come in?"

Lesley nodded, so he went in and sat down on her bed.

They looked at each other for a long time without saying anything, the unspoken words saying plenty.

Finally, Lesley spoke.

"When are you taking mother to Tellus?"

"Soon," he said.

"Do you really think they can save her?"

"I have to try, Lesley," he replied.

Lesley nodded, watching him closely.

"Then what are you waiting for?" she asked.

He looked at her before answering.

"The right time, I guess."

"You mean after I'm gone," she said.

Jonathon looked at her in horror.

"No! That's not what I mean… I want to take you with me, for the same reason I want to take your mother there… But…"

Jonathon didn't know how to voice the thoughts going through his mind: *What if you die during the trip? What if they can't save you? Or your mother?*

And the main one, *what if I am not welcome there anymore?*

Lesley touched his arm.

"I know," she said, agreeing with things not spoken.

"There's Amy to think about, too. And who knows where or when Athanasius, or the Corvidaens, will show up again. I can't risk leaving you both here, alone," Jonathon told her.

"Joshua can be here. He's a good man, Jonathon," Lesley said.

"You like him, don't you?" he asked.

Lesley smiled and nodded.

"Yes, I do, very much… You're very hard on him, you know."

Jonathon looked at her again.

"Yes, I know. He's always so… polite and respectful. It drives me crazy."

"Well, maybe there is a reason for that."

"What? Me being crazy? Yeah, I already know that," he said.

"No," Lesley said, shaking her head, "for why he is always so respectful to you. There may be a very good reason."

Jonathon stood up and thought for a moment before saying, "He'll be back in the morning. Maybe you can ask him."

Jonathon turned and headed for the door.

"Jonathon," Lesley said, making him stop and look at her, "Please fix my letterbox."

Jonathon smiled then left the room, gently closing the bedroom door.

Downstairs, Amy was sitting at the dining room table with the very old book her mother had been given by Katharyn. The book was open, and Amy was busy scribbling notes onto a notepad while checking something on her laptop.

Jonathon came in and sat down at the table.

"What are you doing?" he asked.

"Making notes, translating," she said, not looking up.

"Translating?… You can do that?" he asked, not believing her. "You can read them?"

Amy stopped writing for a moment and looked at him.

"They're not words, Jonathon. It's not like translating Spanish or German. These are all symbols and hieroglyphs, in various ancient languages and dialects. They could mean one word or a phrase or a number or a group of numbers," she explained, then started reading a page in the book again.

Jonathon was equally dumbfounded and astonished.

"How do you know this stuff?"

"I've been fascinated with ancient times for as long as I can remember. I can spend hours on the Internet researching old texts and such," she told him then stopped and looked at him again. "But some of the writings in this book pre-date Earth's documented history… It's an unknown language, not ancient Greek, not ancient Egyptian, none of the known recorded ancient languages resemble anything like this."

"Then how do you know what they mean?" Jonathon asked, still a little skeptical.

"I don't know," Amy said, shrugging her shoulders, "I just do… I look at a symbol or a line of them, and the words and meanings just come to me."

Amy started jotting notes again and Jonathon was staring at her.

"Like this book," she said, as she stopped writing notes. "Did you know there is a whole other book inside?"

"What? Another book?" he replied, confused even more.

"The story in the front about Aryanna and Adanne and all that stuff, that's like a preface… or prologue to the actual book," she said.

"The actual book?"

"Yes," she replied. "This is not a story book, Jonathon."

"It's not? Then what is it then?"

"It's… hang on," she said, then flicked back through her notepad to find the page she wanted. "It's the Book of Laws."

"What?" Jonathon exclaimed, standing up quickly.

"Where did G-ma get it? I know she gave it to Ma on her birthday, but where did *she* get it?" Amy asked, looking at the stunned Guardian.

"*I* gave it to Katharyn… before she moved to Capitol City," he told her.

Amy studied him carefully.

"Well, then where did *you* get it?"

"I've always had it… for as long as I can remember," he said.

After a brief silence, Amy tapped the old book with her index finger and asked, "Did you write these?"

"No," he replied quickly. "Well, yes, some. There were some blank pages at the back, so I used them to record the symbols and marks from my visions and dreams."

Amy nodded at Jonathon as she turned over several thoughts in her mind, one of which was now confirmed by what Jonathon had just told her.

"The Book of Laws," Jonathon said, "Have you deciphered anything?"

"Um, yes, a few pages," she replied.

Amy turned the old book around so Jonathon could see the writings on the open page.

"This one I've just finished translating… as best as I could. I'm only 14 you know," she said, grinning. "Anyway, this law is 'The Waters of Adamah,' and the first part says, 'If the child of the dove, the mother of the swan, takes no breath'… Weird hey."

She looked at Jonathon who didn't say anything.

"But there's more… It reads 'then from the lake of tears, the,'… I can't figure out the next symbol, 'shall rise and the essence of nature will be reborn in the presence of the one father'… and the symbol for 'father' is in, like, capital letters, like it's really important."

"Mother of Life," Jonathon said softly, realizing.

"Pardon?" Amy said.

"Mother of Life," he said, looking at her, "The symbol means *Mother of Life*."

"Yes!" Amy exclaimed, looking at the symbol again. "That's it. Mother of Life… How did you know that?"

"It's part of an ancient prophecy," he told her.

"Wow! A prophecy. That is so cool," she said.

Jonathon started to walk out of the dining room.

"Wait! Jonathon," she said. "There's one more I've done."

He stopped near the doorway to listen.

"It says 'Only the first child can reveal the true king.' Who is the *true king*?" she asked. "Is that a prophecy, too?"

"No idea, Amy," he said, then left the dining room. "No idea… But I think I know who does."

Amy never heard this last statement because Jonathon had said it to himself.

TWENTY-SIX

Capitol City

Jonathon had just called Joshua telling him to come to Henleyville in the morning because Lesley was asking for him. While heartened by this request, Joshua also knew something else was troubling Jonathon from his tone of voice.

Maybe he is still angry about what happened to Katharyn, Joshua thought. *Maybe, but I can never seem to please him.*

Joshua stared at the lifeless body of Lenora Jackson lying on the floor. She was wrapped in several layers of thick plastic, and she had already started to decompose.

"Take a photo of the burn mark. Send it to all the security clowns," Joshua said to himself, mimicking Jonathon's instructions, "Get rid of the body."

"It's not that easy in a city of millions with eyes and cameras everywhere, Jonathon," Joshua told him, even though he already had a plan.

"Figure it out, Joshua," Jonathon said, then hung up.

Joshua went to the front doors of the penthouse and opened them both.

"You two," he said to the two guards with no necks, "take the body down to the basement incinerator facility. Stay there and make sure there is nothing left, and nobody sees you. I'll shut off all the security cameras in the entire building."

The two guards came in and picked up the body and exited without saying a word. Joshua closed the penthouse doors then went to the monitoring room and watched as they entered the staff service elevator before he shut down the security feed.

Down in the basement facility, one of the two security guards carried Lenora's body while the other made sure nobody else was around.

During the day, the facility was a hive of activity with numerous workers operating the laundry equipment, dry cleaning suits and garments for the residents, or disposing of rubbish into the three large incinerators and various recycling containers.

But this late at night, the facility was a ghost town, the perfect time and opportunity to dispose of a dead body.

The guard not carrying the body opened the large door to one of incinerators while the other one tossed in the lifeless corpse and stood back so the door could be closed. One of the guards then turned the setting up to max and they both watched through the thick heatproof glass window as the flames engulfed the body. Mesmerized by the spectacle, the two guards didn't notice the three individuals sneak up behind them.

Hearing someone clear their throat behind them, they turned around just as Haruto Tanaka and the Romanian man morphed into large Corvidaens then quickly killed the guards.

Simon O'Reilly opened the door to the incinerator and the two Corvidaens tossed the dead bodies of the security guards inside on top of the charring remains of Lenora Jackson. Simon closed the large door then watched the fires consume the bodies as the creatures changed back into their human forms.

"Let's go," he said, and the three of them headed off and took the staff service elevator to the top floor.

There was loud knocking on the penthouse doors.

"Good," Joshua said. "They must be done."

But he carelessly didn't check the security monitor to see who was at the front doors. The staff service elevator was the only lift that had direct access to the top floor, and he assumed it was the two no-neck guards reporting back.

"That was quick," he said, opening the doors.

The three men burst in through the doors, morphing in Corvidaens, and knocking Joshua backwards.

Joshua was surrounded.

The creatures split up and were now circling him in the large entry foyer. Thinking quickly, Joshua flashed into the kitchen, grabbed one of the large knives out of a holder on the bench then went out onto the rooftop terrace. The three creatures were on him in an instant. Joshua slashed, kicked, and punched them as they attacked him with their talons.

Joshua sustained several deep gashes but also managed to slice open the neck of one of the creatures which backed away and fell to the floor screaming and growling. The other two stopped momentarily watching the howling creature and Joshua took the opportunity to stab one of them deep into the heart, killing it.

The remaining Corvidaen bared its fangs at Joshua and began lashing at him furiously with its talons. Joshua took several more blows that opened deep cuts on his arms and torso.

Bleeding profusely, Joshua collapsed to the floor still holding the knife.

Sensing a victory, the Corvidaen launched itself onto Joshua, but he managed to raise the knife just in time and plunge it deep into the chest of the creature, piercing its heart and killing it instantly.

Joshua kicked the dead creature off him and slowly got to his feet. Looking at the other creature with the deep gash in its neck, Joshua stumbled over to it, knelt down beside it and watched as it morphed back into its human form.

It was Simon O'Reilly.

"We meet again, Simon," Joshua said.

"You won't stop him," Simon said, his words gurgled due to the blood in his throat. "He only needs one more immortal."

Joshua didn't know what Simon meant, and Simon saw it in Joshua's eyes.

Simon started laughing at him.

"Well, it won't be me," Joshua said, then plunged the knife deep into Simon's heart.

....

Joshua knocked on the front door of the Cooper house just before midday the next day. When Jonathon opened the door, Joshua collapsed unconscious.

About an hour later, he was lying on the bed in Jonathon's old room, still unconscious, but with most of his wounds cleaned, sealed, and dressed. Lesley had done everything, insisted, and was now sitting on the edge of the bed watching Joshua's bare chest rise and fall slowly with each shallow breath.

"Wounds caused by an immortal take much longer to heal," Jonathon told her. "He needs rest now… and so do you."

But Lesley refused to leave Joshua. She was determined to remain by his side until he regained consciousness.

Throughout the rest of the day and into the evening, Jonathon checked on them both. Sometimes, he saw Lesley lying down on the bed next to Joshua, asleep, and had to sneak in to make sure she was breathing too.

Jonathon had let go of his anger towards Joshua the moment he collapsed in the doorway. Jonathon knew what Joshua's injuries meant: he had fought with Corvidaens. And Jonathon's concern now for Joshua was genuine. He needed him to recover, for his own sake, and for Lesley.

It seemed like Lesley had gained some strength and a new purpose, putting aside her own health issues to care for Joshua.

But Jonathon knew it was false hope.

He only had to look at her to know the reality. He just hoped that her obvious but unspoken love for Joshua would give her the will to hang on for a little longer.

If only I could get her to Tellus, he thought, standing in the doorway of his old bedroom, watching Lesley asleep next to Joshua.

They have no illness or disease there. Maybe they can save her too, he thought. *Maybe their medical technology can get rid of the tumor.*

Medical technology.

Suddenly, an idea came to his mind, and he raced downstairs, out to his pick-up and drove away.

....

In The Darkness, Athanasius was furious because, once again, the Corvidaens had failed him. Jonathon had killed his most trusted and loyal of all the creatures, the one who had been by his side since the start of his exile. And Joshua had killed another three of his best also.

None of them would be returning to The Darkness this time. Not like before.

Not like all the other times when the Guardians thought they had killed the creatures.

No. This time they were never coming back.

Athanasius felt like he had lost a family member, but the other creatures in The Darkness had seen how Athanasius had treated his own family since the beginning, so they were trying to escape the growing anger and rage of their eternal master.

But there is nowhere to hide in The Darkness as they soon discovered when Athanasius went on a murderous rampage, killing all the remaining Corvidaens, the effects of which echoed across all the realms.

. . . .

Jonathon pulled up in front of the hardware store and got out. Main Street was empty.

His was the only vehicle on the entire street, and usually was at this time of night when he slept at his own place, the small flat above the shop. He unlocked the front door to the store, then stopped when he heard a loud continuous thundering sound coming from the night sky. He looked up thinking a storm was coming but the sky was clear.

There were no clouds, only stars.

The thunderous sound continued for a few moments more, echoing off the silent buildings up and down Main Street.

Jonathon kept looking at the night sky and listening until the rolling thunder turned to silence, then he checked the street once more before going inside his store and up to his flat.

He opened the old wardrobe in his tiny bedroom, the same old cupboard that was there when he first inspected the flat after inheriting it. He kneeled and removed the false bottom floor panel inside the cupboard, revealing the medical case he had brought with him from Tellus.

Inside it was the device he hoped would help save Lesley.

TWENTY-SEVEN

Saturday October 21ˢᵗ

'……. A consortium of billionaire business tycoons has tabled a proposal with the World Economic Council, requesting approval to build a space defense operations base on the moon… The proposal has sent shockwaves around the globe, with reports of growing unease in Eastern Europe and Asia… More on this story in tonight's bulletin….'

"What are you watching?" Lesley asked, coming into the living room.

Jonathon had been so fixated on the television news program, he hadn't heard Lesley get up and come downstairs. Seeing her now, he muted the TV then quickly got up and went over to help her.

"Oh, nothing. I just had it on for background noise. Here, let me help you sit down," he said.

"Thank you," she said.

It was only seven am.

Jonathon had barely slept at all after returning from his flat last night. Amy was still asleep, as was Joshua.

"How's Joshua?" he asked.

Lesley looked up at him.

"No change," she said.

"Coffee? Would you like a cup? I was going to make some anyway," Jonathon asked.

"Please," she replied, nodding.

A few minutes later, Jonathon came back into the living room with two cups of hot coffee and placed them on the coffee table next to the medical device he had retrieved from his flat.

Lesley picked up her coffee and noticed the unusual object on the table.

"What's that?" she asked.

"It's a healing device," Jonathon said, "from Tellus."

"Healing device?" she asked, looking at it.

"Yes. I don't know why I didn't think of it sooner," he said, with a little excitement in his voice. "There is no disease or illness on Tellus. It has all been eliminated thanks to their advanced medical technology."

"Do you think it can help Joshua?" Lesley asked.

"Joshua?"

Jonathon hadn't thought about using it on Joshua, but looking at his left leg now, where Francis had healed his burns using the very same device, he figured it might be a good idea.

"Yes. I Think it probably will," he said.

Lesley put her cup back on the table and picked up the hand-held device.

"Then let's try," she said, getting up.

"Lesley, I…"

"I know," she said, cutting him off, "Joshua first."

They went upstairs to Joshua's room.

That's what it was called now.

It was no longer Jonathon's old room.

Joshua was still asleep and would be until his body had fully healed.

Lesley gave Jonathon the medical device and he turned it on and operated it the same way Francis had on his left leg and knee a long time ago. Lesley watched in amazement as the wide blue beam from the device moved over Joshua's wounds, healing them within seconds and leaving no marks at all.

Jonathon waved the device over Joshua's entire body and head one more time before shutting off the instrument and looking at Lesley.

"Now we just wait," he said.

Lesley sat down on the bed next to Joshua and held one of his hands. After a few long moments, Joshua opened his eyes and looked at Lesley, then at Jonathon.

"Joshua!" Lesley exclaimed with excitement, then rested her head on his chest and hugged him.

"Good to have you back, immortal," Jonathon said sincerely then smiled.

A little while later, the three of them were down in the kitchen. Lesley had made Joshua some breakfast and he was busily eating it and drinking the large glass of juice she had given him. Jonathon was eager to find out what happened in Capitol City two nights ago, but his concern now was for Lesley and whether the healing device could help her like it had helped Joshua.

"Your turn," Jonathon said, holding up the medical device.

Lesley sat upright in her chair and remained still as Jonathon came over and stood behind her. He turned on the healing device, and slowly moved it over and around her head.

Joshua watched in fascination.

Jonathon repeated the process three times before shutting off the device.

Nobody said a word.

Jonathon went back to the other side of the table to watch Lesley. Joshua remained still and silent, his eyes focused on her. She stood up, then slowly walked around the kitchen, moving her head from side to side at times. Finally, she stopped and turned to face both men.

"How do you feel?" Jonathon asked.

"Okay, I guess," she told them. "I feel… a bit stronger maybe. And I don't feel so unsteady on my feet now."

"What about your head?" Joshua asked.

Lesley moved her head around and from side to side again.

"Well, I don't have any head pain," she told them, but with hesitation in her voice.

"That's great news," Jonathon said, and Joshua nodded as well.

"Let's just make sure, first," Lesley said, holding up a hand to settle the growing excitement. "I'll call Doctor Mac and make an appointment for an MRI. Let's wait till I get the results before we give Amy any false hope. Okay?"

Both men nodded.

"Agreed," they said in unison.

．．．．．．．．．．．．．．．．．．．．．．．．．．．．

The appointment was scheduled for Monday morning.

Doctor Mac was eager to get more practice using the new MRI scanning machine the Henley family had donated to the hospital a few months back. He'd still have to send the scans to Doctor Jurgensen in Capitol City to be analyzed though, he told Lesley, and it might take a few days or a week to get the results.

Lesley knew the drill.

Over the weekend, Jonathon had found out what happened at the penthouse apartment and that his suspicions were correct about the Corvidaens.

"Yes, I stabbed them through the heart," Joshua told him. "And yes, I disposed of the bodies."

Jonathon had laughed at Joshua's mocking of him, and this had confused Joshua a little before he too laughed.

It seems the men have finally bonded, Lesley observed, and this made her happy.

Amy had noticed the sudden change in her mother, too, but she hadn't said anything about it. She was also glad that Joshua had recovered and was staying with them, because he made her mother happy.

That was another thing that Amy had noticed.

On Sunday afternoon, Amy was sitting on the front porch with her notebook when Jonathon pulled up in the driveway after being gone for several hours.

....

A few hours earlier

Jonathon stood on the shore of the lake.

Everyone calls it the lake but technically it isn't one.

It is a dam.

A dam that was built around sixty years ago in honour of, and named after, one of Henleyville's first settlers.

"They have some strange names for people and places here," Katharyn had once remarked to Jonathon.

He smiled now at that thought because he had said the exact same thing to Francis not long after arriving here.

This part of the lake never existed before the dam wall was built. Before then, there *was* a lake, but it was a few kilometers further back in the catchment area and Jonathon knew it was once a very sacred place to the people of a long-ago era.

The large body of water in front of Jonathon had swallowed up a vast rich valley which was surrounded by forests and hills and the mountain he now stood looking at. The foot of the mountain on this side lay deep under the surface of the water, approximately fifty meters down courtesy of the William Broadhurst Henley Dam.

But this didn't worry Jonathon.

The place he came to visit was on the other side of the mountain, not submerged under the dark water.

He arrived at the area of the mountain that hid his secret cave. It was covered with trees, vines, and dense vegetation that had grown there over thousands of years, and as he had done late one night last week, he was careful not to disturb the covering growth too much.

It took him a while to remove some of the rocks and boulders away from the opening so he could get inside. Once he'd removed enough of them, he grabbed the shovel he had brought with him and climbed in through the small opening he'd made.

There inside the cave lay the body of the dark-skinned man. The man who was supposed to be dead forty years ago but had returned with a vengeance the other night to kill Jonathon and Lesley and Amy. Fortunately, he had failed, and now Jonathon had returned to the cave to bury the body.

A little while later, having interred the dead man deep in the ground, Jonathon stood on the freshly packed down dirt and looked around the cave.

The book was still there.

The Book of Laws.

His book.

His journal.

It looked very old now, almost as old as the one Amy was now fascinated with. He went over and looked at it then picked it up and flicked through some of the pages. The bark paper still smelled the same, he noted before closing the book and looking at the back cover. He saw where he had restitched it together thousands of years ago on Adamah, then remembered the notes he had scribbled down and concealed between the leather pieces of the cover.

Francis had said they couldn't figure out what the third line of symbols and markings meant. Then Jonathon thought of Amy, and her remarkable ability to translate pages from this very book. He thought about taking the book with him, but he stopped himself and put it back.

If I take the book then it won't be there for Francis to find it, he thought.

What would happen then?

Would I be standing here right now, he thought.

Would I have been on Tellus?

Would any of this have happened?

Would Athena be dead?

Would we still be on Adamah?

The child can help, Joshua had told him.

It was a message from them, Joshua had said.

Amy?

Is she the child in the message?

I don't know, he thought, *but maybe she can help.*

Jonathon looked around the cave once more, making sure nothing else had been disturbed, then spotted the marking on the cave wall. He went over and raised his hand up to the wall and placed it over the symbol.

At that moment, he had a vision.

In his vision was a presence, an entity shrouded in bright light with a radiant glow emanating from the center. The entity seemed to be speaking but he couldn't understand it because it was just a whisper. He closed his eyes to concentrate, and, in the vision, a face began to form in the entity, but it was out of focus. He listened as the words it was speaking became clearer.

He couldn't be certain, but he thought the entity was saying, "Remember who you are, my love."

Jonathon opened his eyes and quickly took his hand off the cave marking. His hand was warm, as was the marking on his chest.

He didn't understand why.

He looked around the cave. Nobody else was there, but he already knew that.

What was that? he wondered. *Did I hear that correctly?*

He shook his head and left the cave, concealing the entrance again as it had been before, then headed back to his pick-up.

....

Amy watched Jonathon get out of his truck then come up the stairs and onto the porch. He looked at Amy for a moment and she thought he was going to say something, but she spoke first.

"Hey. I think I've figured out what those symbols on the back cover of the book mean," she said, watching him closely.

Jonathon touched the mark on his chest quickly before removing his hand. It still felt warm under his shirt.

"Symbols?" he said. "Plural?"

"Yes," Amy said. "At first, I thought it was just one symbol. I couldn't get a read on it… then something, a feeling I guess, made me focus on it more and that's when I saw them."

Jonathon leaned against the porch railing in front of where Amy was sitting.

"You saw them?" he asked.

"I was staring at the symbol for like five minutes, then in my mind, it lifted off the cover and went back down in place one at a time… It's three," she said.

Jonathon said nothing.

"There are three symbols, one on top of the other, and the third one on top of that," she said, smiling up at him.

"Do you know what they mean?" he asked.

"Yes," she said, "Do you?"

"No. Why would I?" he asked.

"Because it is *your* mark, Jonathon. *Your* symbol, or symbols actually, but they are you," she said. "And that book belongs to you because you wrote it."

"No, I didn't, Amy," he said, feeling uneasy. "I am responsible for some of the pages in the back part, but I didn't write the book."

Amy stood up.

"Can I show you something?" she said, then went inside.

Jonathon followed her.

Lesley and Joshua came out of the dining room and into the living room just as Amy, and then Jonathon, came inside.

"Hey, Ma, you might wanna hear this too," Amy said, grabbing the old book off the coffee table then sitting down on one of the lounges.

Jonathon sat down next to her.

"Hear what, Amy?" Lesley asked.

"I've been doing my thing with this book, and I realized something about it," she said, opening the book at the front then looking at Jonathon sitting next to her. "Here. Check out the writing."

Joshua was very interested now.

"The story? Yes, I know what that is," Jonathon said to her.

Amy shook her head.

"No. Not the story, the writing. Look at the writing," she urged him.

Lesley was intrigued now and came over and sat on the other side of Amy.

"Yeah. Okay," Jonathon said, not sure where Amy was going with this.

"Now look at this writing," she said.

Amy went to a page in the book where Jonathon had himself written some passages in ancient symbols and hieroglyphs.

Jonathon stared at his own writings.

"They look the same," Lesley said.

Nobody was looking at him, but Joshua was nodding his head slightly.

"Now look at these," Amy said, and scrolled back to some pages near the beginning of the book where she had found the Book of Laws.

Amy looked at Jonathon, who was studying the pages, then she looked at her mother.

"It's the same. The writing is all the same. The story, the pages at the back, the Book of Laws, it's all the same handwriting, Jonathon. This is your book. You wrote it," Amy declared.

Jonathon looked up at Joshua who stopped nodding.

"I wrote it?" he said, still looking at Joshua who said nothing, "I wrote the ancient Book of Laws?"

"Yes. That was the original book… Look at these," she said.

Amy showed them the pages with the story of Adamah and then the pages at the back Jonathon said he had added.

"See, the paper is different to the Book of Laws pages, but not the writing. The story of Adamah and the other stuff at the back were added after the laws were written. But everything in here was written by the same hand… Yours, Jonathon," Amy said.

"Oh my god!" Lesley exclaimed, putting her hand over her mouth.

"Yes. Exactly, Ma," Amy said.

Jonathon got up, went back outside and stood at the top of the stairs. Joshua followed him outside and leaned against the porch railing. Jonathon glanced at him then looked back out across the front yard to the big tree at the end of the driveway.

A new letterbox had been attached to the tree where the original one used to be.

A new letterbox from Millers Hardware.

"Did you know about any of that?" Jonathon said, still looking at the new letterbox.

Joshua didn't answer, which, in itself, was an answer in Jonathon's eyes. He looked at Joshua and nodded his head.

"If I wrote it, why can't I remember?" Jonathon said to him.

Joshua came over to him.

"Because you are punishing yourself."

Jonathon faced Joshua.

"How? Why?" he asked.

Joshua put up his hands.

"I am forbid…"

But Jonathon cut him off.

"Yeah, yeah, I know. You are forbidden to tell me… I am getting tired of hearing that, immortal," he snapped back.

Joshua placed a hand on Jonathon's shoulder then turned to go back inside.

"Remember who you are, Jonathon," he said, as he entered the house.

To Joshua's back, Jonathon called out, "And I'm getting tired of hearing that, too."

TWENTY-EIGHT

Jonathon was grumpy for the rest of Sunday and into Monday and beyond. So grumpy that he had stayed away from the Cooper house for several days.

He'd gone back to his flat.

He didn't reopen the shop though. Instead, he spent the time packing the few things he owned then took them down to the ship, in preparation for his departure to Tellus where he was hoping the DNA genetic modification treatment would save Katharyn.

Unbeknownst to Lesley and Amy, he had spent several nights sleeping on the ship with Katharyn, Francis, Mariangela and his other four friends.

Joshua, however, knew where Jonathon was.

Joshua always knew because, as an immortal, he had the ability to sense other immortals and locate them.

And to Joshua, Jonathon wasn't an ordinary immortal or Guardian. He was much more than that, but he was forbidden to tell. He just hoped that Jonathon would end his self-inflicted punishment and remember who he was.

Lesley went to her Monday appointment as scheduled and Doctor Mac sent off the scans to City General Hospital where Doctor Jurgensen examined the images then sent his findings back to him.

It was Friday when the results came back and Lesley had tried calling Jonathon numerous times, but he hadn't answered her calls, because he was still down on the ship.

On Saturday morning, Jonathon left the ship and emerged from the depths of the lake to find Joshua waiting for him near his pick-up truck.

"Lesley wants to see you," Joshua said, when Jonathon got close. "The scan results came back."

Jonathon nodded and got in his truck, started it up then looked out the window at Joshua, who was still standing there.

"You need a lift?" he said, and Joshua smiled then walked around to the passenger side and got in.

Nobody said anything to Jonathon about his absence over the past week. But he noticed Amy had been unusually quiet since he'd arrived there from the lake, and, shortly after, she had gone up to her room without even saying hello to him.

"They said the tumor is getting bigger," Lesley told him.

"So, it didn't work," Jonathon said, deflated.

"Yes, and no," she told him, touching his arm. "Doctor Mac did blood tests as well, Jonathon. My red cell count is back up to normal again. I'm not anemic anymore. And my glucose and vitamin levels are all up too, which is why I'm feeling much better."

Jonathon could tell there was a 'but' coming so he said it first.

"But," he said.

"But…" Lesley said, her eyes getting moist, "your device had no effect on the tumor."

Jonathon hugged Lesley, understanding the implications.

The medical device had helped her general health, but it did nothing to stop the tumor. In fact, as Lesley had told him, the tumor is getting bigger. The medical device was only good for superficial wounds and general health issues. Not for major diseases or complicated issues like a brain tumor.

"I should've realized that," he chastised himself.

The device had healed the burns on his left leg, but it had no effect on the internal damage to his knee.

While Lesley was quietly sobbing in his arms, Jonathon confirmed in his mind a decision he had already made during the week on the ship. He looked at Joshua, nodded, and Joshua nodded back.

Jonathon released Lesley, held her at arm's length and looked her in the eyes.

"Pack your things. Essentials only. We leave tonight," Jonathon told her, then looked at Joshua. "You too, immortal."

Jonathon left them and went upstairs to Amy's room.

Her door was open, and she looked at Jonathon when he appeared in the doorway.

"Amy," he began to say.

She raced off her bed, ran to him and hugged him tightly.

He hugged her, too.

"I love you, Jonathon," Amy said, her words muffled because her face was in his chest. "Don't leave me again."

"Hey," he said, "What's going on?"

Amy pulled out of the hug and said, "I missed you. You left and I didn't know if you would come back."

Jonathon felt terrible now because he'd hurt this beautiful young girl by avoiding them all for almost a week.

"I'm sorry, Amy," he said. "All that book stuff really threw me… But that's why I came up to talk to you."

"Why?" she said, getting a tissue from her bedside table.

"I need to know what my symbols mean," he said.

Amy brightened a little when Jonathon said this.

"Okay," she said, then grabbed her notebook off the floor and sat on her bed.

Jonathon went and sat down on the bed next to her.

"Well, there's three symbols. Remember?" she asked, looking at him and he nodded. "Cool… They are overlaid on top of each other, which I have since figured out is also important… Anyway, first, there is the symbol for the god father, or the father of the gods."

"Godfather?" he queried.

"No," she replied, shaking her head, "not Godfather, like in the mafia. No. It's god father. Two words."

"Okay," Jonathon replied, clearly not comprehending.

"The next one is the symbol for… well, it's like a triquetra. You know what that is, don't you?" she asked.

Jonathon shook his head, and Amy rolled her eyes at him.

"*Everyone* knows what a triquetra is, Jonathan," she said, but he shrugged his shoulders and shook his head again.

Amy rolled her eyes again and shook her head.

"Okay… well… a triquetra is a trinity symbol, and it can mean a few things. Your triquetra represents family, *a* family, *your* family."

"My family?" he asked. "What family?"

"Hey, I just interpret them," Amy said, putting up her hands.

"How do you know it represents *my* family?" Jonathon asked.

"Because when the symbols are all together," she told him, "And this is the cool part I figured out the other day, they mean father, mother, and daughter of the gods."

Jonathon sat in silence for a while, trying to process this new information along with the other things Amy had told him a week ago.

Was he the Guardian of the Book of Laws?

Did the Creators choose him to be their biographer?

And did he have a family he didn't know of?

If so, why does he have no memory of any of it?

His first memory is of the day he and Athena arrived on Adamah to care for Medora, after Aryanna returned to the sacred waters. And thinking to himself now, he has no memory of transcribing the story about 'The Beginning.'

Amy let Jonathon stew in his own thoughts for a while.

She could tell that he was struggling to make any sense of it, and she was almost certain he didn't believe anything she had told him.

Eventually, Jonathon looked at her and said, "You need to pack your things. Essentials only. One bag. We're leaving tonight."

Amy nodded.

Jonathon stood up then added, "And no electronic devices. Where we are going, they'll just be paper weights."

"Jonathon, the third symbol… Do you want to know the name of your family?" Amy said, softly.

Jonathon stopped at the doorway of her bedroom and looked at Amy.

"No. It's not important," he said then, went to leave but stopped and turned back to Amy who was still looking at him.

"I love you too, Amy."

Amy smiled at Jonathon, then he left and went downstairs.

She looked at her notepad where she had written the name that had come to her in a vision recently. It happened while she was studying the symbol on the back cover of the old book, the same symbol she had seen on his chest.

She'd written the name of his family in capital letters because it was important, very important. That is what she had determined from her vision, and as she looked at the words she had written, she, too, wondered what it all meant.

On the page she was staring at were two words: THE PURE.

....

'…. Tensions are escalating in Eastern Europe and Asia after the WEC rubber-stamped the approval for the Hermes Consortium to commence building its defense operations base on the moon… There are anonymous reports coming in saying that threats have been made against the billionaire founders of Hermes, and if they move forward with their plans, retaliatory measures may be taken…. This is a developing story… Updates throughout the evening.'

Jonathon shook his head and shut off the television.

"Time to go," he said to Joshua, who had been watching the news bulletin as well.

"Everything is in the truck," he said.

"And the weapons?" Jonathon asked.

"Also in the truck," he advised.

"Good. We can't leave anything like that here," Jonathon said. "You go with Lesley and Amy. Make sure everything is shut off here then lock it when you leave. I'll go now and start taking the stuff to the ship."

Joshua nodded.

"Did you settle all of Katharyn's affairs as I instructed?" Jonathon asked.

"Yes. Everything was done as you requested," Joshua said. "We are not coming back, are we?"

"No," Jonathon said, looking at the television even though it was now switched off. "There'll be nothing to come back to anyway."

TWENTY-NINE

In The Darkness, Athanasius had heard every word they had spoken. While he listened, he stood silently waiting for the cycle to begin. He would have more time during this one. He always did during a lunar eclipse because the shadows lasted a lot longer than those during a solar eclipse, and Athanasius very much enjoyed lurking in the shadows.

It also meant he had more time to seek out one, or both, of the immortals. He would prefer to eliminate them both, but one would be sufficient for now, enabling him to escape The Darkness forever.

Athanasius needed to kill three immortals, by his hand, to be released from his eternal prison. It was a secret law written in the Book of Laws, a law he had discovered when Athena had been killed.

Her death had caused rumblings throughout The Heavens, with the Creators talking among themselves about the secret law and how, if Athanasius found out about it, the end of his banishment would allow him to wreak havoc across the realms.

And without the true king, the Creators would be powerless to stop him.

"The time is near, Jonathon," Athanasius said, "when you will stand before me and beg for your immortal life... And I will take great pleasure in ending it."

....

Down in the water cave, Jonathon took the ship out of standby mode, and it came to life immediately. He touched the control panel in front of him and the shield covering the forward viewing window opened.

Amy and Lesley were safely secured in their flight seats. The excitement and amazement on Amy's face had not dwindled since she'd arrived at the ship, and once inside, her only words had been "No way!" and "So cool".

Also, she really loved the form fitting flight suits they all were wearing.

Joshua strapped himself into the other flight control seat on Jonathon's left and looked across at him tapping away on the control panel.

"Are you sure you know how to fly this thing?" Joshua asked, the concern in his voice obvious.

Jonathon kept tapping on the control panel.

"Just like riding a bike," he said.

"I've never seen you ride an actual bike," Joshua remarked, which drew a harsh glare from Jonathon.

"Okay. I've set the navigation system to return us to the starting point of our last trip," he said, looking at everyone. "Actually, *my* last trip because this is your first one but... well, you get the idea."

Joshua raised his eyebrows when Jonathon looked at him.

"Lesley, how are you feeling?" Jonathon asked.

Lesley nodded, but she was clearly extremely nervous.

"Fine, I'm fine," she said, anxiously.

Jonathon watched her for a moment, noticing she was already tightly gripping the arms of her flight seat.

Like mother, like daughter, he thought to himself, smiling at the memory.

"Amy? All good?" Jonathon asked the still very excited young lady.

"This is so cool, Jonathon," she beamed.

Jonathon smiled again then took a few moments before he addressed everyone.

"Alright. When we rise out of the lake, we'll fly up high then circle out over the mountain and come back around over the lake. Then on my signal, Joshua, you initiate the rift sequence on your flight control panel, like I showed you. Okay?" Jonathon said.

Joshua nodded.

"Okay. And I'll do the rest," Jonathon added.

After another quick check on Lesley and Amy, Jonathon said, "Ladies and gentlemen, enjoy your flight."

Everything happened exactly as Jonathon said it would and after they flew into the rift, the galactic starship disappeared, leaving no trace it was ever there.

....

Athanasius stood on the shore of the lake, shrouded in total darkness due to the lunar eclipse, and watched as the starship carrying Jonathon, Joshua, and the two pure-borns, flew over the lake and disappeared into a rift.

He had arrived too late.

"I know where you are going, Jonathon," Athanasius said, as the rift closed. "I'll see you soon."

Athanasius then cut short his earthly visit and returned to The Darkness.

....

TELLUS

A rift opened high up in the mid-morning sky above the mountain where Katharyn and Jonathon had once lived. The galactic starship burst out of the rift at near light speed then slowed as it flew out over the hills that surrounded the main city valley on Tellus.

Jonathon looked shocked as he saw the once lush green forests and hills were now brown and dead, and the lake in the distance that was once full, was nothing but a dry barren dust bowl.

He flew the ship back over the valley and the city, but he saw no signs of life.

The place looked deserted.

Joshua saw the confused look on Jonathon's face.

"What's wrong?" he asked.

Jonathon didn't answer straight away.

He flew out over the mountain again and slowed the ship as he came back around then hovered near the dry lake. The view through the main forward window showed the entire city valley and the mountain at the other end.

There was no movement anywhere, no life, no people.

Jonathon was shaking his head.

"This doesn't make sense," he said, then spotted the landing base.

"Jonathon. What is wrong?" Joshua asked again. "Why does this place look deserted?"

"I don't know," he replied, then headed for the landing base.

There was no activity at the landing base either.

Jonathon put the ship down and put it in sleep mode.

There were dozens of fighter starships on the base, but they all looked abandoned. Everyone on board released their flight harnesses and came over to Jonathon who was still sitting in his flight seat looking at the navigation control system.

"Where is everyone, Jonathon?" Lesley asked, looking out through the large forward window.

"It just doesn't make sense," he said, still focused on the control screen in front of him. "When we left Tellus, we traveled back in time 2960 years… so I programmed the navigation system to return us the same amount of time forward to here."

"Jonathon," Joshua began, "Don't forget. We've been on Earth more than forty years…"

Jonathon looked at Joshua.

"What are you saying? I don't know how to program a navigation system?"

"No. I'm not saying that at all… You arrived on Earth in 1980. Correct?" he asked, and Jonathon nodded. "… but we left in 2023."

Jonathon realized his mistake and slowly nodded his head.

"And the navigation system calculated 2960 years from then," he said, understanding.

"Yes, I think so," Joshua said, then pointed to view beyond the forward front window. "I think we've arrived on Tellus forty-three years after you left."

Jonathon thought about this for a moment.

"Yes. You're right… But that doesn't explain why this place looks deserted," he said.

They all exited the starship and stood on the tarmac of the landing base. Jonathon turned quickly when he spotted a figure emerge from the base command center, followed by at least fifty heavily armed ground force troops, who spread out and surrounded them and their starship.

As the figure got closer, Jonathon recognized the man.

It was the commander, and he looked somewhat older than the last time Jonathon had seen him.

"Commander?" Jonathon enquired, when the man got up close to him.

"Guardian. It's been a long time," the commander said, then looked at the other three people standing with Jonathon. "Why have you returned?"

Jonathon ignored the question.

"What happened here, commander? Everything looks dead."

The commander again looked at Lesley and Amy, then stared at Joshua for a moment before he signaled for the ground troops to lower their weapons.

"Much has happened… as you can see. Come," he instructed, then turned and headed back inside.

Inside the command center, it looked very different to what Jonathon remembered it did forty-odd years ago. Everything was very new, and Jonathon noticed the technology appeared to be extremely advanced, even for Tellus.

All the viewing monitors were gone as well.

In their place was a very large one that covered an entire wall of the center, and it appeared to be almost transparent.

The commander noticed Jonathon staring at it.

"We've had an upgrade," the commander said.

"More future technology?" Jonathon asked, looking around the room.

"It was necessary," the commander replied, then turned to face Lesley, Amy, and Joshua. "Who are your friends, Jonathon?"

"Commander, this is Lesley, Katharyn's daughter, and this is Amy, Katharyn's granddaughter." Jonathon told him.

"Katharyn? Your Katharyn?" the commander asked, acknowledging Lesley and Amy with a nod to each of them.

"Yes, commander," Jonathon replied.

Amy started wandering around the command center, looking at all the future technology.

The commander then looked at Joshua intently.

"And who are you? Another Guardian?"

"I am Joshua," he said, extending his hand in greeting.

The commander accepted the hand and shook it, all the while studying Joshua with much scrutiny.

"Commander, what happened? Why is everything dead? And where are all the people?" Jonathon asked.

The commander pressed something on the large round control board in the center of the room then gestured to the giant wall screen.

"They are all up on those," he told them.

When the screen came to life, it displayed a view of dozens of enormous space habitation stations circling around Tellus in outer space. Jonathon also saw the moon operations base, but it had tripled in size since he'd last observed it from this very room.

"Why?" he eventually asked.

"We had no choice. We haven't had rain on Tellus for more than forty years," the commander said. "In fact, the rains stopped coming not long after you and the young Katharyn left."

The commander touched another small panel on the control board and a full view of Tellus appeared on the big screen. The planet looked brown and dead with very little water visible on its surface.

"As you can see, Jonathon, the planet is dying… Most of the water is gone. We were harvesting ice from the polar caps for water for our habitation stations, but there is very little left. All our water now comes from ice on Europa… When the rains stopped, everything died. Nothing grows here anymore… We built those habitation stations with the help of future technology to save us… And now, they are our home."

Jonathon couldn't believe what he was seeing.

He stared at the giant screen displaying a dying Tellus.

The commander switched the view back to the habitation stations.

"Why are you still down here, commander?" Jonathon asked.

"We won't be for much longer. We are scheduled to depart for the central operations base on the moon in seven days," he told them.

"So, there is just you and your welcoming party left?" Jonathon asked.

The commander nodded.

"That's it," he replied, "Plus a few technical and support staff."

Jonathon looked frustrated and began pacing around the command center.

"What about mother, Jonathon?" Lesley asked Jonathon, desperation in her voice.

"Commander. Is the DNA treatment center still operating?" he asked.

"No. That facility was destroyed by an explosion a long time ago… Why?" the commander enquired.

They took the commander to their ship and into the cargo hold area where he was shown the stasis pods with Katharyn and the others. Jonathon told the commander about the murders in 1981 Earth time, then he explained what happened to Katharyn and why she was now in cryogenic suspended animation.

"The disease is rapidly aging her, commander… draining the life out of her. If I hadn't thought of using one of these pods, she would be dead," Jonathon told him.

"Our medical facility is on habitation station seven, but there's no DNA modification anymore… We lost all that technology in the explosion. Everything Francis and Mariangela had designed and created, it was all kept in that facility," the commander said.

"No records? No back-up system?" Jonathon asked.

"No, Jonathon. The DNA treatment facility had a stand-alone operating system. The only people who had the protocols to create a back-up were Francis and Mariangela… We searched their residence after the explosion, but we found nothing."

This day is going from bad to worse rapidly, Jonathon was thinking.

Jonathon looked at Lesley and Amy.

Joshua came over and stood next to him.

"What about Lesley?" Joshua said quietly to Jonathon, who looked at him and acknowledged his enquiry.

"Commander, can we get to the medical facility on that habitation station?" Jonathon asked.

"The transport ship will be here in seven days, Jonathon. We can go then," he replied.

"Seven days? Can't we fly up there sooner? In our ship… or one of yours out there?"

"None of those starships have the docking systems or entry recognition technology for any of the habitation stations, Jonathon. Your ship is more than forty years old… and those fighter ships outside are just that, fighter ships only," he explained.

Jonathon was silent for a while, thinking, and trying to come up with another plan or idea.

"Seven days?" Jonathon asked again, and the commander nodded. "Okay. Is Katharyn's residence still up on the mountain?"

The commander nodded.

"Yes. It was locked up and hasn't been touched since you both left," he said, then knowing why Jonathon was asking, the commander removed a small thin electronic device from a concealed compartment under the central control board.

"Here, you will need this."

Jonathon took the device and they all left.

THIRTY

The mountain residence looked exactly as he and Katharyn had left it and, standing outside on the terrace again, Jonathon felt like it was only yesterday that he was here. He'd stood in this same spot thousands of times with Athena, then later by himself, watching over the city below and looking out to the lake far in the distance at the other end of the valley.

But the lake was no longer there, its waters taken by the harvesting ships and the harsh sun. All that remained was the dry lakebed and the fossils of the marine life that had once been abundant in its sacred waters.

Jonathon had given Lesley and Amy the grand tour of the mountain residence, and both had been overwhelmed with the realization that their mother, and grandmother, had once called this place home.

Katharyn's presence echoed everywhere inside. All her possessions and cherished treasures were still there. She still had clothes in her bedroom, some laid out on her bed like she had been deciding what to wear.

Or what to take with her, Lesley thought.

Lesley spotted a beautiful summer dress hanging in an open wall chamber in Katharyn's bedroom, so she took it out and held it against her own body.

It would fit me perfectly, she thought.

The dress was made from a light white material with thin shoulder straps. It was delicate and shear, with a plunging neckline and Lesley easily imagined her mother wearing it.

Lesley didn't know, but it was almost the same as the dress her mother had worn to the opening of the new school in Henleyville in 1980.

Joshua had brought all the cases up to the mountain residence. It was an easy task for him, thanks to his immortal speed, which he playfully mocked Jonathon about because of his bad knee.

All the utility systems in the residence were still functioning, including the water supply, which was welcome news.

"But there's no water in the lake," Amy said, a little confused.

"Katharyn's home has its own water supply from the mountain," Jonathon told Amy.

Lesley and Joshua also wanted an explanation.

"This home was built on top of a huge water storage system, which is filled by the rains that wash down from higher up on the mountain. We're more than five hundred meters above ground level up here," Jonathon explained.

"Couldn't they pump water up here?" Lesley asked.

"I asked Francis the same thing," he told her. "He said the governing council thought it would be a waste of resources for just one residence."

"But there is another home like this, a smaller one, below us," Joshua said. "I saw it from the ship."

Jonathon nodded.

"Yes. That is… was… Francis' and Mariangela's home. Their home gets its water from the same storage system. The commander said this place was locked up when we left, so there should still be plenty of water underneath us."

Lesley and Joshua both nodded.

"I'm hungry. What do we do for food?" Amy asked.

Jonathon demonstrated how to operate the re-hydration unit, which turned small, sealed packages of dry ingredients into hot or cold food. With no fresh produce anywhere, he told them that it was this, or nothing.

"That's so cool!" Amy said.

Joshua came out onto the terrace and stood next to Jonathon. He looked down into the valley, seeing a city with no life, and tried to imagine what it would have looked like when Jonathon was last here.

"It's not your fault, Jonathon," Joshua eventually said.

"Everything is my fault," he replied, "Everything since the beginning."

"I meant… this," Joshua said, indicating the dire state Tellus was now in.

"I thought we'd arrive back here at the same time as when we left," he said, shaking his head. "I didn't calculate for the years we spent there."

"It doesn't matter now. What does matter is how do we save Katharyn?" Joshua asked.

Jonathon breathed in and out deeply.

"I don't know, Joshua," Jonathon replied, shaking his head slowly. "I just don't know."

……………………………………

Later in the afternoon, Lesley and Amy were on the terrace looking out over the valley.

The sun was setting, and the cooler evening air was a welcome relief from the stifling heat of the day.

Down in the valley, the lights were coming on in the city and outer areas, giving off a false sense that life was going on as normal. The command center base on the outskirts of the city perimeter was a hive of activity though, with preparations under way for the evacuation and relocation of the remaining defense personnel to the galactic operations base on the moon.

Jonathon came outside and stood with them, then looked up into the darkening sky, where several of the enormous habitation stations were visible, floating in space outside the atmosphere. To him, they looked too futuristic even for Tellus standards.

Lesley looked at Jonathon for a moment, then turned and looked behind her to see if Joshua had followed him outside.

"He's gone to check on your mother," Jonathon said, knowing who Lesley was looking for.

"There's something familiar about this place," Amy said, studying the valley and the hills in the distance.

Jonathon nodded.

"Yes. This valley was once part of a huge dam," he said, "the William B. Henley dam."

"I knew it!" Amy exclaimed. "I knew I'd seen this mountain before, too… At the lake!"

"The dam once filled this entire valley and covered the foot of this mountain with water up to about fifty meters," he said, then pointed to his left. "The lake shore and recreation area used to be over there."

Amy and Lesley both looked to where he had indicated.

It all felt very surreal to them.

"What happened to the dam?" Amy asked.

"Destroyed, I guess. Francis told me there was a world war on Earth in the twenty-first century. Almost everything on the planet was blown up… I think maybe that's what happened to the dam wall," Jonathon told them.

"A world war?" Lesley repeated. "We just came from the twenty-first century, Jonathon."

He nodded but didn't elaborate further, the unspoken reality of what his silence meant, dawning on Lesley.

"The original lake was way out at the other end of the valley, out past the city limits… But it's dry now," he continued.

"The original lake?" Lesley queried.

"Yes," he said, looking at her, "on Adamah."

"From the story in your book?" Amy asked, "That same lake? The sacred waters?"

Jonathan nodded.

"Wow!" Amy said, then looked out into the distance to where the lake should now be but wasn't. "Can we go see it, Ma?"

Jonathon smiled.

"I'll ask Joshua to take you both tomorrow… I have things to attend to," he said.

Lesley studied Jonathon for a while in silence.

She knew one of the things he wanted to attend to was trying to figure out solutions for their problems, and in this strange desolate world, she didn't know how she could help him.

"Jonathon, that DNA modification treatment you asked the commander about… Is that why you brought mother here? Do you think it can save her?" Lesley asked.

He looked at Lesley, then at Amy who was also interested in knowing the answers. He didn't speak for a few moments, while he decided how best to answer. In the end, the truth won.

"Yes," he replied. "Katharyn had her first treatment when she was pregnant with you."

This piece of information shocked Lesley.

"What?"

"Mariangela had given it to her before she left Henleyville and went to Capitol City. Katharyn told me she had to wait until she was twenty-five before administering the treatment," he told her. "I helped her do it. She couldn't inject herself."

"Mother never did like needles," Lesley confirmed.

"The DNA modification treatment basically inhibits the whole aging process. You still age but extremely slow. That's why she still looked so young even after all this time," he told her.

Lesley nodded her head.

"Yeah, that always fascinated me, too," she said.

"I think it had an effect on you as well," he told her.

"Me?" Lesley asked, incredulously.

"Like I said, your mother was pregnant with you… I think it modified your DNA as well," he said. "Look at you. You look no older than that day you first came into my store."

Lesley blushed.

"Mr. Miller! Did you just give me a compliment?" she joked.

He smiled at her, then the smile slowly faded.

"I thought the DNA treatment might stop what is happening to your mother… She is aging rapidly, Lesley. Her life force is being drained from her which is what the 'touch of death' from Athanasius does."

"But the commander said everything in the DNA facility was destroyed," Lesley said. "That's just crazy. Every hospital has a back-up for all their records. It's mandatory."

"Hmm... On Earth, maybe. But here, their back-up was Francis and Mariangela," Jonathon remarked.

"Wait a minute!" Lesley said, holding up a hand. "You said Mariangela gave mother a treatment to take with her to Capitol City. Where did Mariangela get it?"

Jonathon thought about this for a moment.

"They could've taken some with them when they left here."

"Maybe… But what if they didn't?" she said. "What if she made it there? Mother told me Francis and Mariangela made products of their own in Henleyville. Lotions, moisturisers, sunscreens, different types of creams, stuff like that. What if they also made the DNA treatment they gave to mother?"

"They'd need a lab for that. There was no lab at the Cooper house… sorry, your place, and without their research and formulas, how could they?" he questioned.

"The commander said it himself, Jonathon. Only Francis and Mariangela knew the security protocols. I guarantee they made a back-up. I know I would," she said. "Besides, they made those products somewhere, Jonathon."

"Yeah, but their home was searched after the treatment facility explosion. The commander said they found nothing," Jonathon said.

"That doesn't mean it's not there," Lesley said.

Jonathon wasn't convinced.

"I'm not so sure, Lesley… If I had created a marvel of medical science and technology like they did, I'd want to keep its secrets real close to me at all times."

Lesley started rubbing her forehead, a painful expression spreading across her face.

"Yeah," she mumbled, "You're probably right."

As she turned away, Lesley's eyes rolled back in her head, her legs gave out and she collapsed to the floor.

"Ma!" Amy screamed.

At that moment, Joshua appeared on the terrace and saw Lesley lying unconscious.

Jonathon said, "Quick. Take her inside."

Joshua carried Lesley into her mother's bedroom and placed her gently on the bed. Amy rushed to the bed and sat down on it next to Lesley.

"What happened?" Joshua asked.

"I don't know. She just fainted," a worried Amy said.

Jonathon was standing in the doorway.

He knew it was the tumor that had caused Lesley to pass out, and the stifling heat on Tellus may have been a factor too, but the tumor was getting bigger.

That's what Doctor Mac said the scan results had showed.

Six days, Lesley, Jonathon thought to himself. *Just hang on for six more days.*

....

Two days later, Lesley still hadn't woken up.

Amy was devastated, and she hadn't left her mother's side the entire time.

Jonathon and Joshua had heatedly asked the commander if they could leave any earlier, but he'd told them again it was not possible because the transport ship had a sixty-day cycle and never deviated from it.

"Only a crisis of galactic importance would warrant a deviation from its cycle," the commander told them. "And I can't see anything like that happening in the next four days."

Jonathon and Joshua stood in the cargo section of their ship, looking at the stasis pods.

Another four days, Jonathon thought to himself. *But what good would it do for Katharyn? Without the DNA treatment, there was no hope.*

He dropped his head when this thought entered his mind. Joshua saw this and looked at Jonathon, then noticed the electronic device on his wrist.

"Katharyn has one of those," he said.

Jonathon lifted his head and looked at Joshua.

"One of what?" Jonathon asked, not really caring.

"On your wrist. One of those," Joshua said, pointing at Jonathon's wrist. "I brought it with us."

Jonathon was still staring at Joshua, confused, and thinking: *And your point is?*

"Katharyn's is a little different to that one, older, I guess. She showed me what it does," Joshua told him.

"Yes," Jonathon said, wearily, looking back at the pod with Katharyn inside. "She wore it here all the time… It does the same as this one."

He looked at the device on his wrist, momentarily, before continuing.

"It's a security device that allows entry into certain places, and to operate all the systems in the residence."

"That's not all it does," Joshua said. "Katharyn showed me… It's also a storage device that uses holographic computer technology. All her personal, business, and financial information is stored on it."

Jonathon looked at the device on his wrist again.

"Hold your arm in front of you like this," Joshua instructed.

He touched a corner of the device on Jonathon's wrist and a holographic display screen rose out of it.

He then put his hand on the transparent screen and scrolled through all the programs it displayed.

Jonathon stared at it in amazement.

"This one has a very high level of security clearance, and those are all of the programming files," Joshua explained, pointing to an area on the display, "but there's nothing else stored on this one."

Joshua then touched the device again and the holographic display disappeared. Jonathon stared for a few moments at where the display had just been hovering in front of his eyes, then looked over at the pod with Francis inside.

"Francis had one of these, too," Jonathon said. "Come to think of it, he never took it off… But I never saw him wearing it in Henleyville."

Jonathon walked over to Francis' stasis pod and looked down at the face of his very old friend, visible through the tiny, frosted window.

"You did have a back-up, didn't you, old friend," Jonathon said, as a realization came to him, "and I know exactly where you kept it!"

THIRTY-ONE

The next day, Jonathon, the commander, and a huge team of other personnel with massive excavation equipment were all in an area just outside the city limits. It was the edge of the valley where there once stood a range of smaller mountains, giant hills really, some of which were now less than half of their former size.

The war in the twenty-first century most definitely had its impact on this place, Jonathon thought as he surveyed the area.

Last night, Jonathon had figured out where Francis probably hid his laboratory while he and Mariangela were on Earth.

It made sense to him.

Like the Book of Laws in his own secret cave, Jonathon realized that Francis and Mariangela had probably made all their products, and the DNA treatment they gave to Katharyn, in a lab on their ship.

A ship that was hidden deep inside a vast cavern at the bottom of the William B. Henley dam three millennia ago.

A ship that was still there today but was now buried under tons of rubble.

"You'd better be right about this, Guardian," the commander said.

"It's there, commander," Jonathon replied, confidently. "I'm sure of it."

"Where exactly?" the commander asked.

Jonathon studied the hills and topography, trying to remember how it all had once looked. It was difficult though because this area had been deep underwater three thousand years ago. Jonathon spotted a familiar marker near the top of one of the hills then looked down to its base and saw the faint remnants of what once had been the massive underwater cave opening.

"There," Jonathon told him, pointing.

The commander signaled for his team to commence the excavation of the site.

A few hours later, they broke through the blockage and discovered that the rest of the cave had remained intact. The lights on the excavation machines shone deep into the huge cavern, revealing Francis and Mariangela's ship still in its resting place. The crew sent notification of the finding, then Jonathon and the commander entered the cave.

"It's been here the whole time," the commander commented, staring at the spacecraft.

Once inside the ship, Jonathon discovered he was right. Francis and Mariangela had created a small laboratory in the cargo hold of their ship. Some of the products they had made were still there.

The commander was amazed, as was the medical scientist who had come down from habitation seven for the excavation.

Jonathon spotted a wooden item on a table in the makeshift lab. It was a napkin holder, one of the many Francis had made in his workshop. Jonathon smiled and went over to it then saw the electronic wrist device inside.

"Commander," Jonathon said, picking up the device and holding it up. "I told you it would be here."

The medical scientist came over to Jonathon and scanned the device with another instrument then, after looking at its display screen, he nodded to the commander.

"It is all there," the scientist declared.

"You're a genius, Jonathon," the commander said with excitement.

"No, commander, that would be Francis," Jonathon said, then turned to the medical scientist. "How long will it take you to make the DNA treatment?"

"It will take a while," the scientist replied, "so I need to get back."

"Then go," the commander ordered, and the scientist made to leave.

"I'm coming, too," Jonathon said, "and we're taking Katharyn."

Katharyn's stasis pod was loaded onto the galactic spacecraft that had brought down the medical scientist, and Jonathon was just about to board it when Joshua showed up.

"Jonathon, Lesley is awake. She is asking for you," Joshua told him.

Jonathon was relieved.

"Good," he said, placing a comforting hand on Joshua's shoulder. "Stay with them. Tell her I'll be back as soon as I can... hopefully with good news."

Joshua nodded then Jonathon entered the ship.

Within seconds, it lifted off then flew up and away at lightning speed towards habitation station seven which was currently orbiting Tellus.

....

In The Darkness, Athanasius opened his eyes, the flickering of the eternal fires revealing an evil grin on his face.

He had been listening to everything.

"There will be no good news, Jonathon," he said. "I've grown tired of your little planet. I'm going to destroy it... along with you, and everyone you have ever cared about."

Athanasius raised his arms and the flickering flames burst into raging fires. Then, from those fires, thousands of dark shadow beings emerged, and Athanasius was pleased because a new army of demon Corvidaens now stood before their creator.

....

Inside the medical facility on habitation station seven, Jonathon watched impatiently as the team of medical specialists rushed around initialising protocols and systems for the rollout of the new DNA modification treatment program.

The head medical scientist who had been at the excavation site stood at a small upright control station beside Katharyn's stasis pod.

The pod was connected to a robotically operated cradle and when the scientist touched the screen on the control panel in front of him, two robot arms came down from the ceiling and lifted the pod. Another smaller arm attached itself to the pod then a needle type device entered it and inserted itself into Katharyn.

"We have to do a biopsy first," the scientist said, noticing the horrified look on Jonathon's face. "We extract Katharyn's

DNA from it, then create the genetic modification treatment specifically for her."

"How long before you have the treatment ready?" he asked.

"About an hour," the scientist told him. "It's how it was always done. Take a DNA swab, create the profile, then engineer the genetic modification treatment… We can't swab Katharyn, so the biopsy method is the only other choice. But to administer the treatment, she must have all her biological functions."

"What do you mean?" Jonathon asked.

The scientist stopped when the small arm disconnected from the pod and inserted the biopsy sample into the DNA sequencing machine.

"We'll have to take her out of cryogenic suspended animation and bring her back to life," the scientist stated.

"No!" Jonathon said. "She will keep aging rapidly then die."

"The treatment needs to circulate through her body. It takes about thirty minutes and we'll be monitoring her the whole time."

"What if the treatment isn't working?" Jonathon asked.

"I'll put her back into cryogenic suspended animation." the scientist replied.

....

Down on Tellus it was nighttime.

Lesley was up and had showered, though this had been a struggle for her.

Amy had prepared some meals in the re-hydrator, and they were all sitting at a table picking at their food. But it seemed that tonight no one was very hungry.

Lesley still looked tired and run down. Her head was very sore and while Amy and Joshua could see the pain in her eyes, neither of them said anything.

"Any word from Jonathon?" Lesley asked.

Joshua shook his head.

"No. I'll check with the commander later."

"How amazing that they found the other ship," Amy said. "And it's been there for three thousand years!"

Lesley nodded.

"Mmm. It is crazy when you think about it… Jonathon told me that Francis and the others left here when mother was your age, Amy… that was around fifty years ago."

"So, it was already there, even before they left?" Amy asked.

"Yes. Since 1970. They traveled back in time remember," she told her.

Amy nodded.

"Yeah, I know. But it's still crazy when you think about it… It's hard to get my head around it."

Everyone was silent for a while.

Amy was stabbing at her re-hydrated food with a fork and pushing it around. Lesley ate little pieces of her own tasteless meal, and she noticed Joshua hadn't touched his food at all.

Amy put the fork down and pushed her meal away.

"Ugh. I'd kill for a burger and fries!" she said.

This made Lesley laugh.

And Joshua smiled too because he hadn't seen Lesley laugh in a very long time. Even though she was gravely ill, her face lit up and made her eyes sparkle. Amy started laughing, too.

•••

In the medical facility on habitation station seven, Katharyn's DNA modification treatment was ready to be administered. Jonathon watched anxiously as the medical team shut down the cryogenic suspended animation program on Katharyn's stasis pod and initiated the re-animation sequence.

Within a few minutes, all of Katharyn's biological functions returned, but they were not strong. Jonathon stood next to the pod, looking down through the small window as Katharyn opened her eyes and saw him.

"Hurry, please!" Jonathon said to the head scientist.

Two robot arms came down and connected to the pod on either side, then an injection probe came out of each one and inserted needles into Katharyn's neck.

The treatment was delivered.

Now they had to wait.

Thirty minutes later and there had been no change.

The treatment wasn't working.

It had no effect on Katharyn's declining condition and her life signs were getting weaker. Jonathon looked into Katharyn's eyes with a sadness he had not felt since Athena's death. He watched a tear trickle from the corner of one of Katharyn's eyes.

"I'll find a way, Katharyn," he said softly to her, then turned to the head medical scientist. "Put her back into cryogenic animation!"

The sequence was initiated.

Jonathon watched as Katharyn closed her eyes when her biological functions shut down and the tiny window frosted up inside the pod.

What was he going to tell Lesley and Amy?

And what about Joshua?

He has been close to Katharyn for over forty years, Jonathon remembered.

He shook his head slowly as the devastation of the treatment failure turned into a raging anger inside him.

"Athanasius, I'll not let you take any more of the people I love," he declared to himself.

THIRTY-TWO

The following day, preparations were underway to have the newly discovered ship relocated to one of the habitation stations where it would be displayed as a museum piece. It had been declared a treasure of historical significance after the discovery of an immense digital library of vital information and data about Earth and its history.

Francis and Mariangela had been very busy during their time there.

Jonathon had come back down to Tellus earlier but, as yet, he had not been to see Lesley or Amy. He had gone to see the commander first to make sure the transportation ship was still coming the next day. But the commander wasn't at the base. He was inside the ship in the cave, so Jonathon went there to find him.

"Apparently there are more caves like this one in the area," the commander told Jonathon.

They were both standing in the ship's flight control center.

"They are lava tubes that were formed millions of years ago," the commander went on. "This one we're in now goes for miles underground to the west."

Jonathon looked at the commander when he said this because he knew what used to be in that specific area, and finding out that a lava tube ran underneath the area where the town of Henleyville once was had surprised him.

Jonathon looked around the control center.

It was almost identical to his own ship, so the layout was familiar. He sat down in one of the seats behind the two main flight control seats and imagined Francis or Mariangela sitting in it.

Or had it been Raphael or Aniela? He would never know.

Jonathon spotted the console between the two flight control seats and noticed something inside the open compartment beneath the control panel. He got up and went to the console and retrieved the item. It was the piece of bark paper he had written three lines of symbols on, one of which Francis had told him they were not able to decipher.

Jonathon looked over to where the commander was and saw he had his back to him, so he folded the paper and hid it in one of his pockets.

"Commander. When will the transportation ship get here tomorrow?" Jonathon asked.

"Sometime around the middle of the day," the commander replied, coming over to Jonathon. "And we're taking this ship with us."

The commander stared at Jonathon for a few moments.

"Jonathon, I heard the DNA treatment was not successful. I'm very sorry," he said, with genuine sympathy.

Jonathon said nothing.

"Have you told her daughter?" the commander asked.

Jonathon shook his head.

"No. Not yet," he said.

The commander nodded, understanding the gravity of the situation and the dilemma Jonathon faced.

"We're starting the treatments again for the population, thanks to you finding this ship," he told him.

Jonathon nodded but his mind was elsewhere.

"I have to go, commander."

Jonathon left the ship and headed to the mountain residence. He couldn't put it off any longer. It was time he told Lesley and Amy the treatment had failed.

………………………………………..

But nobody was home when Jonathon got there.

They had left earlier to go visit the site of their hometown, Henleyville.

It was Amy's idea.

After finding out that the city in the valley was built where the dam used to be, Amy had begged her mother to go and see if anything remained of where they had lived. Joshua arranged for a flight shuttle to take them.

As they flew over the area where Henleyville once was, they saw nothing but dead trees and thousands of years of old vegetation covering the landscape.

From above, it looked like a barren wasteland.

The shuttle landed and they all got out and began wandering around the empty fields.

There was nothing there.

No remnants of the buildings, houses, or roads remained.

No schools and no hospital.

No landmarks of any kind.

After three thousand years, nature had reclaimed the lands and now it was like Henleyville never existed.

"We were only here less than a week ago," Amy said, as they walked over the grounds.

"In another time," Joshua remarked.

"It's spooky," she said. "I can't even figure out where our house was."

Lesley was looking off in the distance, at something about a kilometer away. She had spotted a tree, a very big tree, and from where she was standing it appeared the tree remarkably still had most of its foliage.

Everything else in the area was either dead or dying.

Trees were now skeletons, and the wild grass was brown and harsh under foot. The landscape was basically barren, except for the big tree in the distance so Lesley started walking towards it.

"Ma, where're you going?" Amy asked, then followed her mother.

Joshua trailed along behind them as well.

As they got closer, Lesley saw that the tree was now much bigger than she remembered.

The big conifer tree that had stood at the end of their driveway was now massive, and surprisingly it was still alive. When they got to the tree, Lesley looked up at its huge trunk and saw where her letterbox had once been attached to it. Just below it was the scar, still visible, where Jonathon had lodged the letterbox lid deep into the tree trunk.

"It was here," Lesley said, looking around to where the Cooper house would have been three thousand years ago.

"What was, Ma?" Amy asked.

"Our home," she replied.

"No way!" Amy said, looking at the vacant land, then turning back to the tree and realizing, "That's our tree!"

Amy paced out the length of their old driveway.

She had done this many times as a kid.

Thirty steps up the driveway then ten steps to the right.

"Ma!" she called. "This is where our steps were!"

Lesley and Joshua went over to Amy and stood with her.

A light breeze was blowing but there were no sounds traveling with it, only silence. It was an eerie feeling. Lesley turned and looked back at the big tree.

How could it still be alive? Lesley wondered.

"It's the tree of life," she heard a voice say in her mind.

Lesley went back to the tree and put her hand on its trunk. She closed her eyes, and she was almost certain she could feel the roots grow deeper into the earth.

"It's time to go, Lesley," Joshua said, startling her out of her mind meld with the tree. "It's getting late."

Lesley looked to the sky.

The sun was getting lower.

Joshua was right.

And Lesley was hoping that Jonathon had returned with news of her mother.

"Amy. Let's go," Lesley called out.

They made the trek back to the shuttle and headed back to the city.

Jonathon was sitting out on the terrace when they arrived home. Lesley didn't need to ask the burning question of him. She saw the answer on his face, his sad eyes betraying him.

Later that night, Jonathon was still out on the terrace.

Lesley had gone to her room after seeing the look on Jonathon's face and had not come out. Joshua was with her. He had given Lesley Katharyn's wrist device and told her about the stuff that was stored on it. He showed Lesley how to make the holographic screen appear, then he showed her a folder with dozens of home movies saved in it.

There were videos of Katharyn when she was much younger, holding Lesley as a newborn. Jonathon was in that video as well. There were dozens of videos of Lesley as a baby through to a young teenager.

Most of the videos were filmed by Katharyn.

Lesley remembered her mother filming some of them when she was older, but in the ones where she was just a baby, somebody else had filmed them because her mother was in the videos with Lesley.

"Who filmed all of these early ones when I was a baby?" she asked Joshua.

Joshua looked at her and smiled.

"You? No way!" she said. "How come I don't remember?"

She punched Joshua softly on the thigh.

"Stalker!" she said, and they both laughed.

Jonathon heard them laugh from out on the terrace.

He remembered he had the bark paper in his pocket, so he got up and went inside to look for Amy.

She was sitting at the table with her laptop open looking at photos she had saved on it. Jonathon saw the laptop and raised his eyebrows at her when she looked at him.

"I know. You told me not to bring it... or my phone. But they have my life on them," she told him.

Jonathon sat down at the table.

He had the folded bark paper in one of his hands.

"I'm just looking at all of my photos and videos again before the battery dies," she said.

Amy continued looking at her laptop.

Jonathon had said nothing since they'd arrived back from their field trip because he couldn't find the words to tell them that Katharyn was not going to survive. He looked at Amy knowing she desperately wanted to ask him about her grandmother and what, if anything, could be done now to save her. But Amy, too, didn't know how to voice her thoughts.

Words can be so hard to say sometimes.

"I'll find a way, Amy," Jonathon said, breaking the silence, "I promised Katharyn I would."

"G-ma was awake?" Amy asked.

"Yes. For the treatment she was," he replied.

Amy studied his face.

"It didn't work, did it?" Amy asked.

Jonathon shook his head slowly.

"They put your grandmother back into cryogenic suspended animation as soon as we realized the treatment had no effect on her condition," he explained.

Amy nodded, understanding the gravity of the situation, then saw the folder paper in Jonathon's hand.

"What's that?" she asked.

Jonathon unfolded the bark paper and put it on the table.

"I'm hoping you might tell me."

Amy picked it up and looked at it.

"I know what the first lines mean… But the last group of symbols, nobody has ever been able to decipher them. I thought you might be able to," he told her, with a hopeful look in his eyes.

"Well," Amy began, looking at the paper, "it's just as well I brought my laptop, isn't it. I have programs saved on it that may help."

Amy tapped away on her laptop, opening the program file she was looking for. She was nodding as she typed something, then looked at the bark paper and then back at her laptop.

"I thought so," she said. "They're symbols from ancient Mesopotamia, Jonathon. Symbols from that era can represent people, objects, words, or phrases. The language is Akkadian!"

"Akkadian? How would I know ancient Akkadian?" he asked, dumbfounded.

"I don't know but that's what this is," she told him, indicating the bark paper writing.

"What does it mean?" he asked, intrigued.

Amy looked at the translator program on her laptop.

"This group of symbols translates to 'The daughter will awaken the true king.' Pretty cool, hey. Just like the prophecy."

"The prophecy," Jonathon repeated, softly. "I wonder…"

Suddenly, he looked up and saw Joshua and Lesley standing there. How much had they heard, he wondered, and more specifically, had Lesley heard them talking about Katharyn?

He noticed Joshua was watching him intently with a strange look on his face, like he was hiding something.

Jonathon stood and went over to Lesley.

"Please don't let this all be for nothing," she told Jonathon, then hugged him.

THIRTY-THREE

The Darkness

Athanasius' new legion of demon Corvidaens were not like his previous minions. No. The old ones were too predictable in their true form and easily detected by Jonathon, and even in their original human form, if confronted, they morphed into their Darkness form to fight the Guardian.

Also, they had failed too many times since the beginning.

Hence, which is why Athanasius needed a new type of Corvidaen. One that was not detectable and could move about in The Light realm in plain sight while carrying out its deadly orders. And so, the demon Corvidaen was created from the fires which burned in The Darkness realm. Spirit demons that could pass from one human to another, inhabiting each body at will, without the need for their master's touch.

The new demon Corvidaens made no sounds either because they had no mouths and they moved swiftly and silently.

Athanasius raised a hand to bring his new army to attention.

"One pure-born is at death's door. Another is fighting for her life… but will fail. The last remaining pure-child is weak. When the third immortal falls, and I am free of this eternal prison, I will take great pleasure in ending her life as well… Go now. Find your hosts and wait for my command," Athanasius instructed.

....

TELLUS

At the command center base on Tellus, the commander was still awake finalising the procedures for the evacuation the next day.

The transportation ship would be arriving around noon or maybe just after, he'd been informed. It will hover above the city upon arrival, then send down shuttles to evacuate the remaining ground and air defense personnel. The ship in the cave will be flown up to the transportation ship and into one of its holding bays. The few civilians in the city will also be flown up in shuttles as well, and after shutting down all the city's systems, the commander and his staff will be the last evacuees to leave.

The commander went over the procedures several more times, making sure nothing would be forgotten. Satisfied that everything had been planned for, he ended his report.

In the sleeping quarters on the base, most of the fighter pilots and ground force troops were sound asleep. They had an early start in the morning because it would be their last day on Tellus. A few were still up cleaning equipment or eating a late-night meal but none of them, not the ones sleeping, or the ones still awake, knew what was coming.

The demon Corvidaens entered the base sleeping quarters silently, like shadows, passing through the walls and ceilings and into the bodies of the sleeping soldiers.

Simultaneously, in the galactic command control base on the moon, and on the seven habitation stations orbiting Tellus, thousands of spirit demons entered the bodies of galactic starship pilots and defense personnel stationed on all of them.

Athanasius had set his traps.

And with Katharyn still on one of the habitation stations, he had the perfect bait to lure Jonathon away from the other pure-borns on Tellus, away from the last pure-child, and away from the other immortal.

"I am coming, Jonathon," Athanasius said in The Darkness realm, "and you cannot stop me."

THIRTY-FOUR

Jonathon had a restless night. The fates of Katharyn and Lesley weighed heavily on him. Sleep didn't come easy but when he finally succumbed to fatigue, he had a dream.

In his dream, he saw the symbol he'd carved into the wall of cave, the same symbol on his battle vest, the very same symbol on his chest, everywhere. He also saw the entity in his dream again, and it was shrouded by an intense light so bright that Jonathon shielded his eyes from it.

But he wasn't afraid of the entity this time.

He felt calm and at peace in its presence.

He felt like he was home.

The entity came closer to him.

It had no face and Jonathon saw his symbol on its body as the entity reached out and touched him.

"Athanasius is near, Jonathon. Remember who you are!" the entity told him.

Jonathon woke up, confused, but alert.

He recognized the voice in his dream. It was the voice of someone he had not seen, or spoken to, for a very long time.

It was Athena's voice in his dream, and he now realized the entity was her.

"True immortals never die," Jonathon remembered Joshua had told him.

Athena had said his name, spoken to him, but he still didn't understand what she meant about remembering who he was.

It was just after dawn, so Jonathon got up, dressed, and went out onto the terrace.

A little while later, Joshua joined him and noticed that Jonathon was dressed in his full Guardian battle attire including his battle sword sheathed in its scabbard.

"Is there something you're not telling me?" Joshua asked.

"What?" Jonathon responded.

"You are wearing your battle uniform," Joshua said. "Are we expecting trouble?"

Jonathon looked at Joshua for a moment before responding.

"It's been too quiet, Joshua. I don't like it. Something is not right," Jonathon said.

"Something meaning?"

"Athanasius… I think he is here," Jonathon said.

He looked up into the early morning sky where one of the habitation stations was visible orbiting high above Tellus, and wondered if Katharyn was on it. He wasn't sure because the habitation stations all looked the same.

"Are you sure? Why hasn't he shown himself?" Joshua asked.

"I don't know. I'm not sure… It's just a feeling," Jonathon told him. "I'm going back up to check on Katharyn. If I'm not back in time, you get the women to the transportation ship when it arrives. Okay?"

Joshua nodded in agreement.

Jonathon started to leave then stopped.

"Keep one of the weapons with you at all times, Joshua. Amy knows how to use it, too. And remember what I've told you… trust no one!"

Jonathon left and Joshua remained on the terrace watching the sky and then the city below. There was already activity at the command base.

If Athanasius is here, why hasn't he tried to get to Lesley and Amy? Joshua wondered.

Joshua now had the same feeling as Jonathon.

It *had* been too quiet, but something inside told him that it was all about to change.

Jonathon went to the command base. He was in luck because the starship he had come down on the previous afternoon was still there, so he flew it up to habitation station seven.

The medical facility was deserted when he got there.

It was early by Tellus time, he realized, so he sat with Katharyn and tried to figure out how he could save her.

The DNA treatment had failed.

"It can't reverse the aging process," he remembered Francis telling him. "We don't get younger."

Jonathon shook his head.

He should've remembered this, but at the time, he thought it was worth a try using a double dosage.

He could think of no other options.

But it didn't work, and he was now out of options.

The only thing keeping Katharyn alive now is the stasis pod, Jonathon thought, *even though in cryogenic suspended animation she is technically dead anyway.*

She has no biological functions.

The pod is basically her coffin.

Jonathon closed his eyes and sighed heavily.

On Tellus, Lesley and Amy were up.

They'd both already packed their things for relocation. Lesley had chosen to wear her mother's thin white dress today, the one she had found when they first arrived at the residence.

It fit Lesley perfectly.

Her hair was tied back as usual, and she was wearing Katharyn's small security device on her wrist.

"Wow, Ma!" Amy said, when she saw how beautiful her mother looked in the dress.

Lesley smiled and looked at Amy who, for the first time in her life, was wearing a dress as well.

Amy looks amazing. Older even, with her hair loose, Lesley thought.

"Wow yourself," she replied.

"Thanks, Ma," Amy smiled. "Can we go check out the old lake before we leave today?"

"Sure, if we have time," Lesley said, then turned to look for Joshua.

She spotted him coming inside from the terrace.

"Is Jonathon still asleep?" Lesley asked.

"No. He left a while ago. He's gone back up to check on your mother," Joshua said, staring at Lesley and then at Amy.

Seeing them both standing there in beautiful dresses, Joshua had a feeling of Deja vu, of a time long ago.

"What?" Lesley asked, noticing him staring.

"Nothing," he said. "You both look stunning."

"Thank you," Lesley said, blushing. "Amy wants to go to the dry lake this morning. Do we have time before the transportation ship comes?"

Joshua nodded.

"Yes. I'll organise a shuttle."

Inside the galactic defense base on the moon, the possessed fighter pilots heard a voice whisper to them.

"The time has come," the voice said.

It was Athanasius, and instantly all the demon Corvidaens woke up inside their hosts.

They took control of fighter pilots who then took out their weapons and began killing all the other personnel on the base, before heading for the galactic fighter ships.

In the command center base on Tellus, the commander watched the transportation ship leave the lunar base and start its journey to Tellus.

It should be here within the hour, he calculated.

He instructed the remaining operations staff to shut down the city's control systems and prepare for the shuttles to arrive. When everyone else had left, the commander was just about to shut down the large transparent wall screen when he saw dozens of galactic fighter ships take off from the lunar operations base.

He watched as some headed towards the transportation ship while the rest dispersed and headed towards the habitation stations.

"What the hell," the commander said, then opened a communication line to the moon command center.

"Command One. This is Tellus Command. Why are those fighters in flight?"

No answer.

"Command One. This is Tellus Command. Respond."

No answer again.

On the screen, the commander saw the fighter ships start attacking the transportation ship, firing continuously at it, until it exploded and was destroyed, sending debris floating off in all directions in space.

Outside, all the fighter ships on the base took off and headed for the habitation stations, at the same time as six heavily armed soldiers burst into the command center and began firing at the commander.

He quickly took cover and withdrew his sidearm weapon.

He looked at it.

It was small compared to the weapons being fired at him, but it was all he had so it would have to do.

On habitation station seven, which was currently orbiting beyond the moon, an alarm started sounding. Jonathon went to a viewing window and saw a squadron of galactic fighter ships coming towards the station firing their weapons at it. More fighter ships were attacking the other habitations stations as well.

As he stood watching the mayhem, several defense personnel came storming into the medical facility and started firing at him. He ducked down behind a machine and withdrew his fighting sword.

He needed a better weapon.

Jonathon stood quickly and threw his sword at one of the soldiers firing at him. It struck the man in his chest, and he stumbled backwards before he collapsed and died. Jonathon ran as fast as is bad knee would allow him, miraculously avoided the weapon fire of the other soldiers, rolled on the floor, grabbed the dead soldier's weapon, and came up firing.

He killed the other two soldiers quickly.

He watched as the shadow demons exited the bodies of the dead men and flew up through the ceiling of the facility. He then retrieved his sword from the chest of the first dead man and sheathed it in the scabbard on his back.

"So that's how you're doing it now, Athanasius," Jonathon said to himself.

The habitation station was suddenly rocked by a massive explosion. It was being destroyed by the fighter ships and by other defense personnel inside like the men Jonathon had just killed. Jonathon looked out the viewing window again just as another habitation station met its demise.

Jonathon needed to escape the habitation station before it, too, was destroyed by the fighter ships.

He looked at Katharyn's stasis pod, went over and detached it from its cradle. He checked the pod operating system to make sure the suspended animation program was still running.

It was.

He picked up the pod and headed for his ship, hoping it would still be there, and hoping he wouldn't be confronted with anymore of Athanasius' soldiers along the way because the only weapon he had was his sword, and his hands were now full.

On Tellus, Lesley and Amy were wandering around in the middle of the old dry lake. Joshua was standing about one hundred meters away on what used to be the shore, watching them, with the weapon by his side as Jonathon had instructed.

Amy was looking around trying to imagine the lake that was once here, teeming with life, the same lake that had been on Adamah, Jonathon had told them.

The dry lake area was vast and deep.

Looking back to where Joshua was standing, Amy noticed it was a steep incline to that point. She wandered around some more and spotted a triangle shaped object protruding out of the lakebed. It was small. She went over to it and bent down to pick it up, but it was stuck.

Amy started digging with her hands, and realized it was much larger than she first thought. It took her a few minutes to dig it out and when she did, she saw that it was a metal plate about fifty centimeters long and maybe twenty-five centimeters wide. She wiped her hand over the face of it and discovered it was a plaque.

The words on the plaque read: *The William B Henley Dam.*

Joshua had seen the fighter ships take off and when he looked up, he saw the transportation ship explode high above the planet. Several moments later, one of the habitation stations blew up as well. He was so shocked and stunned at what he was looking at, that he didn't see, or sense, the shadow figure coming up behind him.

Out in the middle of the lake, Lesley looked back to where Joshua was standing and saw him staring up into the sky. Lesley looked up as well and saw the devastation high above Tellus. She looked back to the lake shore and saw a figure standing behind Joshua. The figure seemed to be shrouded in a dark mist, but it was moving closer to Joshua.

Without warning, something pierced Joshua through his back and lifted him off the ground.

"Look at this, Ma," Amy said, referring to the plaque.

Then she heard her mother's scream.

"Joshua!" Lesley screamed. "Noooooo!"

Lesley started to run but stopped in her tracks when something inside her head exploded. The tumor had burst, the pain instantly immense and unbearable. She grabbed her head as the tumor burst again and she fell to the ground paralyzed, unable to move.

"Ma!" Amy screamed, dropping the plaque.

She ran over and fell to her knees next to her dying mother.

"Ma! Ma!" Amy cried.

Lesley could only move her eyes.

Her breathing was labored and shallow.

She looked at Amy.

"Ma. Please don't die!" Amy cried.

A tear trickled from the corner of one of Lesley's eyes as a deep sadness filled her.

Her time had come.

The tumor had won.

She was leaving Amy, her beautiful daughter, and this broke her already dying heart.

Another part of the tumor burst inside her head forcing Lesley to close her eyes to the excruciating pain. She opened her eyes for a moment and tried to say something to Amy, but the words would not come.

She felt her heart stop, and Amy watched in horror as her mother closed her eyes for the final time and expelled her last breath.

"Ma! No!"

Joshua could feel his life fading quickly.

Athanasius had pierced his heart and if he withdrew the steel stake, he would surely die within seconds.

Athanasius laughed as he lowered Joshua onto the ground.

"That was too easy, immortal," Athanasius said, then withdrew the stake.

Joshua saw Lesley collapse and Amy rush to her mother's side. He knew Lesley was gone so he looked up to the heavens as the last moments of life drained from him.

"Remember who you are, my brother," Joshua said as he died.

Athanasius stood back as Joshua's body lifted off the ground and transformed into an intense bright orb of light that hovered for a few seconds, appearing to look at him, before shooting upwards into the sky and disappearing.

Jonathon reached the starship just in time to lock Katharyn's stasis pod into a transport cradle as the habitation station started exploding all around them. As he lifted off, more soldiers inside the station began firing at the starship. Jonathon released one of the blue wave explosives then flew the ship clear of the disintegrating habitation station just as another massive explosion destroyed it entirely.

While he dodged debris floating in space, and fired at the other fighter ships attacking him, Jonathon heard a voice come to his ears.

"Remember who you are, my brother."

"Joshua!" Jonathon exclaimed, then immediately headed for Tellus.

Lesley was dead, her life ruthlessly taken by the tumor and the heartbreak of seeing her beloved Joshua killed by Athanasius. Amy was sobbing uncontrollably, and her tears were falling onto her mother's lifeless body, with some dripping onto the dry lakebed. As more of her tears fell, the skies above Tellus quickly darkened.

Massive storms quickly formed, covering the entire planet, and plunged Tellus into an eerie darkness. Within moments, lightning and thunder filled the skies, the symphony of light and sound both mesmerizing and deadly. Torrential rains began pouring down drenching the lands of Tellus and replenishing all the rivers and oceans.

The flooding rains continued relentlessly.

Amy was terrified but she refused to leave her mother's side. She lay down next to Lesley, rested her head on her mother's chest, held her hand, then closed her eyes knowing her fate.

With a tremendous roar, a great wall of water came rolling though the river catchment and over the hills. The massive wave engulfed the dry lake, filling it within seconds and washed away both Lesley and Amy, ending the life of the last of the pure-borns in the flood caused by her tears.

THIRTY-FIVE

Inside the command center, the commander had managed to send an alert to the harvesting ships which were also roving galactic fighter bases. As he tried holding off the soldiers firing at him, he glanced at the massive wall screen which was still turned on and hoped the alert had been received.

He'd managed to kill three of the soldiers but several more still had him trapped in the command room, and they were closing in on him. His small hand-held weapon was running out of fire power and, looking at it now, he knew it was only a matter of time before it would be useless.

From his starship high above Tellus, Jonathon saw enormous hurricanes and cyclones rapidly swarm the entire planet, hiding it from view. The massive storms swirled and circled Tellus violently, with lightning flashing continuously inside them and stretching for thousands of kilometers.

More fighter ships were now attacking him, and Jonathon was using all his piloting skills to evade their weapon fire while firing back at them.

Suddenly, a rift opened, and a massive starship emerged from it directly in front of Jonathon's ship. It was one of the enormous ice harvesting ships from Europa and it must have responded to an alert from the lunar base, or maybe the command center on Tellus.

Jonathon guessed the harvesting starship was at least a hundred times bigger than his galactic starship and he had to perform drastic evasive maneuvers to avoid crashing into it.

The harvesting ship started taking weapon fire from the fighter ships, but its shields were impenetrable, preventing any damage.

Jonathon circled back around and began firing at the fighter ships again just as a huge fleet of larger galactic starfighters emerged from the harvesting ship and began firing at the smaller fighter ships. Jonathon took this as his chance to head down to Tellus, so he broke away from the battle and headed for the storm covered planet.

His ship burst through the thundering storm clouds just as the rain stopped. He saw the once dry lake was now full and waves of water were crashing onto its shore and rolling into the valley.

Jonathon landed his ship at the air base, retrieved a weapon from its holder and exited. He stood on the base landing area for a moment watching the skies as they began to clear, then heard weapon fire coming from inside the command center.

He rushed over, with his weapon at the ready, and saw several soldiers inside command center firing into the control room. Jonathon entered, firing his weapon at the soldiers, killing one as the other two pivoted and returned fire.

But they were not quick enough.

Jonathon took them down in quick succession.

From his vantage point, Jonathon scanned the command center in all directions, making sure there were no other soldiers coming, then entered the control room.

"Commander?" Jonathon called out.

"Jonathon?" the commander responded, slowly emerging from his hiding place.

The commander stood and saw Jonathon was dressed in his battle attire.

"What the hell is going on?" the commander asked.

"No time to explain commander. Are you ok?" Jonathon enquired.

"Yes. Yes. I'm fine," he said.

Jonathon nodded and threw his weapon at the commander who caught it with both hands.

"Take this, commander. Trust no one. I've got to find the others," Jonathon told him, then ran back out to his ship.

Athanasius stood with his arms wide open, eyes closed and his face to the skies, smiling as the rain soaked him.

He was no longer a shadow being.

He was now released from The Darkness realm having killed Joshua, the third immortal to die by his hand, and he was marveling at the feeling of the rain hitting his face.

He breathed in and out deeply, taking in the cool air and smelling its freshness. He had not felt this whole, or this real, since the beginning when it was just him, his sister, and his beloved mother.

The rain stopped, and the skies began to clear.

He opened his eyes and watched as the water receded from around his feet and into the lake.

He remembered this lake.

He and Adanne had played in it, and near it, as children while their mother had watched and laughed at their antics.

As the lake waters calmed, Athanasius thought of Adamah and the day he lost his mother by his own hand. Sadness filled him as he remembered how his mother had died in his arms and her essence had flowed into these very waters.

But there was still a rage inside him.

A jealous rage for his sister, Adanne, who had always been his mother's favorite.

The skies had cleared, and the sun was shining brightly as Jonathon took off from the command base and flew the starship up and over the valley.

The city was undamaged.

All the flooding water had receded, and Jonathon saw in the distance that the lake was now full, replenished after forty years by the torrential rains.

From somewhere high up in the sky, lightning started hitting the lake. It seemed to be coming from everywhere in the now cloudless sky, but only hitting the lake.

Jonathon saw this and headed in that direction.

Athanasius moved back further away from the shore as thousands of lightning strikes hit the lake. He looked up but there were no storm clouds anywhere.

The sky was clear.

Confused, he looked at the lake again and saw its waters start to bubble, caused by the electricity from all the lightning strikes. Then the lightning stopped, and the lake waters stilled and became glassy smooth.

"Athanasius," a voice called from the lake.

Athanasius stared out at the lake because he knew that voice, the way it spoke his name.

From the sacred waters, replenished by the tears of The Swan, a being slowly emerged, a woman, reborn in The Light, pure and with ageless beauty, her hair long and flowing, and in her arms, she carried the lifeless body of her daughter, Adanne.

Aryanna, the *Mother of Life,* had returned and Nature had once again returned all her essence.

"Mother?" Athanasius gasped as Aryanna walked up onto the shore of the lake. "No! This can't be!"

Jonathon landed his ship nearby and exited just in time to see Athanasius standing near the shore of the lake, as Lesley walked out of it carrying Amy.

"No!" he exclaimed, as he rushed towards them.

Aryanna put Adanne softly down on the shore and touched her face.

"Athanasius," Aryanna said, walking over to her son. "See what you have done?"

Aryanna pointed to Adanne lying lifeless, having drowned in the floods caused by her tears of sorrow for her dead mother.

"Adanne is dead because of your jealousy," Aryanna said, "That cannot go unpunished."

Jonathon saw Lesley put Amy down and when he got to her, he found she was not breathing. He checked for a pulse, but Amy didn't have one, and realizing she must have drowned, Jonathon commenced the emergency resuscitation procedures Lesley had taught him.

"Come on Amy," Jonathon said, pumping her chest.

"Mother, I'm sorry," Athanasius said, still in shock at his mother's return.

Athanasius watched as the symbol of the 'Mother of Life' moved from the back of Aryanna's neck and down to her chest, over her heart, where it glowed. Athanasius stared at his mother as he realized what had happened.

"You have The Pure!" he exclaimed.

"Yes, my son," Aryanna said, then reached out and placed a hand on his shoulder.

Athanasius fell to his knees as all his powers were ripped out of him by his mother's touch. He screamed in pain as they tore out of his eternal soul and watched in horror as their essence burst into flames and vanished.

Aryanna removed her hand from his shoulder and stepped back.

Athanasius felt different.

His head pounded with a pain he had never felt before.

He felt drained, weak, and nauseous.

He looked up at his mother, his eyes barely open because of the throbbing in his head.

"What have you done?" he mumbled to Aryanna.

"You are no longer immortal, Athanasius," his mother declared.

"No!" he wailed.

Jonathon was performing the rescue breathing method on Amy when she started gagging. She turned her head to one side and expelled a huge amount of water from her lungs. She coughed several times as she opened her eyes and saw Jonathon looking down at her.

She didn't recognize him at first because she felt different.

She felt like someone else was in her head.

She sat up and looked around, then spotted Aryanna standing over Athanasius.

"Ma!" Amy called out, getting up.

Aryanna turned to see her daughter, alive, with Jonathon now standing next to her.

"Adanne!" Aryanna cried out and rushed over to them.

Aryanna hugged Amy and cried into her hair.

"You're alive, Adanne! You're alive!" Aryanna said.

"Ma," Amy said, unfolding herself from her mother's hug, "It's me, Amy."

"Amy?" Aryanna asked, confusion on her face.

Jonathon was staring at Lesley and, noticing the 'Mother-of-Life' symbol on her chest, he realized the ancient prophecy had been fulfilled.

Lesley was Aryanna, and Aryanna was Lesley.

How could I not have seen this before, he wondered. *And Aryanna had called Amy 'Adanne' because Adanne was Amy.*

This all made sense to him now.

Lesley had the birthmark on the back of her neck which was now over her heart, and Amy had the mark of the swan, the same as Adanne.

"Aryanna?" Jonathon hesitantly asked, staring at her.

Aryanna looked at Jonathon, and recognition filled her eyes.

She stood in front of him and smiled, looking up into his eyes.

"Father," Aryanna said, "Remember who you are."

Aryanna placed her hand over the symbol on Jonathon's battle vest and immediately they were both engulfed in a huge ball of light, its brightness so intense that Amy and Athanasius shielded their eyes as they watched.

Lightning emerged from the heavens, striking the giant globe of light surrounding Jonathon and Aryanna hundreds of times. After a few moments, the lightning stopped, and a wave of electricity slowly dissipated into the ground around them.

Athanasius stood up and moved further away from the electrified orb of light. Amy looked around at him then noticed Joshua's weapon lying on the ground nearby.

The intense ball of light slowly spread out and dissipated, revealing Aryanna and Jonathon.

Jonathon looked different and Aryanna smiled at him.

Jonathon's hair was now longer, sitting just on his shoulders and his beard was a little thicker but still outlined his jawline and chin. His battle attire was gone, replaced by an elaborate white and bright gold toga that covered his thighs, torso, and shoulders. A large new burgundy colored breastplate covered his massive chest and, on the breastplate, etched in gold, was the same tree of life motif Jonathon had carved into the front cover of the Book of Laws. In the center of the motif was the symbol he had carved into the wall of his secret cave, the same symbol on the back cover of the Book of Laws, the same symbol on his chest.

Together, the symbols meant: The Father of The Pure, The Family of Gods.

Jonathon remembered everything now because Aryanna had transferred The Pure to him, her father, her creator, and fulfilled another prophecy: The daughter will awaken the true king.

Aryanna smiled with love at her father then closed her eyes and collapsed to the ground.

Amy picked up Joshua's weapon and checked it was armed and ready to fire.

"Athanasius!" Amy called out, causing him to turn around and face her.

"Adanne!" Athanasius gasped, seeing his sister standing there.

Amy fired the weapon at him and watched as the bolt of blue energy entered his body and started to engulf him. Athanasius looked at where he had been shot then looked again at Adanne, shock on his face as he realized his fate.

"That," Amy/Adanne said, "is for killing my mother."

Athanasius screamed out as the blue energy evaporated his body and turned him into a cloud of ash that blew away in the light breeze that had come across the lake.

Amy dropped the weapon and rushed over to her mother, who was lying on the ground.

"Ma!" she said, as she knelt down beside her mother.

Lesley opened her eyes, looked at her daughter, and smiled.

"She will be fine, Amy" Jonathon said to her, his voice booming and echoing all around them. "Take her home. There are things I must do."

"Are you coming back?" Amy asked.

Jonathon looked into Amy's eyes and smiled, then a halo of light surrounded him, and he shot straight up into the sky, disappearing into the heavens.

THIRTY-SIX

Several months passed. Tellus was teeming with new life. The once barren and lifeless lands were now lush and green, and all the rivers, lakes and oceans on the planet were once again full of marine life.

The return of Aryanna - the Mother of Life - had transformed the planet into the thriving haven it had once been back in the beginning, when it was known as Adamah.

Many of the people who had escaped the habitation stations before they exploded had returned to Tellus and the city in the valley.

Not all the habitation stations had been destroyed in the attacks. There were still a couple left, but they had sustained significant damage that would take months to repair, and they were now orbiting the moon while those repairs took place.

The ice harvesting expeditions to Europa had been terminated considering water was once again plentiful on Tellus, and both mammoth galactic vessels now orbited high above the planet as the new global defense stations.

When Amy killed Athanasius, all the demon Corvidaens that had infected the thousands of defense personnel, instantly disappeared from existence, leaving their hosts as they had previously been before they were possessed.

Thousands of soldiers had been killed during the battles, some by Jonathon, some by soldiers not infected, and others by the galactic starships that came from the enormous harvesting ship that had arrived just in time, after receiving the commander's alert.

The fighter pilots and soldiers who survived were ordered to the command center base on Tellus where they were examined and questioned extensively before being put to work under the watchful eyes of the commander.

The DNA treatment program was reinstated, and a new medical facility was built inside the cave where Francis and Mariangela's ship had been found. The cave and ship were declared historical sites of world significance due to the vast digital library of information that was discovered on board and the DNA genetic modification files Francis had stored on his security device.

Francis, Mariangela, Raphael, Aniela, Samuel, and Laila were all posthumously awarded hero status and their pods were taken to their ship and housed in the stasis chamber, after which the room was sealed as a memorial to the six of them.

Lesley, Amy, and Jonathon were invited to the award ceremony, but Jonathon had not returned to Tellus.

The DNA treatment unit had been busy since its opening and its first patient had been the commander himself, followed by the surviving members of the governing council.

Everyone was happy again.

Life on Tellus was returning to normal.

But not for Lesley and Amy.

Nothing would be normal for them anymore, not since the events at the lake that day.

Lesley and Amy were different now.

They both knew it and they both felt it.

Lesley was Aryanna, and Aryanna was Lesley, and she still felt her presence inside her. Lesley remembered things that only Aryanna could know. She remembered life on Adamah, her death by Athanasius' hand, and her rebirth from the sacred waters many millennia later.

And when she looks at Amy now, she sees Adanne and knows she is the image of Aryanna's first-born daughter. Amy remembers it all too because Adanne is inside her.

They are the 'Mother of Life' and the 'Swan'.

Lesley visited the new medical facility, and they told her the tumor was gone, no longer there with no trace of it.

She was in perfect health they informed her.

In fact, her genetic makeup had changed, they'd said.

She was no longer aging.

Katharyn's stasis pod was now in the new medical facility and the scientists were working on ways to stop and reverse the rapid aging disease that had infected her. She was still in cryogenic suspended animation but, unfortunately no cure had been found yet.

Jonathon had not returned and both Lesley and Amy wondered if they would ever see him again.

Lesley knew who he was now.

She'd known since she'd emerged from the depths of the lake as Aryanna, and Amy had worked it out as well. Neither of them had spoken a word to each other about any of it. It felt like a taboo subject but each of them was desperate to talk about the events of that day and how they both now felt.

They both stood looking into Katharyn's stasis pod, at the hollow and aged face of their mother, and grandmother.

"Have there been any developments?" Lesley asked the director of the facility.

The director shook her head.

"I'm afraid not, Lesley. Nothing we have designed can combat the rapid cell degeneration."

Lesley nodded her head slowly and Amy grabbed her hand and squeezed it.

"It will take nothing less than a miracle to save your mother," the director said.

....

Time passes in the blink of an eye in The Heavens.

Weeks, months, and years on Tellus are just fleeting moments, and Jonathon, the Father of the Gods and true king, had been busy since his return.

Athena, his eternal partner, was pleased to be by his side again, together as the father and mother Creator entities they had been in the beginning.

Jonathon had taken no time in eliminating all the remaining demon spirits in The Darkness realm, something only the true king could do. He had also extinguished the eternal fires that Athanasius had created ensuring they would never burn again.

Jonathon and Athena were both pleased with the transformation of Tellus. When they gazed upon it from The Heavens, they saw it as Adamah had been when it was first created: new and full of life.

Jonathon was also pleased to be reunited with Joshua, his brother, now that he remembered everything.

But he noticed there was a growing sadness in his brother, and he often saw him staring down at Tellus. Athena knew the reason why and had whispered it to Jonathon.

Peace had come to all the realms again, but there was one last thing that Jonathon needed to do, and for that he wanted Athena with him.

. . . .

Lesley and Amy returned to the residence high up on the mountain. The sun was setting, and the sky was filled with a beautiful red and orange glow that touched the horizon. When they both came out onto the terrace, they noticed two people standing there.

It was Jonathon and Athena.

Amy rushed to Jonathon and hugged him tightly, tears welling in her eyes.

"I've missed you," she cried.

Jonathon put his arms around her.

"I've missed you, too, child," he replied.

Lesley came over to him, smiled at him and put her hand on his chest.

"I'm glad you came back," she said. "I hoped you would."

Jonathon smiled at Lesley and said, "This is Athena."

Lesley looked at Athena and smiled.

She was beautiful and radiant and dressed like Jonathon, in magnificent new battle attire but without weapons.

"Yes, I know," Lesley said, then embraced Athena. "You are the mother of Aryanna."

"We created her, yes," Athena said, referring to herself and Jonathon. "But like Jonathon, I didn't know until I returned to The Heavens… We punished ourselves for our failures with

Athanasius. As Guardians, our true selves were hidden, even from us."

"Tellus has been reborn, thanks to you, Lesley," Jonathon said.

"It is beautiful, isn't it," Lesley said, looking out over the valley and the lush green hills.

"And so have you been reborn," he told her. "The essence of Nature has been returned to the Mother-of-Life. That's you now, Lesley and wherever you go, new life will flourish."

"You are immortal now, too," Athena told her, then turned to Amy. "As are you, Amy. It is a gift from the waters of Adamah, which were replenished by your tears."

"Immortal?" they both said at the same time.

"Yes," Jonathon said.

"Wow!" Amy exclaimed. "That is so cool."

But Lesley looked away, and both Athena and Jonathon saw the sadness in her eyes and her demeanor.

They knew the reason why.

"I wish mother was here," Lesley said, overcome with emotion.

Jonathon and Athena looked at each other and smiled.

"Lesley, Amy!" Katharyn called out from the doorway to the terrace.

They both spun around hearing Katharyn's voice and ran into her open arms, hugged her, and cried with absolute joy.

Katharyn looked magnificent.

Jonathon and Athena had given back her life by taking away the death touch inflicted by Athanasius and reversing all its damaging effects.

They had also made her immortal.

Jonathon and Athena smiled with pride as they watched the three generations of pure-borns reunite and form a new bond, deeper and greater than they ever had before.

Jonathon looked at Athena, and they both knew it was time for them to leave and return to The Heavens. The pure-borns were now safe, forever. They no longer needed Guardians because Athanasius was gone.

"We must go," Jonathon said, breaking up the tearful, loving reunion.

Katharyn, Lesley, and Amy came over to them and hugged them both in turns.

Kathryn put her hand to Jonathon's face and smiled.

"Thank you, Jonathon," she said, as a tear trickled down her face. "I will always love you."

"As I will you," Jonathon said, overcome with emotion.

"Jonathon," Athena said, getting his attention.

She glanced at the sky.

Jonathon nodded, knowing what she was indicating.

He raised his hand, and a wide beam of intense light came down from the heavens and onto the terrace.

Inside the beam, a being emerged.

Jonathon lowered his hand and the light beam disappeared revealing the being.

It was Joshua.

Joshua nodded at Jonathon.

"Thank you, brother."

"Joshua!" Lesley cried out and ran into his arms.

Joshua picked her up and hugged her like he had never hugged her before, just as a bright halo of light engulfed Jonathon and Athena then zapped them up to The Heavens.

....

Some time passed, and the commander was standing at the shore of the lake, in front of a small monument with a plaque attached to it. The plaque had been found washed up further inland by the waves of flooding waters that had temporarily swamped the low-lying areas of the city.

The plaque was a piece of history, and the commander felt a sense of nostalgia as he looked at it.

The plaque read: The William B Henley Dam. Opened on this day, March 1st, 1958.

"You've been holding out on me, commander," a voice said behind him.

The commander turned to see the owner of that voice and smiled when he saw the familiar face.

"Jonathon, what brings you here?" the commander said.

"Your name commander. What is it?" Jonathon asked, already knowing the answer.

The commander turned back to look at the plaque.

He pointed at it.

"My ancestor was a close friend of one of the founders of the Hermes Consortium. He was wealthy in his own right and was afforded a place in one of the underground bunkers... The founders didn't last long underground, Jonathon. They'd caused the destruction of the world. Even their own people weren't happy... My ancestor, and many generations after him, prospered and helped the people underground survive the isolation... When people finally returned to the surface, the Henley name was a powerful and widely respected name. It was actually a Henley who renamed the planet Tellus."

Jonathon nodded.

"Your ancestor, he was Walter Henley, wasn't he?"

The commander looked at Jonathon.

"Yes. How did you know?"

"I met him. I knew him. He was a good man, commander," Jonathon told him.

"When you left Tellus the last time?" the commander enquired. "That's where you went?"

"Yes." he said. "Walter's grandfather founded the town of Henleyville not far from here."

"William Henley, yes," the commander said, nodding. "I am named after him. My name is William W Henley."

Jonathon extended his hand, and the commander took it with thanks.

"Well, Commander Henley," Jonathon said, "I suggest you've got some rebuilding to do."

Epilogue

Lesley sat in the new recreation area at the lake, shaded from the morning sun. The heat wasn't harsh yet, but it was building, and the humidity was rising.

The summer rains will be coming soon, she thought to herself.

She looked down to the shore where her mother and Amy were and watched them for a while. Katharyn was different now. She was no longer guarded or worried about the safety of herself or her family, and Lesley loved her mother's newfound joy for life.

In the distance, Lesley spotted two white doves flying across the lake gliding, diving, turning, and weaving in unison like they were playing a game. Near the shore she spotted a mother duck and her four ducklings paddling in the water towards the eastern side of the lake.

Probably where their nest is, she thought, nodding to herself.

Then a large butterfly flew around her and flitted about before landing on her stomach, her very pregnant stomach. The butterfly seemed to be looking at her as it opened and closed its large colorful wings several times before flying away when someone came near Lesley.

"Lesley" the person said, "Look at this."

Lesley smiled and looked up at the person who had called her name.

It was Joshua.

She loved his melodic voice and the way he said her name.

In his hand he held one of the ancient artifacts from Jonathon's secret cave. It was an amulet carved into the simple shape of a fish and attached to it was a strong chain of long braided hair.

Athena's hair.

Lesley looked down and touched her stomach when she felt a kick. She stared at her stomach for a moment, nodded, then smiled as she looked up at Joshua.

She said, "I think it's a boy."

www.ingramcontent.com/pod-product-compliance
Lightning Source LLC
Chambersburg PA
CBHW061337310726
48974CB00001B/87